How fish got there

got there

and forty-nine other tales about the departed

to Harriet & Mat

How fish got there

and forty-nine other tales about the departed

Charlie Berridge

Enjoy (or else!)

Charlie

BROWN
DOG
BOOKS

Published under licence by Brown Dog Books and The Self-Publishing Partnership, 7 Green Park Station, Bath BA1 1JB

www.selfpublishingpartnership.co.uk

ISBN printed book: 978-1-78545-330-4

Cover illustration by Hannah Carding
Cover design by Kevin Rylands

Printed and bound by CPI Group (UK) Ltd, Croydon, CR0 4YY

For ORB, AWB, BCB and CDB, mes enfants,
who also strive to grasp life's opportunities
in their own beautiful styles.

Charlie Berridge has always been possessed of a creative streak that manifests itself in outpourings such as *French Letters, a journey to at least three places* (AuthorHouse 2007), *Building a billion, the story of John McCarthy* (Harriman House 2011) and more recently, a cartoon and verse collaboration with artist Hannah Carding, *Nude Commute* (Matador 2016). He acquired an MA in Creative Writing from Bath Spa University in 2005 and is a member of the Poetry Society. He lives in England's most "woke" town, Frome in Somerset. You can contact him by email at charles.berridge@virgin.net

The author seated centre of Banksy's *The woman attacked by seagulls* photographed on 7th September 2015 at Dismaland Bemusement Park in Weston-super-Mare.

Contents

IN THE BEGINNING.... When you die it's never the end of things. Not one bit of it. When your life comes to an end and you finish with your body, something about you remains; a blueprint, an impression, some thoughts and words. Some call it your spirit. It's something vital about you from which your code is extracted. This process unravels in the appropriate Chamber where what happens next is decided. The Chamber is the last stop before eternity kicks in. It's an important stopover with a brief examination under the critical microscope by those whose job it is to sort out the wheat from the chaff...

They call me Eliza. I am the list maker, and in attendance for all who pass this way. I sift the spirits, cause the sublimation; arrange the phase transitions. I take an amorphous material and give it structure, turn it into sense, so that the masters can judge what to do next. I examine the spirit, extract the detail and give it form. I can smell bullshit as soon as I unzip your files and away I go. A particular perfume permeates petty philosophers, potential poets, perverted priests, presumptuous prima donnas, pathetic plebs, puffed up philanthropists, pettifogging paedophiles, pained pagans, pale Paiutes, prestressed palaeontologists, proud pall-bearers, poisonous pen-pushers, pampered pundits, pushy panellists, puritan papists, paradoxical paradigms, the petulant paramilitary and pusillanimous paratroops; paranoid prostitutes, parasitic pygmies, putrid paupers, peaceful pimps, peaky publicans, psychic pedestrians, peculiar psychopaths, pseudo-politicians, provisional peeping Toms, peevish Protestants, psychokinetic poachers, pubescent plutocrats, plumy plump pilgrims, pleased pessimists, protective parents, prudish penfriends proscribing prostrate penises or perpendicular phalli, penurious pensioners, Pentecostal prosecutors, prosaic prophets, piqued peers, promiscuous promoters, perfervid Procrustes, profane padres, perfunctory prizefighters, periodic prisoners, pert priestesses, perverse Peter Pans, poisonous Pre-Raphaelites, preposterous Pharisees, pestiferous pharmacologists, precocious Phoenicians, picky pickpockets, precarious pilots, praiseworthy pirates, pragmatic plaintiffs, pissed proxies, procrastinating professors, political police, professed pranksters, profligate profiteers, punchy pupils, perspicacious pillocks, pernicious pacifists, purblind practitioners, Precambrian prats, predictable preachers, proud protagonists and protesting powder puff popinjays. A pyrrhic purdah perhaps, but then paradoxically, I'm the one minding your P's and Q's. I am, I think, the best examiner there's ever been since man first said, "I want." And I do it all in silence. Not a word. Not even a squeak. Do you get my drift? If not, it doesn't matter. You'll perhaps be nearer to understanding once you've browsed the fifty codes I've chosen. There are of course many, many, many more than fifty communications about the departed, but I have selected some that should not send you to sleep, unless you're in that state of mind where passing words on the page are like counting sheep. So jump to it, and hearken, my friends, so you might understand eventually!

áɕ̀-àã ɕ̀-àã : **Those rolling hills**

It's late July and the sound of harvest tolls over those rolling hills. He walks with the excited dog; swings his stick with the air of someone happy to be out in the countryside; the dog as inquisitive as ever and puzzled at the new landscape. The moving, growing crop that hid the rabbit and the rat has disappeared and in its place newly arrived is open, prickly stubble; black crows picking over what they might, and newly planted, big, round monolithic and motionless plugs. The stubble appears shocked and stands to attention, bolt upright, stunned and cut off in its prime, its head and shoulders sliced away, reaped and threshed with a suddenness that has turned a gentle, waving crop into a confusion of frenzied, dusty carnage. The stalk is slashed at the prescribed height and the grain-bearing head is thrust by the cutter backwards between the jaws of the revolving drum and fed into the machine. The hard, dry grain is shaken violently within the bowels of the harvester and forced from its husk, piled high, tens of thousands upon tens of thousands to make bread or biscuits to dunk into tea so that man may not live by bread alone; or for animals to eat. Of less worth and separated from its host, the straw is excreted out of the dusty back-end of the combine, laid on the ground in a thick, neat, fluffy row ready for the baler to suck it in; bind it into a tight roll and plop it out like giving birth to a truckle-shaped tombstone. The bales sit like straw meteors fallen to earth with others, in a shower randomly spread across the field, weighty rounds waiting around for what will happen next.

The sunshine raises the spirit and he walks into the field away from the normal headland track and comes alongside a giant bale, as tall as him but many times more stout. A boyhood thought flashes through his mind conjured up by the shape and direction of the slope away off down the field. Childish winter slides and the kicking of a ball summon back a feeling of well, why not? Wouldn't it be fun to roll it some? Push it to see if it would move. Its half-ton bulk won't budge at first nudge and so he puts down his walking stick and as the dog barks and dances around him, the thing he is trying to shift, does. Very slowly it moves and, encouraged, he puts his back into the job and pushes some more. The bale starts off down the gentle incline and like a giant straw wheel it turns faster and faster. Gravity and weight drive it on as though it's trying to escape and the man picks up his stick and calls his barking dog to heel and the two of them watch as the bale takes flight.

It is at first such fun. The man laughs to himself and then out loud as his schoolboy prank turns into something beyond his control. The momentum of the turning shape grows faster and faster and down the hill the giant bale bounces as incongruous as a straw tsunami on a July field. The man's mirth moves to nervousness and he looks around to make sure that only he and his dog are bearing witness. He calls his dog with an anger meant for himself and the dog wonders why his master's mood has changed; the consequence of action way beyond the comprehension of canine concern. The bale rushes away and on, taking its course from the contour of the land. It flings itself down the slope in urgent silence and nothing will impede its progress. A flock of alarmed pigeons flap away and clatter for the safety of the trees. On it goes and the man turns and walks to the headland wishing that he hadn't wandered off the beaten track, hadn't ordered what he couldn't command. As he reaches the safety of the headland, he thinks he hears the sound of something unusual as the bale reaches the end of its terrifying run in those rolling hills. He quickens his pace and heads for home.

Way down at the bottom end of the field, at the bottom of the hill is a thick hedge and a bank; a haven for bee and butterfly, songbird, badger and vole. Then there is a ditch before the narrow country lane. None of this provides a barrier for the furious bale and it careers and forces its way down and into the lane and, almost with cartoon calamity, lands on the roof of a passing vehicle, turning it into a wreck of bent tin, broken glass, ripped leather, rubber and chrome, the contents of a handbag and some groceries from the village shop strewn around; the detritus of a car crash served up with oil, diesel, water and blood. A plastic school lunch box with a pink princess emblazoned on its lid lies open in the road with a half-eaten KitKat, an apple and some silver paper, testament to a snack partially enjoyed. Mother and child don't know what has hit them. One moment they are on their regular way home from the village school chatting about Mrs Thompson's guinea pigs; the next obliterated by a force unleashed in a moment of playfulness by the man they both love and the man who loves them more than life itself. He was husband to the eldest victim and father to the youngest. It's a brutal harvest in those rolling hills.

Indeed it is a brutal, inevitable harvest and neither is it too easy reaching ripeness through the labyrinth you have set yourselves. Nevertheless, it is I who am expected to sort out your next steps once you have found your way to my Chamber. I do other things; keep the place looking tidy. Well, you never know when the masters might drop in; unannounced. It's interesting work. Variety. That's what's good about it. From one day to the next you're not sure what you're going to come across. All sorts. All dead, but all sorts that matter; actually all sorts of matter. You see, ancient wisdom had it that there were three types of matter: solids, liquids and gases. Recent science has determined that ninety-nine per cent of the visible universe is plasma. So plasma could be described as the fourth type of matter. The fifth is the spirit. When a spirit leaves its body and arrives here as a source of magnetic energy, I'm the trigger for creating a host guest structure or a code. In the same way that a solid can convert into a gas without becoming a liquid, the spirit goes through a phase transition. Let me try and simplify it. Imagine when you go to your freezer to get some ice. You want some ice cubes out of that funny tray that's divided into segments. The one you've put the water in to make the ice. Well, you know when you eventually get the ice it's never full. I mean each ice cube has shrunk. And the longer you leave the ice in the freezer, the more it shrinks. The ice sublimes away in the freezer. It doesn't turn back to water but nevertheless it slowly disappears and reappears elsewhere in the freezer. It's a bit about quantum mechanics, I suppose; all to do with wavelength and possible vibrating estates; that sort of thing. Heavy positive nucleus surrounded by charged electrons. Collective or collision. Pull them back and all the electrons will rush back and oscillate without colliding. Collisions are to be avoided!

áɕ̀-àã ɳ : **Nice Noose**

Why did I hang myself?

Take my life from those that would have me

hanging around. Perished and spidery.

No good for me. Good for nothing

except their sympathy.

I gave pleasure. Once or twice. I never really loved.

Never really lived.

Apart from that time, those precious moments

of childhood,

when astride Daddy's knee, I galloped to anywhere

and back safe again.

We are equal with all things, no greater or lesser

my darling girl,

he whispered to me.

"…we are equal with all things, no greater or lesser…" Some are poets but most are a long way from that ethereal state. The distillation process puts all spirits through the mangle. Now there's an old word you don't hear very often. Mangle: a machine with two or more cylinders turned by a handle, between which wet laundry is squeezed to remove water. Greek manganon, meaning axis or engine. Odd that the same term is used to describe the destruction or severe damage by tearing or crushing or for spoiling something, doing it badly. That's the French for you, though; mahaignier or maim. I wring the essence from the spirit and every spirit has at its nucleus over three and a half million atmospheres, a density greater than that found in the centre of your planet Earth. Three and a half million atmospheres! To give you some idea that's the sort of pressure they can achieve under laboratory conditions by forcing two diamonds together until they reach cracking point. Can you conceive of that? Cracking a diamond! And they have to be done, all processed in the order of their arrival. You can imagine that sometimes are busier than others. A disaster, an earthquake, landslip, tsunami, volcanic eruption, flood, tempest, fire, drought, plague or explosion will fill the Chamber in a moment. This is one of many… 'mansions with many rooms' and all that…don't know how many, but many. Chambers for domestic animals. I remember those. 7566000 to 7596000. Easy number. More difficult is Animals/Other. Can't remember the numbers, but

there are more Chambers and, even though you'd think the processing was straightforward, it's difficult because how can you judge if a hyena's laugh is sincere? How can you even see that chameleon? Here I take them as they come. Process them in strict order. Spirits of babies and infants up to six Earth years go straight through. Well, there's little data to be had. Everything else I get is stored in T>B>P (To Be Processed) and then once I've done what I'm trained to do, I place the results, the marked code if you like, under one of three graded sectors. G>R>E>E>N is Granted Request Entry Examination Needed, or as we sometimes say, Good Result for Ever and Ever Nema. Nema? It's Amen on this side for lots of those with belief and hope. So it's Nema for the successful spirits. P>I>N>K is Pending Investigation. Not Known. And there's R>E>D of course. It doesn't follow that the masters will accept this arrangement. They check everything, well, nearly everything, and G>R>E>E>N doesn't mean you're in. Put it this way. More from G>R>E>E>N get transferred into R>E>D than the other way round. Most from P>I>N>K end up in R>E>D. It's R>E>D you want to avoid, if you get my drift. R>E>D is Refer Eternal Damnation. And, by the way; in case you're interested: Code á́-à̃ ɱ I've just given to you was graded as R>E>D. Suicide, you see. They don't like the taking of one's own. Don't like it at all. I'm not the judge. Please understand that. I have this ability to actually get into the spirit. Get into the spirit, they say! I certainly do. There's plenty of evidence of that. Our biggest coded sector is H>B>P. Have Been Processed. Filed by date, name, cause and all, in the Chamber's databank. So if the masters want to look back, compare one decision with another perhaps, they only have to scan in graded sector H>B>P to check for consistency. I am the list maker. I never make mistakes. I'm an angel in that respect. You'd think it would be easy to process the 9,343 refugee spirits, half of them children, from the sinking of the MV Wilhelm Gustloff, or those from crematory 1 at the Stammlager in Auschwitz, or the eight hundred thousand hacked to death in Rwanda because they were born in the wrong tribe. Compassion and a free ticket to G>R>E>E>N is not even a consideration. Each code is examined on its living merit and the method and manner of despatch are of little real consolation. The vibration of the collision (here I go again getting all scientific) is of little concern. I am looking into the filamentary estate. It's the glow and not the wire; the software not the hard disc. There is no x-ray for the soul but I can see enough to make that preliminary judgement. You getting the idea?

áś-àã Ǹ : **Plain Song**

Breathless Smify. His escarpment exertion restricted striding out and humming at the same time. When he walked, rambled for pleasure rather than necessity, he often hummed a tune inspired by his intimate proximity to the great outdoors. He stopped so that his lungs could catch up and, with bowed head, like a man at prayer, he let them harvest what they needed in answer to his supplication. The scope of the Plain spread out before him like a relief map and from his elevated vantage point he glanced at the ancient contours, the rolling landscape and the field's boundaries. Some had been recently and positively punctuated but others had inherited historic dotted-lined question marks. For a landscape that gave the impression of wide open space, it was well stocked with trees. They mostly stuck together like bushy green whiskers on the face of a giant; woods and spinneys sprang and clung within the dimples, the rises and falls of the topography. On occasion a big tree had broken rank and stood singularly and untidily out of place. Old pasture grew and flowered and flowed over distinctive terraced steps cut long ago into the hillside, put there when agriculture was in its infancy. Litter-like, dark green pom-poms of tight bush exploded randomly where nature had intended their detonation. Modern acres of growing cereal grasped at eddies of wind which sent the standing crop into a turmoil of water-like motion, a frantic Mexican wave of barley from headland to centre field and then back again. The tractor's tramlines marked out where the sprayer had been dragged through the growing green stalks, and delivered its medicine. Like vaccination marks on a child's chubby arm, Smify could see exactly where the chemical cocktail had been administered.

There were infrequent properties but no communities; like the far-off farmhouse and its outbuildings nestling in a protective fold surrounded by trees. If Smify held up one finger at arm's length, the tip would blot out the entire farmstead. A solitary sugar lump-sized cottage, way off towards the hidden railway line, leaned up against its glass conservatory, constructions from different eras thrown together for now. Its panes reflected the sun's rays like a Red Indian flashing messages to his waiting warriors. New barns competed with old ones: the new with stark, precast slabs and metallic corrugated roofs: the old with weathered stone and worn slate. The MOD road, an incongruous white ribbon, marched its military way off through the countryside. Regimented wooden posts with painted white tops stood like sentries alongside, guarding the concrete route so the half-tracks and tanks and men in machines could rumble past on manoeuvres without fear from the ranks of trembling wild oats. A red flag hoisted on a pole like a nodding poppy in a field of green indicated danger and, as if any corroboration were needed, the hammering of distant gunfire pock-marked the soundtrack from over the hill. Clouds let their shadows slip across the yellow-green ground so that dark crows clattered in their shade and then burst out into the sunlit pasture playing a game of hide-and-seek. Skylarks, too, were heard but not seen: not by Smify's rheumy eyes screwed up by the brightness and watered by the wind. His hearing caught their trilling, fortissimo, exultation of distinction from above. The reception of their merry chorus was only interrupted by the staccato crack of distant small arms. Butterflies didn't give a toss and went about their gentle business noiselessly. Bees hummed over clover and nervous rabbits hid and twitched. Distant sheep stuck to the sward like motionless woollen clouds.

Smify's breath came back and he stood up straight, like an observant brown hare from the scrape, and looked. Onwards and upwards, he thought, onwards and upwards and he resumed his climb and his simple hummed tune. The hillock, his target, was perched at the top of the escarpment and could be seen from miles around. It stuck out like a proud bosom; more like a single pert tit belonging to a young woman who'd not yet had a child. He could again breathe through just his nose, rather than gulping air in greed through an open mouth of necessity. Now the rich scent of wild flowers and pasture mingled with damp rot and pollen, not unlike freshly laundered shirts, he thought; the smell of early summer on the Plain.

Approaching the top of the hillock there were three proud trees, now in full sail with their new leaves a cacophony of wind-prompted exclamation. The gangs of hard thorn bushes clung grimly to the ground, whilst beneath them bracken waved fronds in salute while giving cover to the cavernous workings of the badger's sett. Holes that burrowed into the sunny side of the hillock were like the extensive excavations of cave dwellers. Some were old, gaping but hidden and undisturbed, and others new with the signs of recent digging littering the entrance. A few steps further up was the summit where ashes were spread, prayers muttered and small stones, pieces of wood and dried-up flowers arranged in such a ritualistic way as to indicate man-made monuments. It was a wild place with the markings of civilised futility. Like a window pane only momentarily frosted by a breath. Smify stood on top of the tit, right on its nipple if you like, and turned and stared for the three hundred and sixty degrees dropping away around him. The view wouldn't have changed for decades; the actual contours since the ice age. Smify revolved and like an unsteady compass needle seeking its North, he completed his circular tour. This special place, focal point, look-out was where he, too, might like to end his days. Although he hadn't written anything down, left any instructions, he'd often thought that maybe his ashes could be spread where he now stood. He thought about that when he was there but when he left, walked back to normality, he soon forgot about it.

Below there was sudden movement. He noticed the two soldiers down on the other side of the hill, one toiling urgently with a shovel and the other crouched, guarding the trussed-up body. Too late Smify realised that what he was seeing was strictly forbidden. He took in the tableau vivant and because of its shocking seriousness he ducked so as to avoid discovery or implication. He thought he heard the soldier's exchange and knew that he'd been seen. Quickly and with a heart pounding through fear, he crawled and slid back off the tit. His common sense told him that if he legged it across the open ground down the escarpment, the fitter soldiers would soon catch him up. He circled around the base of the summit and crawled his way back up the southern side until he reached the thorn bushes and the open scars of the badger's sett. Feet first he squeezed his way through the covering ferns and into the biggest, darkest, yawning hole and pushed and wriggled until his body was tucked right into the chalky soil. He dearly hoped that the smell of badger was greater than the presence of the beast. His heart raced and before he could calm it, he glimpsed the flash of a black leather boot with the khaki camouflage above it. He heard the military voices in urgent consternation; expletives as every other word. He held his breath and prayed that his hiding place would prevent his discovery. He sensed there was doubt, dissension between his pursuers as one questioned the other. Was he fucking sure he'd seen some civilian prick or wasn't he fucking sure? The soldiers barked at each other above Smify's hiding place and then because of the urgency of their unfinished task, they jogged from the top of the hill and returned to their own burial site, leaving Smify to his.

He didn't move until it was nearly dark. His body ached to be released from hillside internment and returned to normality. He had had time to consider his predicament as badger-like, he lay embedded. He hummed as he hid; probably for self-assurance. His low tune a sort of comfort blanket with which he could wrap up difficulties. He hummed a tune he didn't readily recognise, something that seemed to come from deep within his soul. He hummed and thought, thought and hummed. What were the squaddies up to? Why the motionless body? In Smify's opinion the trussed body was a lifeless one and the two soldiers were up to no good. Why else would they come after him? Why else would he be fearful of his situation? Why else would he squeeze himself into an old badger's sett? He had seen those telltale warning signs sprinkled around in the partially militarised zone: "Tank crossing", "No access for military vehicles", and when you shared the Plain with the military, you got used to seeing them. What he had witnessed might have been some army exercise; but then the whole brief incident he'd photographed in his mind had had a sinister flavour to it. They were definitely up to no good. His train of thought was interrupted by an explosion of angry snarling coming from somewhere inside the ground around him; the sound of animals fighting. It was time to move. He clawed his way out of the hole and cautiously eased himself back into the dusk on the hillock. Suddenly another dreadful noise like a football fan's rattle sent him flat on the ground again. It was the distinctive cackle of a lone magpie he'd disturbed and sent flapping off. The villainous bird had sounded like a machine gun in Smify's current mindset, and he was sure, in that moment, he'd been shot. As if the bird's vocal assault wasn't surprise enough, the undergrowth only inches away from him trembled and shook as two alarmed badgers scurried off, greatly shocked and disturbed by the human interloper. Smify again stood up and furtively brushed the dirt from where it had started to take hold of him. Like a totem pole, his incongruous form rose and took root on the side of the hillock. The sun had gone west and the Plain was in mourning with a sombre palette. Smify ascended to the summit once again and cautiously peered in the direction of where he'd first seen the soldiers. He was half-expecting to see lights, torches maybe, but the gloom confirmed that they had departed. Smify swept his surroundings on the lookout for signs of life, but the Plain was slipping into slumber apart from the pinprick of shimmering light from the distant farm. He took off down the slope and with big, steady strides soon reached the place where the two soldiers had been. He knew the spot when he reached it as the turf lay sliced, folded over like neat portions of layered cake. He could see the signs of where the soldier had started to dig but it looked like the job had been interrupted. Near to the freshly cut clods of turf was a far more disturbing blemish. Although he couldn't be sure, Smify felt that the stain on the meadow, the brownish blot of something spilt on the grass, was blood. He turned and with all the haste he could muster, headed off down the escarpment and back from where he had started earlier that day.

The big badger with fresh gore smeared about his jowls watched him go; an owl hooted from its lookout and Smify quickened his pace in a race against the chasing darkness. From way above him a humming drone registered his growing body heat and sent the information back to its controller.

Not many know that the badger can sing. A badger's song, his pitch if you like, is as you'd expect, earthy. In the same way that a badger cannot chew, neither can he attempt to reach high notes. However, the extended shape of the skull and its construction means that the Melinae or the Eurasian variety of the badger family are better equipped to tackle the bass parts, leaving the treble score to the Taxideinae, its American cousin. The badger on the Plain, Michaelmas Meles Meles, was head boar. He had the wisdom and cunning and a fearless ferocity that gave him the respect he deserved on the Plain. It was through his tenacity that the clan had become established at the top of the hill on the escarpment and it was his forward-thinking that had moved them away from the encroaching danger on the other side of the railway line. Michaelmas Meles Meles had found a route under the terrible tracks. His father and uncle hadn't been so observant and a three-carriage passenger train had taken them, cut through their distinctive markings, leaving them like discarded bloody pelts on the track side. The high ground was an obvious vantage point, but the new headquarters didn't come without a fight. Michaelmas Meles Meles was just short of four feet from nose to tail tip and weighed nearly fifty pounds. He was a formidable creature with the battle scars to prove it, and he could still demand the attention of any sow in his clan and was father to many, many cubs. He also had the deepest, lowest hum of any other badger. It was so low that the vibration issued created in the listener a feeling rather than a sound. But, like all at the top of their game, the pinnacle of their power, for Michaelmas Meles Meles there were younger, more feisty boars pushing hard to unseat his supremacy as head honcho of the hilltop sett.

They'd decided to get him by ganging up on him. In that way they'd either chase him off or, better still, kill him. They knew he'd be in the sett that afternoon and had worked out a plan of attack. One of them would take him head on while the other two would approach from the old entrance and come up behind him while he slept. It was a desperate plan that involved perfect timing, serious bravery and maybe even sacrifice from the boar that was going to lead the assault. It was agreed by the three conspirators that whoever took on Michaelmas Meles Meles face to face, would be the next head boar of the clan. However, the best-laid schemes of badgers and men often go awry. Michaelmas Meles Meles was in that state of half-sleep and half-wake. He was aware of a low humming in a tone which he hadn't heard before. He thought it might be the wind playing tricks thorough the underground chambers or the clamour from a bees nest, but as he slumbered the humming took on more significance. The humming was even lower than his own and it was clear to Michaelmas Meles Meles that not far from where he now lay, there was another bigger intruder. He immediately sat up and sharpened his senses ready for action. When the assault came, Michaelmas Meles Meles was fully ready and had little trouble in breaking the neck of his single assailant as he came at him through the narrow doorway. Once he had made sure that the attacking badger was dead, the old boar cocked his head on one side and listened for signs of life. The humming had ceased and so he headed up and out of the sett. His wisdom was such that when he saw a stumbling human shape emerging from the old workings and two badgers hurrying off, he realised that the plot to get him had been foiled. He didn't know why but undoubtedly the human had prevented the coup by blocking up the assassin's intended point of entry. Michaelmas Meles Meles didn't stop to ponder the reason for his good fortune and knew that the best form of defence was attack, and when the human had gone, with steely resolve and deadly purpose, fired up with the red mist of bloodletting, he took his bearing, sniffed the darkening air and sallied forth in earnest pursuit.

Smify wasn't sure what to do. As darkness descended he, too, left the escarpment and walked back along the footpath and across the railway line to join the defence road which ran parallel to it. The whiteness of its ribbed concrete acted as a guide. Whilst it kept him on the straight and narrow, it didn't lead him into any obvious conclusions. He wasn't sure if he should report what he'd seen and if so to whom? The police were the obvious choice and he reasoned that they would have a line to their military counterparts and the issue, if there was one, would be investigated. The proof, such as it was, was out there on the Plain. Forensic investigation would be able to establish any foul play. His street wisdom and public-spirited nature told him that he really should head straight for the police. And so he strode out and moved with purpose along the military road.

The lights came towards him. They were travelling at speed

and Smify could hear the familiar sound of chunky rubber tyre treads eating into the concrete road. It was a humming; the urgent, purposeful humming of a lightweight military four by four going for it. Smify continued to walk towards the two dancing, circular, distant headlights but moved from the middle of the road to one side so the vehicle would pass him in its hurry. What happened next did so in an instant. When Smify replayed it, however, the whole episode was in slow motion. As the Army Land Rover approached him with gusto, it suddenly veered off its route in the road and headed straight towards Smify who leapt onto the rough verge. At the same time as the vehicle's change of direction, two badgers intent on crossing the road emerged from the rough between Smify and the wayward vehicle. The Land Rover instinctively swerved but caught one, then hit the other badger with such force that its front wheels bounced and the driver lost control, catapulting the vehicle across the verge only yards from where Smify was fixed. It then gathered momentum on its out-of-control downward journey and, scything through cow parsley, young nettle and a flimsy fence at the bottom of the steep bank, it flipped like a tossed coin onto the railway line. Smify watched in frozen horror as the two familiar soldiers inside the front seats fought to get out. They struggled as their vehicle spun on its roof, and one of them managed to climb halfway out just as the three-carriage passenger train smashed into them. There was a deafening bang with the sound of metal being forced and bent and broken against its will. The peace just before the explosion was like no peace Smify had ever experienced before. Then the night air was filled with flames and the smell of burning fuel and flesh, and the distressed shouts from some of those on the train.

Smify put his hands to his face as he sank down on the grassy embankment. It was as though he hoped that when he removed them, the scene he had just witnessed would be a dream; a nightmare at worst. On his knees, at last he lowered his hands and the heat from the fierce fire burning on the track below him hit his face like sunburn. There was another, more gentle, sound to his left. He turned his head to look and, standing between the twisted and lifeless bodies of the two badgers, was the biggest badger Smify had ever seen. Crouching man and standing beast stared at each other long and hard. Neither moved as eye to eye they were pinned, held fast, like a laser onto its target. They searched for explanation and in that religious moment of calm that arced between them, like primeval kinesis, there was a vital communication so that when eventually the badger, having sniffed the shocking night air, disappeared down the bank and back to his position on the Plain, in that precise moment, with that extraordinary exchange of understanding, Smify knew that he needn't say anything to anybody.

It's the dimensions that are always most difficult to comprehend. You are capable of making comparison because of your senses and what they have become used to. But how do you compare what has incommensurability? How tall is keeping silent or how broad is a badger's understanding? Although I must not let it show, sometimes I struggle with my own dimensions. I don't mean that I have a weight problem! Good heavens no! I delve into the cornucopia of spirits and try to remain impartial. Impartiality is easy when the spirit doesn't move me. But when it does, my emotions, those long-forgotten feelings, haunt me as a shadow. Like the discovery of ignorance, I need to remind myself that death is an inevitable destiny and that, even though humankind will go to extraordinary lengths to seek eternal life, try as they may, scientists will never ever create Heaven on earth.

áʃ-àã Ṕ : **German invasion**

The battlefields of Europe churned with the toing and froing of quarrelsome forces. It was a constant struggle for supremacy with, in the main, Brit pitted against German as each fought for territorial advantage.

"Donner und Blitzen," sang the Germans almost in perfect unison. The dark sky responded as though ordered and a flash of lightning reached from a place up there in the foreboding cloud and came down to earth with a bang. Like applause, big raindrops followed.

"Vee shell haf to mauve," they agreed. Their successful campaign to capture their objective that morning in the promising bright sunshine was short-lived. Retreat looked inevitable. While the enemy hadn't really put up much opposition, the weather was turning against them. It was always the weather that beat them back and stopped them from achieving their goals. They retreated, hurriedly gathered their things and left as the white raindrops danced around them like machine gun fire. On the water to whose edge they had come so close, excited rings blurred the surface to prevent meaningful reflection. The disturbed pool itself could have been inches deep or it could have gone down to the Earth's core.

"Bloody hell!" said Amy and she reached for her towelling top; the bumblebee tattoo bobbed up from where it had been hiding on her buttock. If it was going to rain she didn't want to be caught out in just her bikini and besides, now that the Germans had run off, she was going to grab a sunbed much nearer to the poolside and on the edge of the scene of her eventual drowning later that same afternoon.

Never had a day off in my life. No lazing by a pool for me. Well, the job demands full-time attention. Percentages have come down and crude spirit rates have halved in the last sixty Earth years, but numbers go up and up so they add more and more Chambers. I can tell you everything there is to know about the figures. The top ten reasons for spirit arrivals are 12.6 per cent Ischaemic heart disease, 9.7 per cent cerebrovascular disease, 6.8 per cent lower respiratory infections, 4.9 per cent HIV and AIDS, 4.8 per cent chronic obstructive pulmonary disease, 3.2 per cent diarrhoeal diseases, 2.7 per cent tuberculosis, 2.2 per cent trachea, bronchus or lung cancers, 2.2 per cent malaria, and 2.1 per cent road traffic accidents. I can tell you that from the United States of America on Earth in the last full period session, we had 38,364 spirits sent to us as a result of intentional self-harming. Do you know which country on Earth sends us the most spirits as a percentage of their population? Why on Earth would you? South Africa. Over seventeen per cent. Next is Ukraine at over fifteen per cent. And then there is a list of countries in Africa that I couldn't point to on the map. Afghanistan is at number seven with over fourteen per cent, but I guess that has something to do with all the fighting they do in that part of Earth. Syria, too, is up there as a recent provider: its dusty past has caught up with it and its ancient ruins lie in ruins and its children cry, stung and choked by your chemical nightmares. I've had a legion of suicide bomber spirits from there and I put them straight into R>E>D. They often attach prayer mats or photographs of their children as an appendix to their codes, unless they are children themselves. I'm afraid that doesn't really help them much. R>E>D it is. Always R>E>D for the witch doctors of death.

áǵ-àã p̃ : **Alphabetical disorder**

"African bedfellow Cynthia?!"

"Doing English friendliness."

"Gracious heavens I..."

"Just kissing like mendoza. Nothing overly provocative."

"Quite revealing seen together undressed! Vacuous; wrong; xenophobic!"

"Yeah! Zulu!"

As the old adage goes, people who love in grass houses shouldn't get stoned. So maybe you're beginning to understand what it is I do here. Getting the picture. And apart from the idea of a sort of judgemental holding station, does the Chamber itself surprise you? All the Chambers put together would sit very comfortably on the head of one of your perceived pins. I guess with all the millions of transactions you'd expect a complex the size of the large Hadron Collider. Not surprising if you're looking for the God particle. Not a bit of it. All those boffins gathered in CERN searching for the Higgs boson. I could have saved them decades of paper-work and a vault full of currency. I snap my fingers and behold God's particle. Just like that! By rubbing my thumb and middle finger together with the sort of gesture a maître d'hôtel would use to summon one of his waiters, I could call upon a host of tiny techni-quark particles. Squarks, selectrons and neutralinos are lurking in the universe. Physicists on Earth continue their search for what they call supersymmetry. It's the idea that every known particle has a yet-to-be-discovered sister particle. They have no evidence but they will catch up eventually. They've a long way to go! Imagine, if you will, that we are sitting on a chessboard. The brightest of the brightest human minds is on the square in the far corner, the black square where the black castle starts his game. We are sixty-three squares away on the opposite side of the board where the white rook sits ready to play on a white square. If you were to place two marrow seeds on the first square I mentioned and multiply them, so two by two equals four and put four marrow seeds on the next square and do the same sum, so four times four equals sixteen and so on, and so on; the resultant number of marrow seeds you would get to is not as much as the number of years we are ahead of current human thinking ability. Work it out for yourself! By the time you reach the fifth square you're into a ten-digit number of four-thousand-two-hundred and ninety-four million marrow seeds. That's way more than enough marrow seeds to produce way too many fat marrows for far too few green fingers. What I'm saying is that Homo sapiens as we know it will never catch up, and the day it does is the day the system will crash. Down will come Cynthia, Zulu and all. And not in any smug and neatly arrayed alphabetical order either!

áś-àã Þ: Darkness

It's the darkness that gets to you the most. Light is something only hinted at in dreams. Either that or you have to acquire it on the black market. Funny that, buying your light on the black market. Twenty fellons for fifteen minutes. Outrageous but then the recharged cells do the job, bring back the light, albeit in a faltering, pathetic display. For those who don't remember, it doesn't really matter too much. For people like me, the old stagers who can remember seeing the sun and the moon for that matter, then the cells don't really do the job. Well how could they? Man-made light is always going to be just that. "Let there be light," we chant at every gathering but there is none, other than that provided by the wax from the beekeepers. Wax; there's a thing! My grandmother used it to provide lustre to her wood. Now it's the most valuable commodity around, the same price as water and look how that has gone through the roof. It is, so they say, all our own doing. We did too little, too late and poisoned the planet beyond repair. The sceptics said it would never happen. Nature will right itself, they said. But they were wrong. Nature didn't and now we exist in the dark. Fumble about like moles. There may be hope from those that left, took off in search of another place beyond our hidden moon, but we haven't heard a word, so maybe they didn't make it. I hope and pray they did. Not for me so much as for the young who really shouldn't be subjected to this existence. Many of them are already blind and it breaks my heart to hear them feeling their way around; scratching and sniffing, sounding like the sharpening of knives rather than human beings. "Let there be light," we chant at every gathering because it's the darkness that gets you the most.

The sharpening of knives. What a beautiful sound that is. The reassuring scrape of steel on dry stone or metal. A precise action that has a definite purpose. Just like NDEs. Ever heard of NDEs? Near-Death Experiences. A drowning person's life will flash before their eyes. A falling body might experience the same phenomenon. It's a five-stage continuum: Peace, body separation, entering darkness, seeing light and then entering light. Sixty per cent may experience the first stage but only ten per cent will enjoy the last. Some think they have seen the other side, visited those that have gone before; some see Hell or think they have. Others proclaim Heaven. Con merchants transmit messages from great-aunt Ivy or recently departed Jack. NDEs are just that, though. Near-death experiences and not actual death experiences. The first rule of NDEs is that you do talk about NDEs. The second rule of NDEs is that you don't talk about NDEs. The third rule of NDEs is that no matter how much you do or don't talk about them, there is no proof that they exist. But are NDEs real, I hear you ask? I think you know the answer. Would the paparazzi protect the people's princess? Is the soap a prophylactic? Do mayors sit in hoods or something like that?

áǝ̀-àã Q́ : **State Secret**

It's quite extraordinary that only a handful of people know that the coffin borne so majestically didn't contain what it was supposed to.

It's not often that I record my interviews. I tend to scribble frantically in my notebook as the speaker speaks, and then when I get back to my desk rush a first draft onto the laptop, adding my own recollections of person and place. The only time I used a tape recorder was when I was asked to do so.

"Please make sure you get things down as I tell them to you," he said. "It is important. It's so important that it could change the course of history."

We met a few months before he died. He made his living out of the dead and so seemed quite matter-of-fact as he drew towards his own end. He sat there in his worn armchair with a tumbler of whiskey and a few ice cubes that sang out, tinkled like a peal of tiny bells. They bounced off the cut glass and collided into each other, dissolving. He didn't look well and when he sipped the strong drink he licked his thin lips with an effort that seemed to take the sort of concentration the watcher joins in with. He needed time to savour the complicated distillation in his glass. His taste buds were no longer certain. He was frail. Like the ice in his drink, he, too, was slowly dissolving.

"She was as white as a ghost, as cold as a fish. She looked dreadful lying in that stark hospital room. No hint of that famous smile or those sparkling eyes. The colourful front-page model had become a smudge, an unrecognisable grim waxwork copy of what she had once been. There was one picture on the wall, a Renoir I think, a print of course. People by the river having fun. So sad." He paused and looked as though he, too, was a part of that impression.

"The call came through early on the Sunday morning," he continued. "I knew what it would be about but I didn't know who. It was a shock. Of course it was. You expect the old ones. You almost have to act surprised when it's someone you know who's past their sell-by date. But she was only thirty-six, still in her prime. Very much in the public eye. So I reassured them that I'd do everything I could to help. I'd give the grim job the very best attention to detail that I knew would be required. Of course you try to treat everybody the same. I've done more than my fair share of notables, peers of the realm and old royals. But it's not every day that a young princess comes along."

He ran his left hand over his corduroy-covered knee, up and down, feeling the lines in the material to make sure that they were running smoothly.

"Apparently if she'd been wearing her seat belt in the back of the car, she might have survived. As it was, her injuries were terrible, but I'll come to that." He took another sip and the ice cubes again rang their little bells, sang their high notes in the silence.

"I was in the air to Paris within, oh, about an hour and a man from the embassy met me at the steps of the plane. I didn't need to go through passport control with my bag of tricks and we were driven through the light Sunday morning Paris traffic to the hospital. There was no need for sirens and the police outriders seemed unnecessary. The city was quiet. I guess that everyone had gone to the seaside or the country for their summer holidays. So we drove without any real hold-ups to the Place Marie-Curie. Every street corner seems to have the name of somebody who was somebody written on a sign. The Salpêtrière where we were going was originally a gunpowder factory. Saltpetre or potassium nitrate, I guess. Once upon a time it was a dumping ground for the poor of Paris and a prison for prostitutes. It became rat-infested, or so the embassy man told me, and I thought how appropriate. There were, once again, soon going to be plagues of them with their cameras outside waiting for an opportunity to snap at something. The man from the embassy sat next to me, making occasional polite conversation and filling me in on some details. Sir Michael would be there to meet us, he said. The black car swept through the Mazarin entrance to the hospital. Through its darkened windows I could make out the narrow route. Even though the traffic lights were on red, the gendarmes waved us through under the elaborate stone arch with its carved coat of arms and, somehow grimly prophetic, a large urn perched on its apex."

The old man coughed. I stayed silent. I wanted to hear every word he had to say. The green recording light of my machine shone like a twinkling cat's eye.

"There was a brief but firm handshake from the diplomat. He was tall and distinguished just like our man in Paris should be. But he was obviously very shocked by the accident and the particular turn of events was something quite new in the repertoire of ambassadorial responsibilities. He and the doctors concerned showed me into the hospital room where her body lay. The small room with the Renoir. The awful accident that had taken away her young life had also left her beaten and bruised. Four hours of what must have been heroic effort to save her life had left her in a state and, even though the doctors had done their best, had even massaged her heart with their bare hands to try and keep her from death, her body now needed my attention before the other dignitaries arrived. I went to work and I must say that with my skill and patience I turned her back into a Sleeping Beauty. There was no visible sign of any drama on her serene face and those that wanted, needed to say goodbye, could do so without any hesitation. She was once again the Princess Diana asleep."

The ice sang again as the glass was raised and lowered. The cough interrupted the more urgent tinkling and this time I got up from my seat to grab the glass from his well-preserved soft hand and placed it on the little table, next to my tape recorder, so he could carry on without fear of a spill. He coughed and shook with little control, a building twisting and buckling in an earth tremor, until the spasm had passed, and he settled and continued to speak.

"Later that morning, a monsieur Chevènement or something like that, who seemed to be in charge of the arrangements, together with the French Prime Minister, Jospin; the French President's wife, Bernadette Chirac, and the French Health Minister, visited the hospital room and paid their last respects. After their visits, the Anglican Archdeacon of France, a Father Draper, said commendatory prayers from the Book of Common Prayer. Everything was dignified. There seemed to be an unnatural hush around the place. The hustle and bustle of a busy hospital was a million miles away and in the quiet room the princess lay at peace. At around two in the afternoon The Prince of Wales, and Princess Diana's two older sisters, Lady Sarah McCorquodale and Lady Jane Fellowes, arrived. We left with her body an hour and a half later. All that is very well documented. There was nothing out of the ordinary. It was when we had returned to London, when we had placed the coffin in Kensington Palace, that the next instructions were given to me."

He paused again and I nodded in agreement and encouragement for him to carry on. I wanted more and it came.

"Apparently among her final wishes was the specific request that her body was not to be buried. She didn't want to be put in the ground, you see. Nor did she want a grand send-off. But she had become the people's princess. The outpouring of public grief was going to create a mountain range of flowers and the nation was moving towards mass hysteria. The press were demanding royal acknowledgement. The Queen was forced into returning from Scotland, had to go on TV to show her sadness at Diana's death. But the dead princess's wishes had to be carried out. There also had to be a national farewell with a satisfactory burial; a suitable full stop, a final resting place and somewhere geographical that the public could find on a map."

My interest was well and truly fired up. The old man hadn't apparently lost any of his ability to recall detail. His style was like that of a professional storyteller. He sipped some more and went on.

"So very late one night I took her to the West London Crematorium at Kensal Green, about twenty minutes from the Palace via the Edgware Road. Obviously I needed help and two other gentlemen, strong men in dark suits, were sent to lend a hand. We drove in a smart van, more like one of those executive transporters with blacked-out windows, to the crematorium where the job was done. No fuss. No witnesses, just the three of us and the guy who worked the furnace. He had no idea who he was cremating. There was no paper trail that I'm aware of and we were back in Kensington within the hour replacing the coffin from where we had taken it."

I was flabbergasted.

"You cremated The Princess of Wales? So, what, who on earth was in the coffin for her royal ceremonial funeral?"

He bared his old teeth, showing a flash of gold filling, and ran his tongue across them as though he was feeling for an intruder, a morsel of food perhaps.

"I did exactly what she wanted. But I couldn't have those guardsmen carrying an empty casket. I filled her coffin with the very things that had probably caused her more trouble than anything else in her short life. Newspapers and magazines. If you cram a coffin with those it can feel like you are carrying eight stone or so."

"So you mean to tell me that the whole world, millions of mourners were watching and crying over a coffin filled with newspapers and magazines?"

"Precisely," said the undertaker as he took another, longer sip from his glass. The ice, apparently just like the royal body, had disappeared.

"When her brother buried the coffin on that island retreat, he was simply burying old news. I've thought about it lots and it seems to me that my improvisation was most appropriate. Those that hounded her to the grave were ceremoniously buried in it for her."

"And what happened to her ashes?" I said, still trying to take in what I'd just been told.

"Oh I'm sure she's very happy where she is. I'm afraid I can't possibly give you any more detail. Underpasses are full of very dangerous speeding vehicles. So I'm afraid that will always remain a State secret."

The recording device I had taken for the interview didn't work for some reason. Even though the green light was on for the entire time, when played back the little tape remained the same from start to finish; silent apart from the sound of white noise, like wet tyres on tarmac or dancing flames burning paper.

It seems that the living think about sex a lot. Like interest in that fairy tale princess, it certainly prompts more than its fair share of exposure. And sex is the number one item searched for on your feeble systems. Shelter, food and sex; you rate them in that order. Sex. Not gender. Somebody said that a man thinks about sex eight thousand times in sixteen hours or once every seven seconds. I can tell you it's more like ninety-nine times a day. These measurements are never precise but they're not far off the mark. Women are more selective with their thinking, but not always so immune to the tremendous outside forces they can encourage. It's mostly silly man speak when it comes to getting your end away, having a bit of how's your father, getting laid, having a jump, getting your leg over, piercing the bearded clam, shagging, screwing, having a quickie or a knee trembler, a spot of rumpy pumpy, a bit of slap and tickle, some nooky, playing with the little man in the boat, giving a good seeing-to, getting laid, putting Percy up Pussy, dipping your wick, humping or pumping, feeding the sausage into the slicer, givin' er the bone, getting it up, putting it in, letting the dog see the rabbit, poking, doing the business, going all the way, making the beast with two backs, stirring up the pond, making whoopee, getting jiggy with it, slipping her a length, having it off, making love, kissing the pink, feeding the one-eyed monster, polishing the python, making a deposit, splashing the gash, knowing in the biblical sense, bonking like bunnies, having sexual intercourse or relations, boffing, getting some stankie on the hang down, taking horizontal refreshment, pounding the duck, ringing the bell, tickling the G-spot, going up the alley, going in past the welcome mat, copping off, slipping up the Khyber Pass, banging your balls on the buffers, coming together, reaching a climax, making babies, shooting your load, poaching the eggs, splicing the main brace, playing on a sticky wicket, getting a hole in one, planting your marker, sowing your seed, going down the slippery slope or up the chuffer, giving her one, getting your oats, knobbing, coupling, having it doggy fashion, copulating, going up the Arsenal, riding, going to bed with or in through the juicy folds, finding the front bottom, exploring Eve's cavernous crack, putting your things together, nailing it, having full-on coitus or just procreating. Men seem to describe the act as they might a fairground ride. They possess an inability to talk about such things seriously or their collective bravado prevents sensitivity among the senseless. Vivat Vivat Vagina; the male of the species might have acquired a monopoly on the lurid description of the act itself, but females understand the jargon and have become happy participants most of the time. Apart from the many me-too's who have been violated. Men think they have God-given rights to sex whenever and wherever. It takes all sorts from preserved princesses to prostrate prostitutes; lascivious lords to laconic lairds, and, even though I have seen it all, there is nothing that can stir me one way or another. I find it all just crude, rude and disgusting; besides (and say this out loud), Mike Hunt, once a sight for sore eyes, used to be full of surprise. A pretty good cure for losing allure is less work and a lot less meat pies.

áś-àã ǫ : **Travel Bag**

He invites me, helps me to undress so I can lie naked on the bed so that he can then secure my arms and legs, tie them up tightly so that I wonder what is about to happen. But it may give pleasure to both of us. I am turned on by the way he coaxes me, encourages me to yield to his fantasy. He kisses me because that's what I want and, although I try to return the passion, want to kiss him back, throw my arms around him, coil my long legs across his back, plead for him to take me as he has before, this time I won't be able to because of the restraints. He plays with me, runs the tip of his finger around my nipples to make them even more proud. He licks them, bites them gently, the way I like and then moves down to my flat stomach and that little indentation that once tied me to my mother and he explores. He traces the downy, soft hair that trails from my tummy to that place between my thighs where it flourishes into something more abundant. Neat and tidy, like a well-kempt lawn, he runs his fingers and my thoughts in that direction and I respond in my own special way. But stop! Don't stop, I say. But now is not the time. He's other things in hand.

With a little conjurer's flourish he produces a plastic travel bag.

It's one that will fit quite easily over a head. He opens it up and blows some air into it so that it starts to puff up like a clear balloon. He makes sure it's sound and strong with no tears, no broken seams. Then he lets the air out again, pours it over my needy breasts, like an invisible sauce, so that I laugh and say what on earth are you doing, darling?

The mood changes as quickly as turn-on to turn-off and from willingness to get-the-fuck-off-me, as he eases the empty bag slowly over my surprised head. I shake it from side to side with mounting nervousness. I try to prevent him from pulling the plastic over my head but there's little I can really do. I remember the warnings about suffocation and how you should keep plastic bags away from small children. I feel vulnerable like one of them. I start to shout at him, say things like don't be stupid, please don't be a fool. But he is being firm. It is a clear plastic bag so he can see the distress he is causing. He is assertive and tries to be reassuring. He carries the look of someone in control so that he reassures me that everything is going to be all right. I have nothing to worry about, he says. He ignores my pleas, my cries for help and my begging. Like water off a duck's back, he just gets on with the task and isn't worried about the consequences. You cannot make an omelette without breaking an egg, he says. Besides, you're only going on a short journey, just travelling; going to meet your maker. That's all he says with a laugh. I writhe in horror at his suggestion, his intention. Once he's got the bag right over my head, I am nodding wildly like one of those awful toy dogs with a head on a spring that you sometimes see through the back window of anthropomorphic motor cars. He is watching my wide eyes; blue eyes that have looked at him, pored over him and admired him in so many ways. He has seen them at first wide with expectation, just a glint of mischievous expectation, the naughty girl look, and then he has observed them become more white than blue, darting and blinking furiously with alarm. He sees the tears start to roll, not gentle drops of joy or even those that well up and overflow when sadness strikes a chord. These tears are squeezed out with force, like extracting juice from an orange. They are tears of fear. He catches the mouth twist and gape for the good air that is disappearing; that screaming mouth that spoke all those wonderful words, groaned and sighed, laughed and cried. Those lips that did all those mischievous things, blew those kisses, drank him and with him, whispered beautiful things and told lies then and now, are alive with obscenities and unspeakable horror. The words I try to howl when I realise this is not a game only a lip-reader could decipher and then only a part of every other gasp or bagged up shriek. My bright white perfect teeth, the ones I brush every morning and every night, the ones I pick between with the dental strand, the floss, to remove whatever lurks in those hard to get at places, waiting if undisturbed to defile the gums, to breed infection, to bring on the plaque, to bring on tooth decay; my bright white perfect teeth pull at the slippery plastic without impression. He has to be firm. He can't let personal feelings or pity or doubt or guilt step across the threshold of what's in hand; what he has both hands so firmly around. He squeezes tight, tighter than the black bin bag he twists when he puts out the rubbish every other Tuesday or tighter than the pheasant's neck he wrings when the bird flaps when it's still dying from the shot that hasn't despatched it in an instant. Like wringing out a wet towel, he holds onto the plastic with his hands around the neck, both necks, the bag's neck and mine, one pretty one inside, one practical one outside, and he waits. My neck has bulging veins. They feel as though they'll burst but they won't. Smile. At least say cheese or pout like a goldfish. Pretend this is fantasy, not real. Perform for your public. Enjoy the applause. That thrashing beat; the beat of his heart not faster than mine, but stronger. Somehow more assured. A beat with a future. Unlike mine.

And eventually, like a train pulling into a station, everything slows. The energy subsides. The meter runs out. The struggle dies down. My face changes. The dreadful grimace, the pleading look of for God's sake what are you doing to me becomes the still silent stare of for God's sake what have you done to me? The plastic bag has disappeared. Where a few minutes ago it was a floating coat, an outer wrapping hovering over my surprised, excited face, it has now become an extra skin, a film clinging to my terrified stare, the plastic caught tight over my blue lips and in my mouth and over my twisted tongue, my nostrils filled with the man-made layer that stops everything vital from coming and going, going and coming. Only my eyes are open wide, a little wider than normal with still too much white, gazing, but in a way that says it's all over. I can't see him anymore. It's finished. He's been well and truly dumped. And so have I. At the wrists and ankles my skin hasn't shredded with the struggle and those secure restraining knots have turned invisible. My realisation that I'm no longer bound, tied up in fantasy, drowning in a titillating, see-through, travel bag is too late to rescue me, call me safely back home from grotesque self-asphyxiation.

How's your Latin? It ties some in knots. Legions of Latin thinking spirits have come this way. Through the Chamber. Res ipsa loquitur. Elizabethans, too. Came with their nosegays. Not much use here, sunshine! Forseuth and merrily we go amongst our brethren in search of what will be. Gainst all ganders who wilt forsaith that even tide in pursuit of after happiness, straight way unto the disarming nature of the beast. I've had them all. Different languages, different religions, different politics, different colours, different persuasions, different orientations, different attitudes, different ideas. Always the same spirits, though. Stripped down and bare with just a code to throw up some substance. Like a memento from a trip to the seaside. That cheap china boat with Charmouth painted on its prow. Fakers, fornicators, fugitives and failures. You get drones of them. Liars, lechers, levitators and lesbians. Persecutors, perverts, politicians and procrastinators. One and the same. Philby. K or 007. That poor fellow with the squint who hated the hard ball and net practise in equal terrifying measure or cheating baseball player, John McGraw, or W.G. Grace. The leader who declares war because it suits him and not those who put him where he was or Mahatma Gandhi. Notorious Biggie Smalls or Isabella Baumfree (Sojourner Truth) or Jesse Owens. Dr Shipman and Himmler. Mother Teresa or Florence Nightingale. X or Y, Blakelock's aunt or Mo the Lawn. God works in a mysterious way His wonders to perform.

áś·àã Q̀: **Aunt's Legacy**

When Blakelock's aunt is cremated, she goes out with a bang. Not one of her friends or relatives knows that she has been fitted with a pacemaker, and the loud report that it makes when the furnace fires up isn't quite drowned out by the electric organ. The few who have come to see her off are trying to sing along to its music in the crematorium chapel. The half-hearted nature of the congregation's effort is more to do with the choice of hymn, rather than unwillingness to partake. "Onward, Christian Soldiers" or "Fight The Good Fight" would both have diluted the bang. "What Our Father Does Is Well", a rather obscure harvest hymn with a difficult-to-follow tune, does not promote a natural harmony or the vocal gusto to muffle the unexpected sound. The undertakers from the Co-op are given the blame for the pacemaker oversight and its resultant small explosion, but no mention is made to the bereaved about the unfortunate incident and how it interferes with Blakelock's aunt. The operator of the fiery furnace, the guy at the coalface, gets a nasty shock when the lid of Blakelock's aunt's coffin takes flight and the dead aunt herself tries to vacate her last resting place by suddenly sitting up just as the flames are taking hold. The operator needs a cup of sweet black tea to help restore his equilibrium and he is allowed to go home early, entrusting the rest in line that day to one of his colleagues. Some say he will never be quite the same again.

The explosion of Blakelock's aunt's pacemaker is attributed by the congregation to a coincidental vehicle backfire on the busy road outside, where life carries on as normal as Mohammad, the driver of the A1Lawn at Bargain Price van ("green shoots r us") speeds past the crematorium gates unaware that Blakelock's aunt is being burnt to a cinder and her pacemaker is about to explode. The six-year-old green van is long overdue its service, and as Mohammad pushes his booted foot to the floor, the tired engine responds with a noisy and fume-fuelled hiccup that sounds like an old blunderbuss being fired. Mohammad curses as Blakelock pretends to sing the words, "Though nor milk nor honey flow, in our barren Canaan now," and the Good Lord takes the exclamations from both men in His stride as Blakelock's dead aunt briefly sits up, shocked in her tracks, on her way to meet Him herself.

Blakelock hasn't really bothered with his aunt and so it is a surprise to discover that she has left him a bequest of £100,000. Blakelock decides that his inheritance, his aunt's gift, should be marked in some appropriate way. The old lady would probably have liked that. So Blakelock thinks about the various options that are now open to him. He could purchase some rather fancy piece of antique furniture or a work of art with which to commemorate his aunt. He could invest in some fine wine, something he thinks that would have been close to and given succour to his aunt's heart. It was said that she had enjoyed the better part of a half-bottle of red Burgundy every day and that had, together with the pacemaker and the pills, kept her heart condition on the right side of wrong until the very end. Blakelock considers the leg of a racehorse but agrees that this might lead to bad money after good no matter how swift the particular leg.

About two and a half weeks after receipt of his late aunt's money, Blakelock decides on a Hummer. Of nearly all the things he might have chosen to spend his aunt's money on, a Hummer is not the most obvious. The Hummer is not just an ordinary vehicle but a rugged statement that tells everyone who sees it that here is a car that is much more than a car. Blakelock is not concerned about miles per gallon. He jokes that it is more a case of gallons per mile. The Hummer wags two rude fingers to the carbon footprint, and on the basis that Blakelock's aunt hadn't apparently shown any signs of believing in the existence of global warming, Blakelock is happy that his expenditure would have met with her approval.

Blakelock's aunt had lived in an old house without the benefit of many modern trappings. Insulation and double glazing were just words as mysterious to Blakelock's aunt as Higgs boson or Quantitative Easing. Her old radiators were left to rumble on, winter, spring, summer and autumn, at a steady sweltering eighty degrees, and the coal fires that burnt furiously in her various grates added their considerable pollution to Blakelock's aunt's personal volume of greenhouse gases.

As if to add further arrogance to the Hummer statement, Blakelock chooses a brand new red vehicle which is in marked contrast to the old green van driven by Mohammad of the A1Lawn at Bargain Price franchise ("green shoots r us"), a vehicle which doesn't let the grass grow under its wheels because Mohammad (Mo the lawn to those that know him from the local mosque) runs a busy business assuring weed-free, lush swards for his satisfied clients whilst trying to fulfil the increasing demands of his more fundamentalist brethren. The green van is being used to stock-pile a dangerous amount of fertiliser and fishmeal without attracting any undue speculation from nosy neighbours; lawns and fertiliser being natural bedfellows.

The thing about a red Hummer is that it does attract attention, some of it unwanted, a lot angry, some of it resentment and quite a lot based on envy. Blakelock secretly likes the more favourable attention, the head-turning looks he can see in the vast wing mirrors as he hums passed. He particularly likes it when the swivelling heads are pretty and female. Blakelock hasn't enjoyed much attention from the fairer sex and his new red Hummer brings him a ticket, a ringside seat, to a whole new experience that he finds difficult to resist. Sophie is one such but not content with just looking, she wants to touch, and in getting closer to the rugged vehicle, she becomes closer to its owner.

"Would you like a go in it?" Blakelock says to the young woman when he returns to the new shopping centre car park and sees her stroking the bonnet of his big machine.

"If that's OK, yeah, I would," says Sophie, very excited at the prospect of being let into this brash new world of petrolhead heaven. She has enjoyed a Truck Fest or two and the Battle of the Monster Machines at the Millennium Stadium in Cardiff sent her into an unusual trance for several of the following days.

Blakelock takes her for a spin and enjoys showing off around the car park. It is as though the Hummer is patrolling the lines of parked vehicles inspecting them rather like a general might review his troops. The Hummer looks down on most of them, is the king of the lot, loud and proud and majestically red as it rides through the rank and file.

"Wow," says Sophie when, having cruised most of the lanes, Blakelock brings the big machine to a screeching and rocking halt in one of the parent-with-child parking bays.

"You should see it off-road," says Blakelock and immediately Sophie wants to. She agrees to meet Blakelock again the following Saturday when Blakelock promises to take her for a decent run with a bit of off-roading thrown in as well.

Reversing out of the parent-with-child parking space, Blakelock doesn't see the A1Lawn at Bargain Price van and the red Hummer slams into the side of it with the sort of force a fast rhino might employ when hitting a slow poacher. There isn't a big smash but more of a dull crunch and the sound of thin metal being bent and torn. The A1Lawn at Bargain Price van suddenly has a new tattered logo on its battered bodywork. Several of the letters have disappeared into the gaping holes in the van's punctured side. The strapline is distorted and doesn't read any better and the new message seems to be saying something it shouldn't. Mohammad looks like a wild rabbit caught in the headlights as he springs from his assaulted van to confront whatever it is that has interrupted his progress through the big shopping centre car park.

"What in God's name are you doing!?" Mohammad shouts at Blakelock who is already inspecting the rear end of his Hummer. The damage to the big machine is minimal and it does seem incredible that Mohammad's van has sustained such scars without as much as a scratch on the red Hummer.

"You've buggered my van right up!" Mohammad protests loudly. Sophie is full of mirth. She has seen the whole thing and is probably the cause and distraction for the incident. Blakelock was showing off in front of the new admirer by revving the several hundred horsepower under his foot's control into a fever pitch before declutching and sending the red vehicle lurching backwards into the passing van.

"Ha, ha!" laughs Sophie as she reads the new description on Mohammad's damaged vehicle.

"Alla at Bar." She pronounces the strange new words as they have been arranged. She reads them out slowly, in an uncertain, childlike manner with no understanding of their meaning. Mohammad spins around as though he, too, has been struck suddenly. He cannot believe what he is seeing.

"It's Allah ak Bar! Not Alla at bar!" he exclaims, incensed at the female's ignorance. He squints at the letters, takes in the full meaning of the battered new inscription. The letter K could be a letter T, but there is no doubt in his mind about the new message proclaimed on his van. He looks as though he has seen God and certainly feels as though God is at this very moment speaking to him.

"Shoot us!" Sophie sings rather more positively, relaying the only two words in the new slogan on the green van, as under the deformed message of 'A1Lawn at Bargain Price', now reading 'Alla at bar', the words 'green shoots r us' have been transformed into 'shoot us'.

Quick as a bird with a worm, Mohammad wrenches open the rear door and pulls out an old shotgun which he wields and points precariously in the direction of Blakelock and Sophie with such a motion that it looks for all the world as though Mo the lawn is about to perform a top dressing treatment rather than simply comply with his treacherous training and recently radicalised new instructions.

"Allah ak Bar!" He screams his battle cry as the first lethal shot slices its way through his unfortunate quarry. The ferocious impact causes the recipient to dance and spin like a bleeding puppet in an extraordinary enactment. The sound of the shot is, thinks Blakelock, similar to the noise he heard at his aunt's cremation. He doesn't hear the second blast, but as his and the young woman's dying blood drips almost unseen down the red paintwork of the Hummer, Blakelock's last thoughts are along the lines that he really should have gone for the antique, the wine or even the leg of a horse, rather than the big, red American beast.

Clocks tick. Tick-tock. Or quietly hum telling their time. What is time? Does it actually exist? Common sense has it as the fastest thing on your Earth because there is nothing quicker. Not light; nor even a message from God or a speeding bullet. You have made it so but it will depend on where your measurements are taken. Does time travel faster on the top of a mountain? You say that time passes more quickly when you are having fun. But that's just a hidden illusion. People hide behind the respectability of their titles or curtains or hedges in the same way that a clock face covers its movements. The Chamber peels away the layers, the grime, the dirt of years. It smoothes away the craquelure, reveals the blemishes, seeks out the scars and buffs up the true shine of the spirit hidden under all that pretension. That's why the Chamber is so well appointed. We uncover the covered, unless of course there is no cover involved. Nothing to witness here, move along please!

áé-àā Ḿí : **Jehovah's Witness**

Saturday. A Witness from Jehovah arrived on our doorstep this morning, a charming old boy, who after some moments of conversation realised we were playing on the same side; pretty much anyway.

Sunday. He seems to have made some sort of encampment in the hedge and as we pass on our way to church he says, "Say one for me."

Monday. He knocks us up bright and early more out of the necessity for somewhere to dry out (it's been a wet night) than through his enthusiasm to spread the word from the Good (damp) Book clutched so firmly in his hand.

Tuesday. He is rather partial to Lapsang Souchong and gentleman's relish thinly spread on hot white toast with the crusts cut off and says that my wife makes a simply wonderful banana cake ("Man cannot live on bread alone," he quotes from his book) and he also likes the way she carries herself, whatever that means.

Wednesday. Our Witness says that he was sent to us by Jehovah to help us come to terms with the stresses of modern living and that as a part of the process of (as he puts it) detoxification, he'd be willing to throw himself completely at our disposal and he especially wants to help my wife come to terms with her role as the homemaker.

Thursday. At my wife's suggestion ("Pick up thy bed and walk," she said with a tad too much frivolity) he's moved onto the top floor and we can hear him rearranging the furniture to better suit his particular requirements.

Friday. He's persuaded me to take up his cause so I'm out on the streets trying to spread his word and stuffing copies of The Watchtower through people's letter boxes while he's at home presumably spreading my wife's legs in a direction they haven't enjoyed for some years and pushing the senses way past her welcome mat and a long way past my patience. ("The Lord moves in a mysterious way His wonders to perform" and "Vengeance is mine. I will repay, says the Lord.") Alleluia and Amen!

Nema indeed! Man became man when he found tools and shelter. Some had possessions. Some became possessive. Tools and shelter became more important than anything else, more important than his spirit. Take two men out of a total population of twenty-six. A has more about him than B so, nine times out of ten, A will try to have a controlling influence over B. A has the tools and he allows B to use them in return for a fee.

B might accept the position. He might be grateful for it. His aspiration or requirement might be for what is termed a simple or steady existence. As long as he can get the tools and shelter he needs from A, he's content to pay up, so A prospers over B's toil. Along comes C and D, E and F, some of whom have the same attitudes and sympathies as B but some who have more ambition and drive than B: but none of them have the tools. The five of them get together and are persuaded that by joining forces, B, C, D, E and F might get a better deal on the tools they need from A and therefore attain more reward for their work. So if you get my drift, A=B+C+D+E+F. But A was clever and he could see what might happen. He would not allow his tools to be hired out for anything less and he wanted to make sure he had enough of them for those that wanted and needed them. So he got G, a fellow of equal if not better calibre, to join him so he could provide more tools as well as sharing his vision for the future. This threw B, C, D, E and F into turmoil because now there were tools on offer from A and G at the same and established fee; so they set about recruiting more to join them. H, I, J, K and L came along and once again the balance between the two groups, tool providers and tool users, was restored. I think it was C that suggested that if they recruited M, N, O, P and Q to join them, they would have enough united clout to demand better terms and conditions and cheaper tools from A and G. G had a cousin once removed called R, who joined A and G and his youthful vigour and feisty know-how, when it came to providing tools, made him a fellow to be reckoned with. So the formula of balance between tool providers and tool users became:- A+G+R=B+C+D+E+F+H+I+J+K+L+M+N+O+P+Q. Of course you can see what happened next. S, T, U, V and W were coerced into joining the rank and file and, as quick as a flash, X was headhunted to join the tool providers as a tough negotiator and hard-headed tool providing businessman. Y won the lottery so didn't give a damn about tools at all. That left Z. Well, Z just slept all day as Z's do. His lethargy was legendary. He didn't bother about much and didn't need tools, didn't vote either, which was why the formula between tool providers and tool users didn't ever change. Occasionally man needed to be reminded.

áɕ̀-àā M̅M̅ : **Pit's end**

"Put that in your pipe Joe, smok it if you dares!"
I eyeballs 'im, he does same; "You best say bloody prayers."
"They'll never close pit, lad; they'll never shut us down.
Our man will win day, lad, he'll beat the Thatcher clown."
"I'm tellin' you the truth, Joe, coal has 'ad his day
and workin' men like you an' me must look for other pay."
"Yer talkin' through yer arse, lad. Arthur is the king
an' he'll not sell us out, lad, not for anything."

"Go and net that carp Joe, go and catch a pike!
It's no good getting gloomy man. Get out on yer bike."
But peddle as he does, there's nought for miles around,
nothing for a miner who's forced from underground,
who has to join the dole queue, sign up for that long line
and lose the sense of dignity from working down the mine.
It's sad for Joe and t'others from the rank and file;
put out on the slag heap to swell a useless pile.

Just like old Joe, his crooked pipe sits upon the rack,
an implement of yesterday and never coming back.
The pit wheel has stopped turning, the cage is broken up,

the black seam underneath us not worth a second look:
And all the generations who toiled for national wealth
are pages in a history book written out by stealth.
"Put that in your pipe Joe, smok it if you dares!"
I eyeballs 'im, he does same; "You best say bloody prayers."

Friends. Comrades. Spirits don't have them. They are not needed. Only the living cling to friendships like a picket to a factory gate or a limpet to a rock pool's rock. I have no friends, only passing acquaintances. There's no time to forge friendships because there is no time. I think if I was granted one wish, one request, a favour if you like, it would be for friendship. With friendship comes a host of baggage, though. Good and bad. Friends want to chat. Friends want to share. Friends want to involve you. They want to be involved. Some need you more than you need them, and some only need you some of the time. I've heard it said that you can choose your friends. Can you? Do you? Do they agree with the selection process? Isn't it that friends see something of themselves in the friends they make? Love your enemies, someone said, but that was bullshit. It's hard enough to love your friends! Human or inhuman; real or imaginary; fettered or foul.

áɕ̀-àā Ḿm̥ : **Bird talk**

The chickens were restless and some of them were not feeling very well.

"It's inevitable!" Brendahen was brooding on her perch. Her brown feathers puffed up across her breast. "It's coming whether we like it or not."

"Don't be such a clucking scaremonger," Paulinehen wasn't having any of it. "Look what a flap you caused about Last Time," all the others clucked noisily as if in agreement.

Brendahen looked ruffled. "Well, Last Time was serious," she said, trying to win back some sympathy. "Last Time they stopped eating our eggs for months," the shed went quiet. They'd all heard stories about the terrible cull. Brendahen continued. "We mustn't forget what happened to our mothers," the shed issued a collective cluck, an exclamation for the departed. Brendahen was winning them back.

"And our grandmothers and aunts. Don't forget them. And sisters, too. Some of us lost our sisters," Bettyhen chirped up, exaggerating the genocide. She was about to add cousins to her epitaph when she caught Paulinehen eyeing her up fiercely.

"Well, I still think you're worrying over nothing," Paulinehen didn't like the way things were going. She pecked at Bettyhen who scurried off into the crowd. Some chickens were so easily scared.

"This time will be far worse," Brendahen made her pronouncement. "This time they'll take us all out. We'll all go," the shed erupted as though someone had mentioned Colonel Sanders.

"Rubbish!" shrieked Paulinehen above the din. "You don't know what you're clucking about. You'll put us all off laying if you carry on like this."

"I wish it was rubbish," said Brendahen, "But Rufuscock, who as we all know keeps his beak fairly close to the ground, heard things. He heard that it was inevitable," the shed didn't like the sound of Brendahen's certainty. Uneasiness crept through the straw litter like the smell of a passing fox. Hens pecked nervously, twitched and jerked while others clawed at the ground; pretended to look for something or somewhere to hide.

"Well, what did old dry balls hear exactly?" Paulinehen wanted chapter and verse; wanted the others back on her side. Several hundred beady eyes looked up.

"Pandemic," said Brendahen importantly.

"Pan what?" said Paulinehen.

"Demic," said Brendahen.

"And what's a pandemic when it's at home?" asked Paulinehen in that sing-song, sarcastic way she sometimes used.

"Like bird flu," said Brendahen.

"And like worm crawled," said Paulinehen with a repeat of that sing-song, sarcasm to her cluck. Some of the others laughed. The hen's wit had eased the tension. Paulinehen was clever and the best flyer in the shed. She shook her wings as if to emphasise the point.

"How can flying cause a pan-what-you-may-call-it-demic?" She flustered some more and, encouraged by the other hens, leapt from the perch and, half gliding, half flapping tried to make it across the shed to a cobwebbed ledge beside the wired-up window. Her flight was unsteady and the short trip never looked that confident. Paulinehen had been showing off. She had wanted to impress the others as she had once before. Her concentration this time wasn't at its best and her frustration with Brendahen had taken it out of her. She collided with the metal pole that carried the overhead lighting, hit it hard and spiralled to the ground in an ungainly heap, landing in the scattering, noisy crowd, her wing broken and her left leg badly twisted.

That evening when Jack did his rounds to shut them in for the night, he found the wounded hen lying on the straw covered floor. He picked it up roughly and wrung its neck by twisting the bird round and round violently as he grasped its head in his clenched fist. It was a casual act and something Jack didn't bat an eyelid over.

His wife plucked and cooked the bird for them to eat and that was how the first case of Ebola fever came to Kent.

My name is very apposite. Eliza; not unlike Ebola, but a whole lot prettier. Eliza, the list maker. My god is oath. Hebrew. Elisheba. Not the diminutive Bethia which means worshipper of God. No. Eliza. Consecrated by God. A bountiful god. A god of plenty and joy. A god who passeth all understanding. A god who has given the living an inbuilt desire, an obligation, to procreate and that is why Man will eventually destroy the Earth. What was it that was preached? The meek shall inherit the earth. Won't they also bring about its demise by doing nothing about it? But hey. That's not my problem. Enough about serious philosophical thoughts or heavenly hallucinations and stirrings. Talking of which, do you drink tea? I haven't had a cup since, well, teatime. As it was set down on the console in front of me, I observed that there were ripples, tiny ripples, vibrating concentric circles. Difficult to say if from the centre outwards or from the outside in, the dancing waves were reflecting an outside influence. It was nothing from inside the teacup, nothing from the tea itself but rather a liquid canvas upon whose surface a message was being displayed. Imagine being able to take that thin layer, the skin on the top of the tea. Peel it off so that the vibrations, the message if you like, is captured and taken away. Now, even though the tea has lost its top, another will instantly take its place and the ripples will start again. But because you have removed a thin layer, because you have reduced the mass, depleted the volume, the ripples cannot be the same. The message will have a new meaning. It's like that with spirits. Peeling off the thin layer at a moment in time, a moment after life. I get the message and relay it. That's me. Eliza, the cup that cheers! Or as someone said about my namesake, "if you lay on soil of your own heart and sound; if you hear the pound as many suffer on the ground; you have all you need to win a battle but never decline a woman with a belief because we remember then and now." The prediction can be more easily swallowed if the predictor possesses a predilection to prettiness.

áś-àã M̀N: **Bats about the weather girl**

I tried to see her every day and got to understand the way in which she spoke or tried to say what had been and come what may:

How she moved and swept her arms, her sparkling eyes and female charms removed from me all silly qualms and blew away my false alarms.

She never had a face like thunder when precipitations spread around her; her silver lining burst asunder with settled outlook: little wonder.

Her weather words went pitter-patter. I tried to speak, could only stutter. My wings and heart were all a flutter. That smooth, white neck; oh let me at her!

And when she smiled, the moon shone bright (my teeth like stars came out at night) but I didn't care for she's just right and, even though she's not my height, I had to stretch to get the bite.
A vampire with a spider's might.

I love my weather girl.

Get on with your bloody life whatever the weather, whoever's the jugular. Cain and Abel attitudes win the day and piss off all you Good Samaritans. You'll take the law into your own hands, use all the bias claptrap that has been peddled your way by those with vested interests and the power of the people behind them. Beast-like, you'll follow the herd pushing and shoving to get to the front, baying for the sake of it, crazy for something, anything that will satisfy the red mist and allow you to get home and put your feet up; enjoy a cup of tea, dunk a biscuit, watch some telly, go to bed, shag, turn over and go to sleep with a clear conscience. Wake up to a world full of wailing and gnashing of teeth, oh ye of little worth and, even though your religion may allow you lip service to repent, you'll have to take your chance along with all the others in the Chamber, and Eliza doesn't suffer fools gladly.

áś-àā ḾṔ : **Catching the train**

It was the morning after the dreadful night before. He'd gone. Left early. Slammed the front door as if to punish the house for being there. She lay for a moment or two almost enjoying the relief, the calm after the storm. Then her baby cried, a delayed reaction, disturbed by the noisy exit and the shudder from downstairs that shook the whole house. She dragged herself out of bed and went to get the child.

It was a beautiful morning. The sky was flecked with fluffy clouds and a light breeze ruffled the leaves on the overgrown shrub by the front door. She put a fleece jacket over the baby's T-shirt just in case he felt the cold. Not yet a year old, she'd read somewhere in one of the baby books that they feel the cold so need double the layers that she did. She strapped him in the three-wheeled pushchair and manoeuvred its spoked wheels through the hall and out of the front door, locking it behind them.

The road from the village was narrow, a country lane, and people always drove too fast. She pushed the pram on the right-hand side of the road, walked towards any approaching traffic. There wasn't a lot and the three or four vehicles that passed her all slowed down when they saw her on the edge of the road. The blackberries were just ripening in the thick hedge and at a gateway she could see the sheep, heads down, grazing the still green grass. Her baby twitched, looked up at the sky, the top of the hedge perhaps, his mother's familiar outline.

She knew the quickest route to take. An even smaller lane turned right and she joined the less hazardous road, more able to relax without the traffic. The lane wound its way through the countryside following the course of an old drovers' track. The hedges were banked high on both sides and old trees overhung so that in places their branches reached across to touch each other. She was glad she'd put the extra coat on her baby. Out of the sunlight, the chill of the breeze became more cutting. The tramline wires strung out between the pylons crackled overhead, dangerously out of reach. She walked underneath them, heard the static charging down the lines, like a swarm of bees, and thought how it must be harmful to her baby's brain.

The metal gate guarded the route across the tracks and next to it the sign gave its warning. She opened the gate and wheeled the pushchair through. Her baby was asleep. The momentum of the journey had rocked him off. She shut the gate behind them and then, moving the pushchair ever so gently so as not to wake the baby, she parked it directly between the nearest set of rails. She put the brake on and then carefully leaned forward to touch the little boy on his cheek. She stroked the soft skin for a brief moment, then taking her hand away almost reluctantly;

she turned and squatted down next to the pram. She sat there between the metal rails, cross-legged like an Indian squaw. The two of them were waiting, one asleep, and the other out of her mind, waiting to catch the express train.

You could be forgiven for presupposing that my judgements are made purely on religious grounds. But if I tell you it's got nothing to do with religion and everything to do with the state of the spirit, then maybe you'll understand a bit more. It's belief that's important. But the real I.R.A., the Nazis and the Ku Klux Klan all believed with a passion! As the Mau Mau hacked into the white Kenyan farmer, the machete-bearer believed in what he was doing with all his heart. It's not that sort of belief they're interested in here. Not the lust for destruction but the longing for life. A belief in good, to use an old-fashioned term , and the way in which the spirit has shown willing. A spirit can believe all it likes, but unless it believes in a worthy exit then it serves itself poorly. The mother standing over her baby as the little elephant slowly dies because the rains are late; the way she sifts and lifts the dry dust and sprays it over her head in desperate despair and a forlorn hope that somehow the dirt will turn to water. She stands over the last gasps of her dying calf, trying to protect it from something she herself has no control over. She shows a longing for life and if she, too, was to succumb to the rigours of dreadful nature, she would at that moment be in a condition where her spirit would enter the appropriate Chamber with all the right attributes for G>R>E>E>N. So the Chamber doesn't care what label the body wore. There is no right or wrong religion despite what thousands of years, countless battles in the name of God, millions of deaths, have tried to establish. It's the longing for life that counts.

More than that. It's the longing for goodness in life, if I can put it that way. And the goodness of life walks quietly by, often unnoticed like a quick shadow, without fuss or much ado. Goodness has never been worthy of praise. Evil, if I can call it that, captures the imagination of Man on a much grander scale. Evil personifies more readily than goodness, so there are chambers full of 'sinners', but only a few shelves stacked neatly with 'saints'.

áɕ̀-àā Mɓ: **Edmondo's sigh**

Old Edmondo was glad that winter seemed to be at its end. The months of cold and damp had got to him as never before. These days he couldn't seem to get warm. The fire hissed at him, the reluctant logs too sappy, too wet to take up the offer at once, and when the flames did lick into action, beating the thick woodsmoke to bring some flickering, dancing, brightness into the room, Edmondo couldn't feel their warmth until he'd held his worn and wrinkled hands out towards them for a minute or two. Even then and almost stroking the flames, he had to rub his hands together, like dried leaves, to get the coldness out of the joints in his fingers. Those fingers that had gripped and toiled, clawed and wrung, pointed and poked and picked. Dirty, broken nails and cuts and calluses from a life of manual labour; Edmondo's hands were his tools, the tools of his trade and even more than the heavy lines on his face, his deep brow set above those watery old man's eyes, his hands told of his tale as a mountain man.

The lighter mornings meant that he'd be up, the dog fed, and chopping his kindling before seven and then the first cup of sweet, dark coffee and mouthful of bread by half past. It had been a long winter and the snow had covered the hillside for many months. From the back door to the wooden outhouse the ground looked surprised. Edmondo had cleared a path and, even though the snow had tried to take control, the old man and his wide snow shovel had won the battle. The ground was dark, dirty and damp, like a healing scar, and the banked snow hung around at the margins, pockmarked with cold, grey ash from the fire, looking lumpy and off-white heaped there by the old man's efforts rather than by nature herself. The hillside was still muffled, blanketed in white, but Edmondo could just make out the sound of running water, the first sign of the thaw as the hidden stream took itself off down the slopes to the valley bottom. A sigh of relief from the running water that winter seemed to be at its end.

The buzzard mewed somewhere above the tree line, out of sight but up there circling slowly, hunting, looking from above at anything brave enough to break cover and dart across the white ground. A furry snack taken, stabbed to a violent death by the razor-sharp, swooping, hooked beak and carried lifeless but still warm up the hill out of harm's way for the big bird at least. Edmondo heard that call. He stopped and looked up, hugging the logs to his chest as though it was them being hunted, but he didn't see the kill and shuffled back inside to stack the wood beside the fireplace so that it would appreciate its purpose. He'd have that bird before spring was over. He'd have it before it could take any of the newborn.

Edmondo wiped the end of his cold, wet nose across the back of his cold, hard hand. The snail-like trail rubbed off onto the well-worn, faded, blue overall he wore day in, day out and mixed in with the living culture that, like millions of moving spores on a Petri dish, waved welcome to the new arrival. The cocktail of the grime fermenting on Edmondo's mountain uniform comprised snot and dust and grit and smoke from the fire, oil from the chainsaw, grease, duck fat, sheep dip, grass, sweat, red wine, spittle, soot, blood, eau de vie, coffee, nicotine, paint, goat's cheese, white spirit, creosote, diesel fuel, battery acid, urine, kerosene, candle wax, cassoulet, gun oil, dog hair, lichen, rat poison, honey, moss, WD-40, saucisse, earth, cèpe, tree bark, pot-au-feu, sawdust, butter, tobacco, salt, chocolate, semen, whiskey and shit.

There was Brebis, too, and Edmondo cut himself a piece to go with the dry bread, already stale from yesterday's oven. His teeth, like those of an old ram, pushed through the ewe's cheese, broke the bread, and the Madiran, red and rough, washed round their jagged edges, a rising tide of Tannat grape juice off to meet and scuff the old palate just like the start to most days. He spat back at the fire, a piece of reddened cheese rind, and spun another log into the big hearth. A shower of sparks stuttered upwards and disappeared around the greasy, blackened roasting spit and up the dark chimney, up to the clean, fresh mountain air.

The sun came round and over the opposite peak at eleven and the shadows retreated across the hillside in a race to hide from the glare. The reflection of the sun off the snow was as bright as a blast furnace. Edmondo squinted as he sat by the wooden table set up against the outside wall of the hut. The table he'd made served him well. He took his midday meal off it when he was there and not out and about on the hillside. He gutted rabbits on it. He fixed things on it, sawed wood or wired snares. Oiled his gun and drank his wine. He sat and watched as the power of the sun crept nearer and nearer. His eyes gushed, he blinked to clear them and then the rays met him, at first quite gently, and then, suddenly, full on. The warm spring sun-shine, the first for months, bored into him. Edmondo felt the warmth. He closed his watery eyes. The sun burnt its way into his old bones and he sat with his back against the hut wall, his face to the sharp glow, his grey hair pushed back from his forehead, and he sighed. It was a big sigh, a sigh of relief that winter seemed to be at its end.

He daydreams and dozes and the rays wrap him up and carry him away. He is by his fire, the centre of his life, the giver of heat and light and nourishment. Then he stoops in the woods, precariously balanced on the steep slope, his chainsaw shaking and cackling like a dreadful jagged-toothed beast as he cuts what he chooses, slashes years of woody growth in just a few high-pitched moments to give him the fuel for the hub of his life. The oil spits off the flying chain when he guns the motor and makes its dark, wet mark of warning, oil and grease, that vital cocktail for smooth running. He can now smell the fat as it oozes from the duck breast cooking on the home-made metal grill, the two pieces of ironwork he crafted for the purpose between which he can burn his meat in the open flames of his fire. Cook his meat but not his hands. Bon appétit and then down to the penned flock and each animal's submersion in the potent brew that kills everything and even gets to grown men in the end if they aren't careful about protecting themselves. The sheep's reward for the shocking dip is to be let out onto the grass, the mountain sward thick with a million flowers. And while the ewes settle heads down, the sweating labourer takes a sip or two of red wine from the leather gourd and spits at a job well done. The soot that marks the fleece of each and the blood from nicks where the shears have overdone their cutting at their rears are washed away like the end of a good feast with strong, white eau de vie, black coffee and a roll-your-own so strong it can strip the paint off an oak door. A wedge of goat's cheese with the taste of her udders and dry hillside grass is cut with the Laguiole, the one with the bone handle, the one that he's had with him all his life. The next chore to soften the round and stumpy bristles on the brush with white spirit and work in another coat of creosote to the outbuilding's wood. It smells strong like the diesel fuel kept in jerrycans inside the timber building next to the defunct generator. It hasn't worked for years since the battery acid had corroded the lead. He's going to fix it one day. Perhaps. He stands and relieves himself outside before carrying in a tin of kerosene to fill the lamps. He has to light a candle to see what he is doing. The hot candle wax slides down his thumb and becomes firm, sets like a raised white scar. It is later than he thinks; gloomy inside. Maybe cassoulet for supper, out of the tin or maybe the stew will stretch another day. First he's going to clean the carbine and in doing so excites the dog, sulky for lack of gun, jumping with false joy at the thought of the hunt at dusk. Instead he throws a stick and the hound bounds off to fetch and returns with the lichen-speckled branch, a testament to the pure air and the dog's love of attention. He mustn't get to the rat poison that killed his mother and extra care is taken with hiding the deadly bait. She's buried up where the bees make their honey under a mossy bank with a simple shard of rock to mark her faithfulness. As the light begins to fade, the hands are cleaned with the spray from the can. WD-40 smells as though it should be good and if it takes rust off metal, it must make light work of dirty hands, no doubt about it. The lamps are lit and the saucisse unhooked from the nail in the beam and sliced, thinly cut on the table top ready for the evening feed. The fire is stocked up with an earth-covered log the size of a small tree, the one where the cèpes grew and it won't take without the help of the dry tree bark stacked under it to encourage the fire to life again. The pot-au-feu, made three days before, in its cast-iron cauldron, is slid onto the oven top and a handful of sawdust sprinkled into the mouth of the cooker to get the fire up and running under the big vessel. There's rancid butter with the stale bread tonight to make it less so. A cigarette is smoked almost with every mouthful and salt is heaped on everything in handfuls. For afters it's thick, dark, chocolate for the old man's sweet tooth and out comes the dog-eared girly magazine with faded photos of busty Parisian beauties with saucy, come-to-bed looks so that without much fuss he takes himself in hand, gives himself a little treat. Then another, long-lasting one; a glass of whiskey with no water in a strong, chunky, tumbler sipped with content and before bed, defecation.

Sitting in the mountain sunshine, warm for the first time in months, it was his time to go, a change to the routine. They found old Edmondo stiff as the boards he was propped up against.

Down in the village they say that if you're up in the hills and you stop and listen carefully you might hear a sigh, and that winter seems to be at its end. They do say on the first day of spring you can hear Edmondo's sigh.

Nature or nurture, somebody said, trying to be really clever with words that have similar rhythm. Is the code generated from its inception, 'good' or 'bad' or does it become one or the other with the passage of experience? I don't know. The powers that be suggest that infants can do no wrong, so they must favour the theory of nurture. A baby can't be evil so our instructions in the Chamber are to give them a G>R>E>E>N ticket. So let's say the choice is now yours. Heaven forbid! At what stage in his development do you condemn, say, Hitler as a dude with a bad code? Day one nestling in Frau Hitler's arms, is he bad? Was he created bad? Certainly had Herr Hitler, while holding his new-born son and cooing and gooing over him for the first time, slipped and dropped baby Adolf on his still soft new-born skull, the world would probably be a little different. Or would it? Another might have taken his place and all the things that happened as they did, would still have occurred. Aged three when he took his first steps, presumably not goose steps, was the infant Hitler thinking bad thoughts? Was his spirit already calculating the invasion of his neighbours and the launching of a master race? At what age did he take a dislike to the Jews? Did one of them punch him in the playground? So was young Adolf a bad'un from his very first cry? You don't know! You cannot judge! It's easy with the benefit of hindsight. Very easy. Slip his code into R>E>D and that's an end to it. But had his spirit been presented before his first birthday then the rules would have been different. So if nurture is important in deciding an outcome, then there is real scope for influence. Good parenting, exemplary coaching, peer persuasion with positive purpose, all helping to shape that code, point it in the right direction. Come in useful or divert the course a spirit might otherwise take. Now there's the dilemma.

áǝ-àā ḾṔ: **Titanic**

"More ice, please, steward. I say more ice if I may... you can never have too much ice with a gin and tonic, don't you know."

"Couldn't agree more, dear boy. A tip-top cocktail often rests on a bed of the cold, white stuff. That and a twist of something sour. Takes a good man to mix a good drink."

"Takes a good man to down it, don't you know."

"There was this excellent chappie in the Long Bar, an Indian of all the sorts, and he could rustle up a concoction that would really hit the spot. He'd smear the glass with a drop or two of bitters and then shake the thing dry and apply the gin so that the resultant brew looked as pink as a petticoat. It slipped down like a bad girl's drawers."

"Gupta."

"What?"

"Gupta. That was the punkah wallah's name, don't you know."

"I think you're right. Didn't like anything piscatorial or the sea. Made him as sick as a dog apparently."

"Wouldn't have liked it out here, then. Southampton to New York a ruddy long way on the water, don't you know."

"He'd be tickety-boo on this voyage. Big ship like this. Size of several hotels, shouldn't wonder. Firm as a maiden's bedhead."

"Unsinkable, don't you know."

"So they say. Ruddy marvellous what they can come up with in nineteen twelve."

"Very comfortable. Very comfortable, don't you know. But where's that ice?! Steward! Where's the ice, man? Ice, don't you know!"

"Probably gone off to find an iceberg."

You build for yourselves comfortable lives only to have them cut short and, even though you appreciate your own fallibility, you never learn that it's not always you that calls the shots. One minute safely on track, the next completely off the rails or ploughing into the inconvenient buffers of termination, those stalwart marshals at the end of the line. The half-life of facts is a shattering reality. It's when you thought what was, is no longer. The exact measurement in height of the highest mountain on planet Earth turns from one set of figures to another. Makes liars out of those once trusted. Avoidance language tries to explain the change but fails dismally. Secular stagnation as a result of income inequality runs amok, and those in the theatre that have come to hear the great poet's work pretend to understand every word when they can hardly grasp the meaning of every other one. In the Chamber everything is in black or white; green or red, actually, but you know what I mean. There's no room for ambiguity. Bullshit, even in teeny-weeny traces, will be found out. Lies laid bare. Pomposity popped. Ignorance no excuse. Indolence inexcusable. Politics pointless. Hot air as hopeless as hopscotch on water. Hiding behind a mask as futile as standing in front of one. If you get my drift.

áś-àā ḾǪ: **Roots and a whisper**

"Welcome home!" it screams. In his dreams it screams and he wakes, tries to shake the echo from his hurting, pounding head. Not just his bed head. A sound that in the no-surprise, high-rise springs open doors and causes shouts of, "Keep the f'ing noise down!" His usual surroundings are littered with bold and unforgiving man-made solid, sordid urban, suburban trappings. All brick, tarmac, concrete and graffiti. Streety graffiti he calls it. No entry and street signs telling, yelling at those that can read and those that can't what they can and cannot do. Neon splashes, DayGlo dashes and exhaust fumes, the constant hum and buzz of background city noise with the crescendo of over-worked, over-revved Vespas and the deep thump of drum and bass, the big boom boxes set into the tiny go faster, boy racer Astras and silly little, willy tickle, Fords. Oh for a big-bonneted V8 with fat rubbers, a great, big, throbbing, fanny magnet. Need to trade more for one of those. Less up the nose or in the arm, more in the pocket. F'it. Needle up, Nellie, and don't spare the horses!

Baa baa black sheep, to try and break his nasty habit they put him on a bus, a National coach, and it rolled out through the stop-start traffic and onto the motorway until that turned into something like that old rifle, the 303. Go West, young man he hums to himself. And he does. From his grey gangland precinct to the rolling green hills of a distant aunt. Her big-bosomed warm bread kitchen apron smell and Aga smile, like an old fat cat with a lagoon full of fresh milk. Like opening a door to Heaven. How, he wondered, could anybody live so close and yet so far? So tied in and knotted up with express relief just a coach seat away or a cheap day return. The electronic tag of wayward lad snapped asunder, brushed aside and in its place thick, green, ankle-deep grass, the deepest he'd ever seen. Thicker than Carpetright, a shag pile to shag and die for. Better even than a BMW. A low-mileage 7 Series at that.

Kick off the flashy trainers. Walking boots or wellies, leather or rubber to keep out the wet, either daisy root does the job, protects those feet in whose ancient footsteps he traces his route through the fields, along the well-marked footpath to the mound, that great burial hill, where the spirits of the long-dead linger between the roots of the wind-bent thorn bush. What stories they have to tell! They marched them up to the top of the hill and they marched them down again. Sitting on the hillside out of the wind he can hear them whispering. They gossip of Saxon skirmishes and the plague. Ring a ring o' roses, a pocket full of posies. One whisper in particular catches his attention, makes sort of sense as it emerges from the wind, surfs above it, with it, to broadcast a clear message away from all the others. It gobsmacks him in the lughole.

"Welcome home!" it shouts.

He watches a walker with his dog (he carries a stick). How much is that doggy in the window? A young Jack Russell, as vibrant as a leaf tossed by a gale, barks with delight. Their springtime stroll through dripping fields where dandelions roar and shake their glistening, cobwebbed manes and buttercups blaze their yellow streaks between the sodden green blades, the teaming, steaming sward seethes between their legs. Blackbirds hop and flap like competing teams of lazy ballroom dancers and off the excited terrier goes after them with little hope prancing through the meadow, leapfrogging damp tufts in a headlong dash to catch one unawares, the preening, scheming bird. He never does, never comes close, but always runs back to heel as though he had and gets the nod, the look of approval and a smile or a laugh out loud that sets him off again on another wild goose chase to try for murder in the murder. Watching that dog chasing crows, knowing that neither of them will ever catch one; what simple fun it is, what a glorious pastime; not a moment wasted so he could spend all day, a lifelong quest, watching that dog chasing crows. The one with the waggly tail. Nothing is absurd in this beautiful countryside and everything is as strange as life on a Mars.

Certainly the chirrup of grey partridge, a rare English treat, in their covey out of sight but in earshot, refocuses attention. On the hillside the vixen smiles and licks her lips, stops in her tracks, then hurries off, making a note to return at dusk. The rabbits play a game of tag not far from the safety of their bank, their warm burrows tucked into the grassy contours. They dart off with the white tips of their tails bobbing like the youth club's ping-pong balls on a sea of green. See green and white. A beautiful pea green boat. The breeze plays across the fields and takes the growing crops this way and that. That and this. We'll never walk alone. A million waving stems in a crowd acting as one, looking like water but actually wheat or barley or hairy oats, rye grass or oil-seed rape waiting to turn yellow but all still green, too green to combine. Too wet to cut the mustard. Clouds float like dollops of clotted cream on a blue tablecloth with the warm sun the master of ceremonies for a few daylight hours at least. And what's so strange is that he knew he was home. Home in this absurd, over-coloured chocolate box, Disneyesque landscape without a knife to cut anyone who dared to look him in the eye or give a cheeky glance. Diddle diddle dumpling my son John. Back to his roots. Before he even heard that whisper. "Welcome home," the wind cries and he feels that he is.

It's little surprise he finds his name cut into the gravestone in that overgrown churchyard. Down in the hamlet off the moor, stepping back. There it is, just visible through the lichen and ivy, carved, probably, by a West Country stonemason back in 1649 when King Charles had lost his head. Those that plotted against him had it cut off with one quick blow on a cold winter's morning and so as not to shake with the icy blast, shiver so the crowd would think him a chicken, the king had worn an extra shirt. Wrap up warm, Your Highness. Here comes the chopper to chop off your head.

There he was, back then, spelt the same as he is now. His family came from these parts but his roots like those of the thorn bush had been lost, buried in the mound and the churchyard just waiting for the whisper in the right ear to bring the lost son back home.

Like the monarchy, restored.

Incy wincy spider climbs the waterspout. Woven through the years, spun across the decades, spiders work their cords everywhere. The trillion silky strands stretched out from the graves in that churchyard across the country lane, from hedge to hedge, nearly more violent, more destructive than anything on earth. All those spiders work in vain. He can see the lines, fine and glistening when the sunlight catches them just before the white van: there are white vans even in these parts plying their trade, but not a black face anywhere other than the sheep; just before the vehicle slices through the lifelines without even knowing what it's done. He snorts up his own thin white line in the graveyard, crouching behind the old stone to give himself a boost. Life over death. With their eight legs the spiders work eight zillion times harder to trap their prey but white vans will always be a gigantic catch too far, a morsel beyond their comprehension, until they stop their engines and rust away and then the spiders will triumph. When dusk comes the wind will be fumbling in the semi-darkness and brushing off the cobwebs that cling to everything. They blow, billow, like very fine, dusty net curtains drawn to the low harvest moon. Spiders were here before the dinosaurs and their webs will hang around long after all the people have gone. Dead and buried. Night night. Sleep tight. Mind the bugs don't bite.

There's no double take again when another name the same jumps off the war memorial, the inscribed plaque stuck to the limewashed wall inside the honey-coloured church. It swims his way and he makes sense of the familiar letters. When at eleven o'clock on November 11th the guns fell silent and tens of millions sighed with one terrible breath, those with ghastly, black bayonet holes, home to the rat and a place for the bindweed to take root, how does your garden grow from the dark,wet bottom of their muddy, unmarked mass graves, some sculptured by metal bullets punctured and pocked like grotesque sponges, some ripped apart in little pieces hung out across the cruel barbed wire, torn limb from bloody limb by high-explosive blast, some gassed and blinded, racked with a deadly, drowning cough and those missing, erased from the face of the earth, while the rest were driven stark staring mad: pretty maids all in a row. Every year since when the bugle sounds the last post, the Glorious Dead fall in for the ghostly parade that stretches further than the eye might see across continents and generations. Just one in that long, long line, his relative, someone from his family tree marched off from the county town with that 303 over his shoulder, his chest out and a swagger in his youthful stride never to return to the gentle English countryside, bombshells for birdsong, dark Somme ooze for light Devon chalk. All the king's horses and all the king's men couldn't put him together again.

"Welcome, Somme!" the shout went up from the enthusiastic marching men.

"Welcome home," the word came softly back.

At his demise he won't, God willing, be taken by an axe, Saxon, Roundhead or otherwise. The plague won't swell his tongue, nor will bullets or bombs rip him apart or gas and vile noise send him to his grave raving mad. Couldn't put Humpty together again. He won't be road kill, fingers crossed. Nor will he slip away, propped up in some NHS Trust bed, his heart's valves flapping like a Tesco shopping bag in a windy car park before they send him off to the crematorium. Send for the doctor to be quick, quick, quick. His ashes could be spread on that mound where he sat and watched the Jack Russell chasing crows, where the fox takes the partridge poults if she can, barks and skins the young rabbits, where the spiders plot their next webs and where his forebears whispered and will whisper again, "Welcome home."

Instead they find the young man slumped by the stump, his bandana tied around his arm, pumped-up veins ripe for another pricking. He'd over-done it. It was all too much. The tears on his young cheeks leave a telltale trail more heartbreaking than the wounds on his arm or his gang's tawdry stamp. Their mark of approval and sell-by date. Jack fell down and broke his crown. He'd overdone it in the long grass on his day in the country. They took him back to town, back to the familiar places where he had grown up, back home to where the spring showers gave way to city drizzle. The pathetic drops blurred the windows like melting plastic so that no one really knew what they were looking at anymore.

Man has a weakness for stimulation. Snakelike, not satisfied in your own skin, you'll experiment with dubious mantels. Some of them will work; provide harmless extensions, a side-track meander from the dull route march. Music and art some such welcomes. In all its forms a language that every star can share, no matter its degree of sophistication. Outside influence may be controlled. Tears will be stemmed eventually and memory kicks in like an image burnt deep into a disc to be retrieved at will. Inside influence is altogether another kettle of fish. Not to be ignored, waved goodbye, dismissed, put behind you, taken back, brushed aside or flushed away, that which is ingested, absorbed into the vital system, can never be touched lightly. Who can judge that the dry Amontillado the midwife sips after her tiresome delivery is any worse than the hot teaspoonful of heroin shot so urgently into the punctured tattooed forearm of the teenage mother who has just had the child. One puff, one sip, one sniff, one taste and one may do one's head in.

áś-àā Mq : **Dulcet tones**

When Dolcie's head hit the pillow, her torso slid onto the bedroom floor and ended up alongside the old tallboy, the one she'd inherited from her uncle. Her violent killer had despatched her and her partner with such ferocity that it would take the very best that Mr Dulcet's cleaning company could come up with to remove all the traces of the dreadful event and make the bedroom once again habitable. Mr Dulcet had become an expert in such things. What he didn't know about the removal of those tricky bloodstains from the skirting boards was nobody's business. Well, no live body's business.

Founded in 1942 by Reggie Dulcet senior and fairly quickly given a rather useful business leg-up by the Luftwaffe, Mr Dulcet's cleaning company cleaned up in the East End. Its next big break came in December 1951 with the Gillingham bus disaster. The sixties saw a lot of tidying up after the Kray twins, and the seventies bought the IRA to London and more work for the third generation of Dulcets. The eighties provided, as history and Companies House would show, rather thin pickings for the specialist business but thanks to frugal management, fastidious Jewish accountants and an unorthodox approach to supplementing the income, Mr Dulcet's cleaning company survived right through to the present day. Given, as they were, the key to the door, temptation to bolster turnover by plundering the goods and chattels of the unfortunate was too much to bear. The light-fingered habit first experienced by Reggie Dulcet senior became an ingrained and inevitable sideline shamelessly passed down through the generations. What the several Mr Dulcets lacked in take-home pay they more than made up for in takeaway booty.

Mr Dulcet always liked to quote for the main jobs himself. So he was first on the crime scene when the police, photographers and forensics had done their digging. Dressed in the regulation white bodysuit with its built-in hood and wrap-around footwear, Mr Dulcet entered the house looking rather like those that had just left it, but nothing like anyone who had crossed the threshold since Dolcie and her late husband had acquired the place in the nineteen eighties. He left the same premises looking a few sizes bigger, and the white protective suit had filled out to protect far more than its wearer.

Dolcie kept a tidy house. She was what some would term a house-proud person. She liked a place for everything and everything in its place. Her dusted collection of musical instruments stood as good testimony to her willingness to be openly judged as a woman of taste. When she said comfortable or vegetable she always prolonged the sound so that every vowel was pronounced as it was written. "Very com-fort-able," she'd declare as though she was speaking in time to a metronome. Her precision and attention to detail were just two facets that made her an accomplished music teacher. Music, however, was not the only food of love as far as Dolcie was concerned. Since her husband's passing and after a respectable interlude, she discovered that she needed the involvement of a good man or indeed two. Thus it was that unwittingly she stumbled into the path of her murderer. Jealousy, it seems, was a dangerous and unwelcome bedfellow and one that sadly lost Dolcie her organised head.

"I'm sure that Mother kept it there," said Megan when it was her turn to enter and inspect the cleaned property. Mr Dulcet couldn't throw any light on the missing possession and didn't say a word as he showed the daughter of the deceased his handiwork. Megan couldn't see anything different in her late mother's tidy home, which of course was why Mr Dulcet's cleaning company had the reputation it did. From a slaughterhouse to an ordered house, that was Mr Dulcet's unwritten slogan.

But there was no doubt about it. Dolcie's violin wasn't there. More to the point, it wasn't anywhere in the house and so was reported as missing, presumably stolen by the perpetrator of her murder. When in the process of their investigations the police eventually charged a local man with the double killing, it became clear that he only had one thing on his deranged mind. He wanted Dolcie and her partner dead because, as the arresting officer put it, the detained suspect was involved in a complicated and intimate relationship that involved both of the victims of the crime. The local hack would have put it more colourfully had his editor let him loose on the front page. "Music teacher plays love triangle."

The case of the missing violin, or more correctly the missing violin and its case, was puzzling. Megan knew that her mother had thought quite highly of the old stringed instrument. She had called it her "you-hou-dee" after Yehudi Menuhin, and no one was quite sure where it had come from other than from the same uncle next to whose tallboy Dulcie's torso had finally come to rest.

In stuffing the instrument down the front of his white all-in-ones, Mr Dulcet emerged from the home looking even more like the Michelin Man than when he had entered the building. He grabbed the case on his way out almost like a busy mum at a checkout snatching a bar of chocolate just because it was there. There was something else, too, that made him go for the neat, black leather case. He thought he recognised it, was almost positive that he'd seen it somewhere before. The faded rose emblem embossed onto the surface seemed very familiar. So he scooped up the prize almost with a feeling that it should belong to him, if it didn't already. Once safely in the van he extracted the case from out of his uniform and threw it in the back along with the tools of his trade and the paraphernalia of the professional forensic cleaner.

"Should be worth fifty quid," he thought when he finally opened the case in the safety of his own home and pulled out the handsome fiddle. He added it to the small pile of assorted loot he had acquired nearly every day that week. Little and often was what his father had told him. "A good man puts a little into kitty each day." Not one to upset the family code of practice, Mr Dulcet did as he was told. An old violin with catgut strings would, Mr Dulcet smiled to himself, be most apt in satisfying kitty that particular day.

And then he glanced at the photographs he had displayed in their assorted frames. His family looked out at him from the past. His father and mother with him on his father's knee. His proud grandfather surrounded by a ragtag gaggle of smiling children. He was wearing his flat cap and standing next to the horse and cart, and in his hand was a violin case. Mr Dulcet picked up the old photo frame and peered into it. There it was. The same instrument case he had brought home. The rose emblem just visible in the black and white image. What an extraordinary coincidence, he thought. By pure chance he'd stumbled upon something that his grandfather had owned or perhaps borrowed back in the forties. He took another look at the case and decided that he'd hang onto this particular prize. If it was once in the family then it should become an heirloom. He'd keep it.

Nearly every Saturday he took his week's collection along to his usual and willing contact and exchanged the stolen goods for cash. That particular week the contact was asked to pick up the goods because Mr Dulcet was otherwise engaged. Had he been at home when the contact called, Mr Dulcet would probably have hung onto his violin. But he wasn't and because it looked like part of the week's haul stacked up with the other bits and pieces, it was included at £45 as a part of the £649 tax-free payment left in the envelope, in folding, with no questions asked. Actually Mr Dulcet wasn't that bothered. It would have been nice to keep something his grandfather had once had, but never mind. Mr Dulcet went to bed and slept.

The same local newspaper (it also made the nationals) that had reported on Dolcie's murder and the arrest of her killer broke the news about the Stradivarius. There was little doubt about it and the insurance company confirmed as much, namely that Dolcie had indeed been the owner of a rare instrument. Much was made in the tabloids about the sale at the Tarisio Auctions of the Lady Blunt, a 1721 exquisite example of the master's craftsmanship sold for $15.9 million to an anonymous bidder in 2011. The Nippon Foundation auctioned the instrument to raise funds to help the Japanese tsunami appeal.

"Fuck-me-gently!" said Mr Dulcet which was quite a thing for a man who rarely swore. He was beside himself. Forty-five quid for something worth millions. How could he have been so dumb? He hurried off to find his contact and to retrieve his instrument. He felt sick. He felt angry. He felt confused.

The damp, open-air market in the East End was no place to create a scene. Mr Dulcet was determined that he wouldn't accost his contact in an aggressive way but so pumped up was he with anxious emotion that he leapt at the poor fellow and dragged him to the ground by his faded lapels.

"Where is it!? Where is it!?" was all Mr Dulcet kept saying to the terrified contact across whose chest the trembling Mr Dulcet sat like someone trying to cling onto a mechanical bucking bull. Obviously the prone contact didn't have the faintest idea of what his assailant was talking about. But Mr Dulcet was persistent. "Where is it!? Where's the violin!?" The garbled answer hit him like the aforementioned tsunami.

"Who the fuck bought it!?"

From the description he eventually got, Mr Dulcet realised that the purchaser of the priceless instrument was Megan, Dolcie's daughter. It all made perfect sense. She had obviously been trawling the markets and suchlike for her mother's stolen violin and had struck lucky. Mr Dulcet decided to go and see her. He took with him the photograph of his grandfather holding the violin case, rather awkwardly like a just landed fish.

"Yes, Mr Dulcet," said Megan. "I was very lucky. Found it as I thought I might at that big market, you know, in the East End. Got it back for sixty pounds."

Mr Dulcet's mouth was as dry as it had ever been. He had shown Megan the faded photo and she had studied the picture with a broad grim. She pointed to one of the children in the picture, a little girl with pigtails and long, white socks up to her bare knees and below her tatty, drab dress. Apparently her name was Dolcie and the man she knew as her uncle was the fellow holding the violin.

"Sixty quid?" said Mr Dulcet in a robotic tone of incredulity.

"You know it's a Stradivarius and probably worth at least five million pounds. If not more." Megan let the words trip casually, cruelly. "You Dulcets," she went on. "You might be good at cleaning up but you're not very bright when it comes to priceless possessions. Fancy losing the thing twice! I don't know, very careless. Finders keepers, losers weepers. Isn't that right, Mr Dulcet?" And she laughed as she shut the door on the crestfallen cleaner.

Mr Dulcet sat down heavily on the doorstep and felt his incredulity welling up from inside. With his head in his hands he started to nod from side to side and very quietly at first a wail could be discerned and, increasingly pumped by his leaden lungs, the sound grew into something primeval; the sound of despair, an alarm, a lament, a cry for help, a summons, a warning, a siren. It was indeed a dulcet tone, thought Megan as she put her kettle on.

Wooden-hearted makes a brew, maple, spruce and willow, too.
Walking trees have no knees, stalking trees don't need leaves;
stomping through the undergrowth, thin as sticks with little girth,
giant woodland on the march, moving forward, "Come on, Larch!"
Like that wood in the Scottish play, transformed in a magic way;
rootless, branchless, without ties, stretching up before our eyes.
These aren't trees with wood and bark, but aliens landed from the dark
and they will take us one by one, pulp us, bleach us in the sun;
not saw, nor fire, will cease advance, until they have us not by chance.
We'll end up wrapped in wooden box taken from the marching copse
not cleansed or purged from all our sins; still plucking at our violins.
Eliza writes prompted by the codes. Their creation gives inspiration.
That rhymes with anticipation. So wait for it! Hold your horses! It's
never over till the fat lady sings or the fiddle is stroked, coaxed, by a
hothouse whore keen to make melody.

áś-àā ḾQ̀: **Private Dicks**

These days he was never too sure where his wife was or what she got up to when she wasn't with him. Their marriage had been a 'good one' and for ten years they had enjoyed each other. Their relationship hadn't been passionate, although in the beginning there was lust. Sex on the freezer had been quite hot and the dining room table had seen some decidedly intimate and different culinary episodes. But that was back then. Nowadays it was a Sunday morning squeeze if the dogs would allow it, or the occasional grapple in bed when the lights went out if he hadn't drunk too much and she didn't have a headache. Admittedly she would have liked children but he wasn't so bothered by the lack of them and besides, they did have the Labradors.

Recently she had joined a health spa which in itself wasn't a bad thing as it kept her away from him when he wanted time to himself. Time to himself, however, got him thinking about why she had wanted to join a gym. The thought grew and like unchecked ivy spread around the trunk of his thoughts, climbed up the bark of his emotions and threatened to strangle the fruit of his reason. That terrible suspicion brewed up by jealousy began to get at him.

"Oh I won't be long, darling," she sang to him as she almost skipped out of the front door. "See you later," she called as the thing slammed shut, cutting off her cheerfulness and trapping his suspicion.

He wasn't happy. He imagined that she was up to some mischief: being unfaithful, and if that was the case, well, she'd better look out. He'd been toying with the idea of following her, but knew that she'd be on the lookout if she was up to no good and besides, the Range Rover Sport with his personal number plate was a bit of a giveaway.

He grabbed for the Yellow Pages and looked up 'detective'. He found 'detective agencies' after 'design consultants' and before 'dieting and weight control'. There were several listed, most featuring logos with either drawings of a magnifying glass or a close-up of the human eye. One even had the picture of a bloodhound and most were endorsed by something called the Association of British Investigators. He chose one of these and dialled the number, straight away hanging up when he heard a voice answer. He was being ridiculous and he had no reason to suspect his wife of anything.

"Good God, man," he said to himself. "You're becoming paranoid. She's just out getting fit and that's all there is to it."

If absence makes the heart grow fonder, then the husband didn't have a heart. His wife's increased time away was in direct proportion to his increased concern, and the relationship was beginning to suffer.

"I'm surprised you haven't wasted away completely with all that exercise you're doing." It was a combustible comment like the scraping of a Swan Vesta which lit that particular fire.

"Don't be so bloody silly. If you took the time to do some exercise yourself, you'd probably be less bolshy and a bloody sight fitter!"

"There's nothing wrong with my body."

"That's a matter of opinion."

"Oh yes. Whose?"

"Mine. For a man of your age you are getting too fat."

"I'm perfect for my height."

"Not for mine."

"What?"

"Nothing. It doesn't matter."

"It bloody well does."

"It's just that I'm keen to keep fit and you don't seem to care anymore. You're just letting yourself go to seed and..."

"And you want to run about in your bloody skintight leotard with your personal trainer ogling at your tits..."

"Don't be silly. It's not like that at all..."

The row went on like that until she went off to bed, leaving him to Kirsty Wark.

The next day his wife went out after a light breakfast and didn't come back until four in the afternoon.

"Good session?" he asked on her return in a way that implied more than a workout on a treadmill.

"Yes thank you," she replied as though she'd been sitting innocently astride a rowing machine.

Her morning departures and evening arrivals continued and he became as wound up as the grandfather clock that stood in the hall. He called another detective agency listed in the Yellow phone book and arranged a meeting with them that day.

"You can come here," he said undeterred by the response of, "OK, sir. How do we find you?"

The interview was pretty straightforward and the fresh-faced private investigator, who looked as though he'd come straight from college, took notes and a recent photograph of the wife as she appeared in her bikini on a beach in Barbados.

"You'll know her when you see her," said the husband obviously and the private investigator agreed that he would.

After a week there was nothing to report. The private investigator returned to visit the husband and delivered his findings which were that there was nothing to report.

"She just spends all the time at that bloody gym?"

"Yes."

"And there's no hanky-panky with anyone there?"

"Absolutely none at all. I can confirm from someone on the inside and from at least two other reliable sources that your wife spends her time working out in the gym, using the pool and the spa; that is the sauna and steam rooms and twice in the week she had a massage, again kosher, and on three occasions went to the restaurant for the healthy option luncheon. It's all here. Written down by the hour." The fresh-faced private investigator handed over a brown A4 envelope and looked very pleased with himself.

"So she's not up to anything at all?"

"No. Nothing out of the ordinary. She's obviously very keen on keeping fit and I'd say you're a very lucky man."

The private investigator was given a cheque for his company's services and his opinion about his client's luck was noted but not agreed with.

Despite the written evidence the husband wasn't convinced. His wife had the sort of spring in her step that reminded him of their early days together. He knew that she was playing away but couldn't prove anything. So another phone call produced another private detective who was briefed on the job of wife-watching.

"Make sure you keep an eye on her in that gym because I know she's up to no good."

The newly commissioned private detective was an ex-Army type and he was determined to apply his military precision and years of training to the job in hand. His ex-sergeant major's moustache stiffened in anticipation of the new task.

His report, too, confirmed that nothing was going on.

"At ten-hundred hours the quarry was seen entering the hotel spa reception area. At ten-o-three, having signed in, the quarry received a white towel, a standard spa issue white towelling dressing gown and a white pair of towelling flip-flops, and proceeded to the ladies' dressing rooms. At ten seventeen the quarry was seen entering the gymnasium complex where she mounted a static bicycle and proceeded to pedal for a period of fifteen minutes. The peddling started at a fairly slow rate timed at thirty revolutions a minute and this went up to..."

"Yes. Yes," said the husband, completely exasperated by the private investigator's delivery. "I know all that. Was the bloody woman caught with her knickers down?"

The ex-sergeant major confirmed that at no time had the quarry been caught in a "compromising position".

The investigator duly dismissed, the husband considered the latest report on his wife. The description of her as "the quarry" did nothing to alleviate his doubts. The picture in his mind of someone mining in the quarry became rather too vivid, so he called a third agency.

The private investigator arrived (this one looked rather like John Humphrys of the BBC) and he was taken through the same brief that his two predecessors had been given.

"Right ho, then. I'll keep an eye on the good lady for you," he said in a way that sounded a bit like John Humphrys from the BBC.

A week later and the report from the John Humphrys look-alike confirmed that the suspect under surveillance was just keeping fit.

"Is that all?" said the husband in complete disbelief and almost disappointment.

Determined not to be beaten, like a man on a mission, the husband sought help from a top team of private investigators from London.

On the recommendations of one of his chums in the bank, and without actually disclosing the real need for the service (he made mention of a lost Labrador), he got in touch with an agency that advocated the use of "hunting in packs". As the MD of the firm told his new client, "It's our firm's creed that three heads are better than one, that's why we call ourselves Sixth Sense." The husband didn't get it and looked momentarily puzzled. "Three heads equals six eyes and six ears, hence Sixth Sense. With our team you get three private investigators on the job."

The trio were set to work on gathering evidence. They looked like Essex nightclub bouncers with shaved heads and the sort of physique that said, "Don't muck with me."

Two weeks later back in the offices of Sixth Sense, the news about his wife's activities was no different. The black binder with neatly typed script and photographs confirmed that it was keep fit on the agenda and nothing in the form of any unusual extra-curricular activity.

The husband was mortified. He was also getting somewhat concerned about the thousands of pounds he was spending having his wife watched. Money didn't grow on trees, although in his case it did accumulate rather nicely from the hedge fund.

"If you want a job doing properly, do it yourself." The idea came to him one evening when he'd been leafing through "One Thousand Drawings " by Tracey Emin, a fat book printed on thin paper that confirmed to him that he could draw every bit as well as Miss Emin. He decided to join the health spa.

One morning after his wife had left with her usual sing-song, "Byeeee," an hour or so later he set off for the health spa. He parked his Range Rover next to her red BMW and went into the reception for his induction programme.

"I don't want my wife to know I'm here," he said to the pretty receptionist. "I'm going to surprise her with my new keep fit regime." The blonde smiled knowingly. She'd seen it all before: men trying to get fit for their women. Eric, in his smart tracksuit, showed him around and took him through a programme of exercises on the gym equipment.

"In just a week or two you'll notice the pounds dropping off you," said Eric, unaware of the thousands already spent by the new member just watching the place.

Eric left him to master a weightlifting machine and quite soon he had worked up a decent sweat. A dip in the pool would be good followed by a session in the steam room where he'd go and find his wife and surprise her. Just for good measure, he'd take his grandfather's old service revolver from the car, the one that had been languishing out of nostalgic curiosity at the back of the hall cupboard for years. He'd found some bullets, too, that slotted rather comfortably into the chambers. This would show her he meant business.

It was quite a surprise for all concerned. As he pushed open the door to the steam room and the wall of foggy heat hit him, he could just make out the shapes of some other bodies in the hot-house. Sitting on a wooden bench with nothing on at all was his wife, like a queen bee, and around her in a sort of admiring, dripping semicircle were six naked men, her workers. A sweaty, fresh-faced boy, an ex-sergeant major with a very droopy moustache, a damp John Humphrys look-alike, and three Essex nightclub bouncers each with a hard, glistening head.

"Hello there. Always room for one more," called out his wife through the thick, hot steam. "Let's see who he's sent me this time," she sang, sweating in the heavy atmosphere. "You can never have too many private dicks."

Is the anticipation more tantalising than the real event? Is the stalk

better than the kill, the striptease better than the bare naked result?
Death better than torture? Everlasting afterlife better than the here and
now? Who knows blue nose? I don't run Purgatory. There was only ever
one way out until Martin Luther pissed on that parade. Now you have
choice, whether you like it or not. So, my friends; take it without waiting!
How many holes in Blackburn, Lancashire? How many hoops in a
pack?
How many noughts and how many crosses to carry on your back?
How many moles for how many worms and how many wiggling hips?
How many deaths and how many births and how many fingertips?
How many people jump through rings in hope of finding what?
How many fools just sit and wait, content with diddly-squat?

áə̀-àã ɱíˀ: The waiting room

The airless waiting room smelt like grilled kippers and Dettol and could have been the antechamber to a fiery furnace. Every cough brought up more unwelcome flecks of germ. Every sniffle, even into a sodden tissue or handkerchief, oozed green and the slug-like slime trails on the backs of hands were rubbed dry on dreadful coats or anoraks. Children (there were three of them) rooted through the battered toy box without inhibition. The xylophone that clanked away when struck with the scarred wooden hammer made an awful noise. It, too, sounded sick. A brightly coloured plastic fire engine hurried across the patchy carpet and flew through the air for a moment, its chubby controller away with the fairies singing like a siren, nee nah, nee nah, nee nah. The fat mother of the boggy brats (one of them coughed like a coffee-making machine) tried her best to control her brood but soon gave up and hid in a copy of HELLO! She looked at the well-thumbed photos of C-listers, a million miles away from her damp terrace, and dreamed that one day her numbers might come good. Her coughing girl was in distress and she told her that if she didn't stop, the doctor would give her some foul-tasting medicine or, worse, he'd stick a needle in her bum. The child's cough diminished for a brief moment and then intensified with crying and streaky tears that washed down her inflamed cheeks. Everyone else in the crowded room pretended not to notice, quietly cleared their throats and got on with the waiting.

The information posters that overflowed the corkboard hung, Blu-Tacked, to the discoloured woodchip wallpaper. Some of them were straight but most were not, unlike the messages they brought. Smoking kills so give it up. The mother of three tried once but couldn't kick the habit of a lifetime. Have you got a sexually transmitted disease? Chance would be a fine thing, the old man thinks to himself. Are you pregnant? The mother of three might well be on her way to her fourth but she doesn't really know or care much. Do you suffer from prostate cancer? The middle-aged guy in suit and trainers does get up every night to have a pee, sometimes twice, but maybe that's just the beer talking. Do you need a jab for malaria? Not if we're going to Blackpool again this year, thinks the fair-haired woman with the trendy specs. Are you suffering from depression? He wasn't until he woke up this morning. Why not join our young mothers' yoga classes? Not sure they'd have me, but it might be a great place for trying to get my leg over. Do you use all your pills? Most of them, although he did slip some of the Viagra into the dog's food when he got pissed. Are you entitled to free prescriptions? Bloody right he is, worked for forty years in the biscuit factory, paid his stamps, bloody right he is. Do you have a car and want to become a hospital visitor? She thought about it once but tripped and fell so became the visited. Do you keep the appointments you make? We're all here on time, give or take, in the bloody waiting room but there's no sign of the doctor we've come to see. You want to post your own notice on the wall or write it as graffiti with black felt-tipped pen. Do you care about your patients, do you really or is it just a job?

"Mr Smith," says the doctor who appears suddenly from behind the thin door with the frosted-glass window. Mr Smith looks as though he's won first prize and gets himself up and into gear. His time has come. His waiting is over and he follows the doctor through the pathetic door to the consulting room. It is just one of the places where the programme of mass medication is being carried out. It's the government's drastic measure and, so they believe, the answer to the problem for everyone who gets sick and who cannot afford or will not pay for treatment. It will, so the minister responsible for population was reported as saying, effectively bring down the target for waiting room numbers to more manageable levels.

"…more manageable levels…" Now that is a laugh! Ha ha! I manage my lists and very well, too. Mine are dead and gone. Well, most of them. The dead don't cry. They moan a lot. But they don't cry. Well, they can't. It's too late. They don't laugh either but that doesn't mean we can't. I like a good laugh. Who doesn't?

áś-àã ŋṂ : **Having Natasha for breakfast**

As women went, Natasha was OK. She'd do for the time being. She didn't overnag and she wasn't that demanding. She certainly wasn't high maintenance like some other girlfriends that could be mentioned. If the last one had so much as winked at you, it meant a new pair of diamond studs for her gorgeous lobes. Natasha was quite good between the sheets, nothing to write home about, nothing too adventurous, but you wouldn't hurry to kick her out of bed. She was relatively happy with her lot. She had her own money, and a job but not a fortune. She wasn't always the prettiest girl in the room, but she scrubbed up well and you could count on her not to drop you in it or to say anything that would get you struck off the social register. She got on with your mother, which was actually quite something, even though she was N.Q.O.C. Your brother, too, but then he'd get on with anything you were going out with even if it had a broad Essex accent (actually especially if it had one). She'd always drive you home if drinking was the issue and, although she was chatty with other men, she never overstepped the mark and you certainly wouldn't find Natasha in the downstairs loo snogging with the sozzled host. She liked her food but didn't overeat unless it was cheese or olives. She could probably do with losing a pound or two but didn't think about going to the gym. Her taste in music was pretty similar to yours apart from the awful Take That thing and the music from The Mission which was obviously a throwback to something from the past. She also liked EastEnders, which was fine as long as you didn't have to watch it, and she found Ricky Gervais funny when actually he was just an annoying little shit. Like Chris Evans.

Actually it was Chris Evans who brought things to a head. Natasha got up most mornings to go off to work and tuned into the Breakfast Show on Radio 2. She joined it at 7.00 every morning and just as the chirpy, ginger-headed DJ was starting up, Natasha was soaping down in the shower. The lather flow in both locations was full of froth. Over several weeks and months Natasha developed 'a thing' for the DJ, and 'the thing' turned into a habit. Not a weekday went by when she didn't listen to the enthusiastic red-head from start to finish. She would buy any and every newspaper and magazine that featured him, and when his book came out she was third in the queue at the Waterstones signing and the store security staff had to ask her to move on after Chris Evans had said, "Who shall I make this for, luv?" and she'd replied, "To Tache, the woman of my dreams."

Natasha became Chris Evans's stalker. She developed an unhealthy obsession. She hung on his every word. She'd take time off work and go to the stores that he was opening. She'd wait for hours outside theatres and studios, and the entrances to Broadcasting House became as familiar to her as she was to its doormen. She went to his pub in the hope that he'd be there to serve her. The day she actually tipped over the top was when it was announced that Chris Evans was going to marry his new golfing girlfriend, also called Natasha. It was I who took the brunt of her fury. She grabbed the serrated bread knife and took a swing at me. Perhaps I shouldn't have been so offhand about the news, and my comment about a hole in one was probably misplaced. Anyhow the swinging bread knife missed my chest, thank God, carried on its forceful journey, glanced off the kitchen wall and finished its frenzied arc by impaling itself in the side of Natasha's neck. She'd stabbed herself in the jugular. I guess what I should have done was to call 999 right away. The paramedics could probably have stopped the bleeding if they had got to us in time. I didn't make the call. Natasha bled to death on the kitchen flagstones. It wasn't my fault and you couldn't really blame Chris Evans either, even though it was his Breakfast Show; even though he has resigned.

She left a last will and testament which was rather unlike her. She wasn't a great forward planner but had obviously made some recent arrangements in the light of her new attachment to Chris Evans. Her instructions through her lawyer were quite clear. Her body was cremated and I was charged with the task of getting her onto the Breakfast Show with Chris Evans, which wasn't going to be a piece of cake. I had some of her ashes of course and by using them, this was going to be the only way I could comply with her request. I thought about posting them to the BBC but felt sure that there must be some sort of vetting system that prevented crank mail from reaching its target. I could have just left them in the plastic container they give you or tipped them in the garden or over the cliffs on that coastal path walk she loved so much. Every time I looked at Natasha in her little container I felt a twinge of guilt about not calling that ambulance soon enough. I felt that I really owed her something and besides, if I didn't carry out her instructions, I wouldn't get the £50,000 from her life insurance policy. It was £50,000 for me and £50,000 for her parents, which was very kind of her. However, I had to provide proof to her lawyer that I'd done the deed. Getting her on the radio with Chris Evans wasn't going to be that easy, but I guess it was the least I could do for Natasha.

So I thought about it. You couldn't do something like that with his blessing. As wacky as he was, Chris Evans wasn't going to let a complete stranger with his ex-girlfriend's ashes get involved in a macabre ceremony or celebration on the Breakfast Show. How would you do something like that without him knowing about it? That was the puzzle that got me thinking. I, too, started to listen to the show and it dawned on me that the DJ liked his grub. He talked about it, and featured it quite a lot, and so I hatched my plot. It actually wasn't that difficult in the end. I sent round the new, extra-hot, extra-spicy pizza with its extra-special dusted topping knowing that Chris Evans loved a food challenge and sure enough he tucked into the thing on air. So did Jonny and Lynn, and Moira the newsreader described the flavour as "interestingly fishy".

My ex would have been ecstatic as Chris Evans raved about having Natasha for breakfast. I filmed and recorded the whole episode from start to finish so that I could prove that Chris Evans had in fact had Natasha on the Breakfast Show. I wanted to make sure that I'd get the fifty grand. I wouldn't have been able to do it for Natasha; wouldn't have been able to get her quite so close to her hero had I not started going out with my new girlfriend. She's the producer on the Chris Evans Breakfast Show and she's quite good at it, too.

Surfing those radio waves who says we don't have a sense of humour? We do. Laugh? I nearly died. Well, you know what I mean. Once I told them I was R>E>D/G>R>E>E>N colour-blind they nearly wet themselves. You shouldn't make jokes like that, one of them said to me on the quiet, and I realised that I might have overstepped the mark. Then, I thought, they shouldn't take themselves so seriously. Then I thought, eternity isn't just for Christmas. That made me chuckle and all. But if you can't have a laugh at those in authority, then you can't have a laugh at anyone, if you get my drift. Pomposity needs to be pricked every so often and the days of bowing and scraping are over. We move with the times; actually we move ahead of them and we always mean what we say.

áɜ́-àã ŋŋ: The boy who always had money in his pocket and why we turn out the way we do

Bob Sykes was one of the chaps who always seemed to have money to spend. While the rest of us in the 'gang' had to wait for the next letter to arrive from Granny and the neatly folded ten-bob note slotted in between the pages of Basildon Bond, or an exeat Sunday with the parents and the loose change from Father's pocket once the luncheon bill had been settled at the Lamb Inn: Sykes always had money in his pocket.

"How dew do it, Sykesy?" we'd ask him. He'd always reply in that very annoying way of tapping the side of his nose and saying even more infuriatingly, "Take care of the pennies and the pounds take care of themselves."

Someone in the gang, probably Blackett, named Sykes 'Ten-Bob Sykes' because he nearly always pulled a crumpled ten-shilling note from his right trouser pocket at the school tuck shop counter. The rest of us had pennies or a shilling or two if we were lucky, but Sykes, 'Ten-Bob Sykes', always managed to come up with the folding stuff.

It gave him friends of course, but not real friends like me and Blackett. Ten-Bob Sykes's' so-called mates were brown-nosing him just because he had money. Mind you, he wasn't actually all that generous with it. I suppose it's because of that that the trouble happened.

If he'd been the sort of decent chap who'd have divvied up when a bloke was a bit short, or if he'd lent a couple of bob without wanting it paid back the following week with interest, then he'd have been all right. Having the money gave him a sort of power, I suppose. Having Blunt, too. Blunt who was in the upper fifth and boxed for his house; he was a bloke you wouldn't want to argue with. Blunt had bloodied Cunliffe, and Cunliffe was quite a big bloke. Blunt had landed him one on the nose before chapel one morning and Cunliffe's nose didn't stop bleeding until after the last Psalm. He looked a frightful mess and he hadn't got a handkerchief so his shirt was covered and he got into a right state and a bollocking from the head of house, Jones. Blunt was 'Ten-Bob Sykes's; minder and collected the money that was owed to him when it was due. You didn't ever want to borrow money from 'Ten-Bob Sykes' unless you absolutely knew you could pay it back on time and with the extra required.

Mother always said, "Neither a lender nor a borrower be,"

which was all very well for her to say because she didn't have to buy stuff from the school tuck shop every day, or owe Dyer three and six for some quite rare Commonwealth stamps.

Anyhow that's how it was that I asked Sykes, 'Ten-Bob Sykes', if he'd lend me half a crown for two weeks. In two weeks I knew that I'd see my parents and that I'd be back in funds. No worries. 'Ten-Bob Sykes' reached into his right trouser pocket and produced half a crown. He tossed it in the air like a referee at the start of a match and coolly caught the spinning coin after it had arced its way upwards above our heads. He caught it and quickly placed it on the back of his upturned left hand keeping the coin covered with his right.

"Heads or tails. Double or quits," he said in his annoying voice.

"What dew mean, Sykesy?" says I.

"I call heads or tails. If you win you don't have to pay me anything, but if I win you have to pay me back double."

"Five bob if I lose?"

"Nothing if you win," said 'Ten-Bob Sykes'.

"Why don't I just borrow the two and six and leave it at that, Sykesy?" says I.

"It's a toss-up or nothing," said 'Ten–Bob Sykes'.

"Go on, then," says I, at which 'Ten–Bob Sykes' scooped the coin from the back of his hand and flipped it into the air again. Before it had even finished its ascent he shouted, "Heads!" and, sure enough, the half-crown coin landed heads up on the floor. 'Ten–Bob Sykes' bent down and retrieved his coin. "That's five shillings in two weeks' time and don't be bloody late. No excuses accepted." He reached into his right trouser pocket and fished out a half-crown coin and flicked it at me with disdain.

"Don't spend it all at once," he said coldly. 'Ten–Bob Sykes' wasn't a nice person at all and I felt that I had perhaps made a mistake.

I paid Dyer another instalment for the stamps and stocked up with sherbet fountains and Caramac and had some leftover for a couple of Battle Picture Library comics and a trip into town to the Rex cinema to see The Magnificent Seven.

It was a bit of a blow when Father wasn't well and he and Mother couldn't make it for the exeat as had been planned. Actually it was several blows once Blunt had caught up with me and the tooth that the dentist had filled last term needed to be done all over again thanks to Blunt's fist.

"I'll be dealing with you every week until you pay up Sykes what you owe him," was how Blunt left me spitting blood and saliva in the corner of the music room.

As luck would have it, Blunt broke his femur in the inter-house rugby match the following Saturday. It was a bad break and we all heard the snap as it ricocheted around the games field rather eerily. Blunt made a hell of a fuss. He was carted off to the RAF hospital where he was laid up in plaster for months.

Without Blunt's support, 'Ten-Bob Sykes' wasn't much of a threat. He sulked around and barged into me a couple of times, saying, "You owe me," out of the side of his weasel mouth. But that was all. With Blunt out of the way at least there would be no pain and 'Ten-Bob Sykes' would just have to wait until my funds were once again in a liquid state.

'Ten-Bob Sykes' didn't wait, though. He went to Jones, who went to the Head of House to report that some of his money had been stolen. He said that he had seen me take a ten-shilling note out of his blazer pocket and that was that. I was called up before Head of House where I vigorously denied the charge.

"Well. Sykes has said he saw you. You say that you didn't do it. It is a serious charge and we need to get to the bottom of it."

I could of course have told the truth about how 'Ten-Bob Sykes' had lent me half a crown and how I hadn't paid it back yet because my father being sick had meant that I hadn't got any more pocket money and that Blunt had beaten me up and all that. I didn't because you don't tell Jones or Head of House anything like that. You never tell them anything.

Anyhow, the storm blew over. My desk and tuck box were searched but no money was found and the Head of House decided that under the circumstances he would be keeping a close eye on me and that for good measure I'd be gated for four weeks.

"I don't know if you did it, boy," he said to me, "but I don't want any of this sort of nonsense to happen again."

I think it was Blackett, my friend, who discovered that Sykes, 'Ten- Bob Sykes', had a double-sided half-crown. It had heads on both its faces.

"How the hell dew find that out?" says I to Blackett.

"I saw Sykesy using it the other day when he was talking to Sparrow about something. It fell on the floor and rolled off and when Sparrow picked it up he said, 'Hey, Sykesy, this coin has got two heads.' Well, Sykesy wasn't very happy and grabbed the thing back off Sparrow, saying maybe it has and maybe it hasn't. And that was that."

"That bastard," says I.

After lights out one night, me and the 'gang' got around Sykes, 'Ten- Bob Sykes's", bed and we put a pillowcase over his head, dragged him out and off into the bathrooms. Someone kept lookout while three others held Sykesy firmly by the arms. I asked the questions.

"You'll get nothing out of me," said Sykes, 'Ten-Bob Sykes'.

But we did. My father gave me one of those Swiss Army knives for Christmas, the red-handled thing with lots of useful blades. It was with the combination of the sharp knife and the saw that I managed to cut through the tip of Sykes's, 'Ten-Bob Sykes's, little finger; the one on his right hand. He howled like a baby but we put a pair of socks in his mouth. His blood, and there was a lot of it, turned the whole Swiss Army knife red, not just the handle.

The deal was that when he came out of the San, he went to Jones and Head of House and told them that he'd made a mistake. He hadn't seen me take any money and he'd made up the whole thing.

His little finger had been caught in the dormitory window when it slammed shut, and sadly no one could find the tip of it. I flushed that down the bog.

Sykes, 'Ten-Bob Sykes', knew that if he didn't do what he was told he would lose another finger or worse. He did what he was told. I paid him back the half-crown I owed him, but he couldn't put it into the pocket of his trousers because his right hand was still bandaged. He always had money in his pocket but it stayed there for the rest of that term anyway.

I believe he became a nine-fingered investment banker and was run over in Threadneedle Street. I followed my father into the family fishmonger and butcher's business where I always made my bloody mark.

You think it is important that you make your mark. From handprints in damp caves under ancient France to an Arsenal football shirt pinned up and spread out like someone being crucified on a bedsit's plaster. Yesterday's newspaper stuck up on a mud wall of a hut in the wild bush to Hirst's overpriced step and repeat rolls that those supposedly in the know will oowww and arrhhh over. Our taste betrays us. Sorry, your taste betrays you. There is no one who can judge what is right or what is wrong, although there are those that try. The Chamber is not a columbarium. We don't concern ourselves with the paraphernalia of the dead. We ignore the trinkets tossed into the open grave or stacked in the bone store. From golden chariots to paperback books, we brush them aside. The meaningless mementoes that the living think will somehow comfort the departed. At least attest to those gathered around that you knew the deceased, understood them well. Not for you a pinch of loose dirt but rather a half-bottle of Scotch or a flower or something more exotic. The message sent saying as much about the sender as it does about the dearly departed. I am tasteless in that respect and yet, if you think about it, I make the most important judgement based upon the evidence provided. Those impressions stuck fast to the codes of the dead by the dead and not implanted by the living upon the dead. I trust that you're beginning to understand my importance, beginning to get my drift.

áɕ̀àã ŋǸ: **Buy one get one free**

Shopping at the supermarket wasn't much fun. It was a chore that had to be done but Agnes found a way to make it a little more interesting. She shopped mostly at Sainsbury's in her local market town. It was always difficult to make ends meet but Agnes was inventive. She took the grocer's advertising slogans literally and whilst she agreed that 'Good food cost less at Sainsbury's' when it did, she was even more delighted to be invited to 'Try something new today' when the company updated its advertising slogan.

Agnes got her idea from the supermarket's own marketing campaign. Bogofs, they called them. Buy one get one free. It often happened when she was trawling the aisles. She sauntered into the biscuit section and there on the shelf was the point of sale that said quite clearly McVitie's Ginger Nuts 65p. Buy 1 get 1 free. She wondered how the supermarket could afford to do it.

"How can you afford to do it?" she asked the girl on the checkout.

"I don't know, luv," was the reply. "Have you got a Nectar card?" Agnes did have a Nectar card. The points she gathered during the year allowed her to get some more free goods at Christmas, which was a bonus. She liked the idea of being rewarded for being a regular user of the supermarket.

She first tried her idea out on a busy Saturday morning. She did her normal shop, which came to £35.70. With what they called 'multibuys', Agnes had saved £2.08, according to her till receipt. She wheeled her trolley out to the car park where she had found a slot behind one of the architectural trees that the planners had presumably insisted upon. It was out of the way of the CCTV cameras. She unloaded her four bags of shopping into the car, replaced the trolley in the trolley park and then drove home. She unpacked the car and her shopping. She'd put the four empty plastic carrier bags she'd used for her purchases into her coat pockets. She then returned to the Sainsbury's supermarket. The round trip didn't take her thirty minutes. She grabbed another trolley and went back into the store. Using her till receipt as the shopping list, she carefully reloaded the trolley with everything she had bought earlier. She made sure that what she took from the shelves for the second time that morning matched exactly with her original till receipt. In the magazine section where the aisle was full of people browsing, she loitered, too, and at the same time repacked the four empty plastic bags with the goods in her trolley. This was the most risky part of the operation but no one noticed a pensioner fumbling with her purchases, then leafing through The Lady and Homes

& Gardens. She then pushed the trolley back through the fruit and veg section and into the busy café at the other side of the checkouts. She queued and bought an all-day breakfast. She enjoyed the meal and browsed the Daily Mail. Once finished, she pushed the trolley out of the store and back to her car.

No one stopped her. If they had she would have produced the till receipt with the bit on the bottom neatly taken off. She'd doctored it before returning for the second shop. The only evidence on the printout that recorded the time she bought her shopping was in the last two lines. Six groups of digits that she could easily remove with a sharp knife, just below the words that suggested: "PLEASE KEEP FOR YOUR RECORDS. Published Terms and Conditions apply". Agnes got a little thrill, an adrenaline rush, when she pushed the second trolley of the day out into the car park. She'd got away with it.

"Bogof," she said out loud and she chuckled as she pushed her load of stolen goods unchallenged to her car.

Agnes had become a shoplifter. She didn't see it as a crime; after all, the supermarket seemed willing to give away product. All Agnes was doing was extending their generous offer to cover all the goods she purchased.

Having got away with it once, Agnes embarked upon her crime spree every week. She didn't always choose the Saturday. Sometimes she would use Friday and sometimes, when there wasn't a service in the village church, a Sunday. She got bolder and on several occasions added bottles of wine to her two shopping trips. If she bought six, she'd get a twenty percent discount and, more importantly, could carry her six-bottle purchase in a handy cardboard carrier conveniently provided in the wine section.

"You're so thoughtful," she said to the girl on the checkout as she loaded the bottle carrier into her trolley for the first time that day.

Since Agnes only had the occasional sherry, she built up quite a wine cellar. She didn't know very much about the stuff but shopped for bottles around a fiver. She always selected a variety that the supermarket had on special that week. When her purchases and the duplicate freebies started to fill up her garage, she realised that her 'Bogof collection' would have some value to someone who wanted several hundred bottles of wine.

Her first customer was the friend of an acquaintance. She discovered that Bertie liked a drop of wine and let it be known that she had inherited about 200 bottles from her brother who had sadly passed away. Bertie was delighted to part with his cash and at £4 a bottle he seemed well pleased with the deal he struck with the acquaintance of his friend.

"Thank you so much," said Bertie. "We pensioners need all the help we can get. The cost of living today is bloody disgusting and the government doesn't seem to care a damn."

Bertie's words struck a chord with Agnes. She agreed that pensioners like her weren't at the top of the pile. She realised that her "Bogof scheme" was an earner. She lay awake at night dreaming of building a business, a mini-empire even. She could see the day, not too far away, when she needn't worry about money any longer. She fantasised about retiring to Portugal or Madeira with her friend Christine. Somewhere in the sun would be lovely. If she won the lottery that's what she'd do. If the "Bogof business" could take off, that's what she'd do.

At first Agnes, wasn't sure how to capitalise on her new business. She called it a business and realised that if it was going to grow, she'd have to involve others. Agnes had friends. There was Christine, her best friend, and bridge partner most Monday evenings. Elsie was a good friend, too. Recently widowed, poor Elsie had taken the death of her husband rather badly. It had shaken her up so Agnes used to whip round to see her. She'd take her out for a run in the car, go and visit the garden centre or the National Trust place if the weather was kind. Winnie was another whom Agnes counted as a friend. Winnie sometimes appeared rather grand, but Agnes knew that Winnie was worse off financially than she was. Winnie's husband hadn't had a decent pension and they had had to do something about remortgaging their home in order to keep themselves solvent. Then there was Daisy. Daisy had been a schoolteacher, the old-fashioned, no-nonsense sort, very keen on the three R's. Daisy had retired and now gave a little private tuition on the side, coaching children for their entrance examinations. Daisy, like Agnes, had never married and, like Agnes, she loved birdwatching.

Agnes thought about who she'd involve first. She knew that she'd find it easier to persuade her friends one at a time. She'd had experience of committees, and by and large thought they didn't work awfully well. Too much talk and not enough action. Christine was the obvious choice for first gang member, and so she got on the telephone and arranged an evening when the two of them could meet up at her house.

"Come round at about six and we'll have a glass of sherry. I've got something I want to talk to you about."

"How intriguing, my dear. Look forward to seeing you," was what Christine said.

The Bogof Gang had its inaugural meeting. At first Christine looked perplexed. She actually thought that her friend had gone off her rocker. But ever so slowly, like melting ice, and helped in some part by the properties of the sweet sherry, she began to see that Agnes was onto something quite interesting. "It sounds rather exciting to me," said Christine. "And you've actually been getting away with it, dear?"

"Most certainly!" For the umpteenth time, Agnes confirmed she had.

"And there's no way that they can catch you out?"

"No way, José!" Agnes sounded like a Bolivian bandit.

It was agreed that the next morning Agnes would take Christine with her to the supermarket for a first-hand demonstration. They travelled together and Agnes drove them to Sainsbury's.

Christine was as nervous as a kitten.

"You're only going to watch me, dear," said her friend by way of encouragement.

Agnes went through her paces and shopped with Christine stuck to her like glue. The two women went through the checkout and Agnes paid for the shopping: £42.57 with double Nectar points on several of her buys.

"Alright to pack your own bags, luv?" the girl on the checkout asked, employing her customer-friendly training.

"Oh, thank you, dear. I can manage quite well, thank you."

Agnes and Christine loaded the shopping into the car and returned home. They were back again in the supermarket twenty-two minutes later for the repeat shop. Christine seemed to be more relaxed on the second visit. Agnes couldn't feel her hot breath this time as she selected another Greek yoghurt from the chilled section.

"All right, dear?" Agnes asked her friend.

"It's quite exciting, isn't it?" came the reply, which made Agnes smile.

The second visit went like clockwork.

It was outside as the two women approached the car that the man who gathered up the stray trolleys came up to them. His fluorescent yellow jacket made him look like a lollipop man.

"You haven't dropped anything, ladies, have you?" he asked.

"No," said Agnes. "I don't think so." Her heart was racing. She thought they'd been found out somehow.

"It's just that I found a purse over here. I'll take it to the customer enquiry desk. Cheers, luv."

Agnes continued to push her trolley to her car with Christine in nervous attendance once more.

"Excuse me, ladies." It was a security man. There were two of them standing next to the car.

"How can I help you?" said Agnes too quickly.

"We'd like you to come back with us into the store please. We have reason to believe that you are trying to leave with goods you haven't paid for."

"What utter nonsense," said Agnes. "I have the receipt here somewhere."

"That's fine, madam," said one of the security men. "There may have been some mistake but if you'd come with us to the manager's office, I'm sure we can clear up the matter. This way please."

Christine was white with fear. Agnes thought for a moment that she was going to pass out.

"Come on, dear." Agnes took Christine's arm and the two walked back from where they had just come. One security man walked in front of the group, showing the way, while the other followed, pushing the trolley full of shopping. The manager's office was through the store and out the back, through a set of big swing-doors. The two old ladies and their uniformed escort and the shopping trolley processed into the unglamorous world of behind the scenes at the supermarket. Parked in tight rows were big cages on wheels, jammed full with product waiting to fill the shelves. Notices on the wall, some encouraging, "Smile and your customers smile with you", some warning, "Have you washed your hands?" and some regulation small print.

The manager's office wasn't big. The manager was. He looked weary but like a spider that's sensed the tremble of imminent prey. He spoke to the two suspects.

"Well, ladies. I'm sure you know why we've asked you back for a word?"

Agnes stood ramrod straight and still. Her composure was not going to be ruffled by this man.

"I simply cannot imagine," she said after a suitable pause that tried to indicate she was in charge.

The manager gave a groan, which turned into a heavy sigh.

"I think we'd better call the police," he said with a nod to the security personnel.

Christine, who'd been as white as a sheet since their apprehension, visibly jumped and started to shake like a washing machine on spin cycle.

"I thought you said you'd got away with it, dear!" she shrieked at Agnes who instantly knew that on this occasion she hadn't.

Cups of tea were offered as they sat together in the security office waiting for the police to arrive. The hot mugs of brown liquid relaxed them, made them feel at ease and, quite quickly, quite dizzy; lulled off into a happy, soporific state, and wooziness that wrapped around them like a comfort blanket; a warm haze of reassurance that made the miscreants feel like they were both floating off towards something heavenly.

The two security men didn't have any trouble in carrying the two old ladies, one at a time, out of the room and into the rear yard behind the building. In one corner the cardboard crusher had just finished compressing one batch into a tight bale, and Agnes and her friend were carefully lifted into the machine and the green button was pressed which started the powerful hydraulic rams once again.

Agnes would probably have taken some satisfaction in coming back to that very store as part of a cardboard outer for Portuguese sardines in olive oil. Christine, on the other hand, wouldn't have liked her new role as a part of the box for Sainsbury's 85 ultra-soft white tissues. Both brands were on special that week. Buy one get one free.

You get those who think they have an instant right of decent passage. Holier-than-thou pensioners. Just a morsel from the chosen ones. Makes me laugh or more often as not, see R>E>D. If I see R>E>D then they see R>E>D and all. Ha ha! I wrote a ditty. I scribble lots. Tried to explain why it is that it's not always what it seems if that makes any sense. Quite pleased I was. It went like this…
Eliza, Eliza will never be wiser
than Esau who saw daylight first.
Jacob, dear Jacob was hastened to wake up
by Esau with terrible thirst.
Then he gave to his brother (complicit with mother)
the birthright stew he implored
and thus through deception

came Israel's conception,
the favoured one of the Lord.
If you know your scripture, Esau is mentioned all over the see-saw.
And how many s's in that? Genesis, Obadiah, Malachi and in the
New Testament of the Christian Bible, St Paul's Letter to the Romans
and another to the Hebrews. I don't really know my way around the
Good Book as once I did. It's a bit like a Katherine Mansfield short
story or your Highway Code. After the test it gathers dust.

áś-àã ɲP : Standing in a pool of moonlight, Beryl Fairfield undressed herself at least six times

Standing in a pool of moonlight, Beryl Fairfield undressed herself. What an evening it had been. Had Melissa really been so keen? Had the Martini gone straight to her head? The sound of laughter wafted in through the open French windows and Beryl realised straight away that she should have perhaps closed the curtains before removing her tweeds. Too late, she watched Melissa running through the gay group and across the lawn, screaming; her silk dress clinging to her beautifully distressed curves like petals to an orchid. Beryl Fairfield looked on with pity and some remorse as she gently peeled the arachnid-like moustache from her trembling top lip. That was Movember, she thought; what would December bring?

★

Standing in a pool of moonlight, Beryl Fairfield undressed herself.

"Good God, Beryl!" exclaimed Bertie as the olive shot from his surprised mouth and fled across the room like a small green busy bee. "What on earth have you done?" Bertie's monocle swung away in protest from his raised right eye and splash-landed into his cocktail.

"Oh it's the latest fashion," said Beryl, smoothing her hand over the single track of tight, curly pubic hair. "I believe it's called a Brazilian."

"If I wanted to go native I'd book a Pan Am flight to bloody Rio." Bertie was being his pompous self.

The sound of the piano being played and the happy singing from Coward's latest sheet music reminded the Fairfield's that they should return to the party. Beryl in particular was very keen to see what Sebastian thought of her new landing strip, but she'd have to shake off the limpet-like attention of Bertie first of all.

*

Standing in a pool of moonlight, Beryl Fairfield undressed herself. She then undressed her co-pilot. The landing celebrations, the popping corks from the control room, had died away and the crackly sound of piano music came at them from Earth, another planet away. He looked into her eyes and smiled.

"I want to be your man on the moon," he said with cut glass diction.

"Damn it! This will be just one small step for man but a giant leap for mankind," Beryl said with a glint in her eye as she threw herself at the co-pilot like a piranha. It had been a difficult journey and they were both a long, long way from home.

★

Standing in a pool of moonlight, Beryl Fairfield undressed herself.

"Don't do it, darling," Basil implored. "Please, Beryl. Don't!" It was the pathetic plea of a desperate man. "I'll do anything, darling, give you anything your heart desires."

Beryl carried on with hypnotic determination and slipped the last vestige of silk over her head and let it fall, snakelike, onto the moonlit ground. It curled and settled next to the art deco ice bucket in which the empty champagne bottle nestled, corkless and spent. The white curves of Beryl's body in that light made her look Greek. He thought that she had been carved, just for him, by some master mason out of virgin marble. They could hear the voices of the other revellers on the terrace at the party. A piano played a merry tune and a tenor tried to keep up but was lost in the mélange of laughter and happy voices drifting down from the big house, all of them unaware of the lakeside drama unfolding before them.

When at first light they eventually fished the body out of the grey, mist-covered water, it wasn't at first clear to the local policeman why the gentleman still dressed for dinner had drowned. That was for the fish to know and the coroner to decide.

★

Standing in a pool of moonlight, Beryl Fairfield undressed herself.

"Oi!" said the pool of moonlight. "Mind where you put your feet."

"Oh I'm dreadfully sorry," said Miss Fairfield with a startled expression on her pretty face. "I didn't realise anyone was there."

"I come and go," said the pool of moonlight. "One minute I'm there and the next... poof... I'm gone."

"Well, I'm truly sorry," said Miss Fairfield, realising that she had indeed caused some offence. "I'll be more careful next time."

"There might not be a next time," the pool of moonlight spoke with gravity.

"What do you mean?" said Miss Fairfield.

"Just what I say. There might not be a next time." The pool of moonlight spoke with even more gravity.

"But what would I do without a moon?" said Miss Fairfield.

"At the very least no more songs, shine on harvest moon, blue moon, by the light of the silvery moon, moon river, that sort of thing. No more tides. No more seasons. At the very worst no more life on Earth; apart from the spiders of course." The pool of moonlight was being serious.

"No more cocktail parties or going to the theatre with Giles. No more days in Sussex and nights in Hanover Square. No more dancing or beach holidays in Biarritz. No more Royal Ascot or tennis or tea with Buffy and the girls. No more riding to hounds or helping Mummy with her parties. No more allowance from Daddy. What on earth is a girl to do?" Miss Fairfield started to glow.

"On earth a girl like you is to do nothing," said the pool of moonlight and very slowly it started to fade. Miss Fairfield realised with some trepidation that the light in her life was ebbing away.

"Please don't go! Please!" she pleaded as the pool of moonlight slipped away.

Beryl Fairfield awoke with a start. She was undressed and lying beside the bed on which she had slumbered, where she thought she had stripped off her fragile party frock and discarded her dancing shoes, lay her habit. It was time to dress for early matins and Sister Beryl could not be late.

★

Standing in a pool of moonlight, Beryl Fairfield undressed herself.

The man in the armchair moved stiffly, cleared his throat and spoke.

"So, you really think that we should go there, do you?"

"Certainly," said the woman as she slipped into a dark silk dressing gown.

"But it is bound to cause some trouble."

"You can cope with that, besides no one would dare to stand in your way."

The woman walked across the darkened room. The reflection of the moonlight from the snow outside made everything ghostly. She stooped to kiss the man. The piano was being played downstairs and the mood of the background voices was confident, not raucous, but the sound of the elite enjoying a cocktail party. The man reached out his arm and stroked the Alsatian that lay at his feet.

"We'll do it, then, Bee," he said. "We'll go to Poland."

"Good move," said the woman. "And please don't call me Bee. You know I much prefer Eva."

"Right," he said and with that the Führer got up, his German Shepherd stood to attention and the three of them left the room to go to war.

Scalping has been practised since man discovered how to sharpen metal under a full moon. To take the skin from the top of the head and display the result as a trophy was to demonstrate supremacy. To wage war with seriousness that spreads fear. You have come to see it as a sign of savagery. What could be worse? The top of the head used by the Scythians whose soldiers used to scrape off the flesh and rub the skin between their hands until it was soft so they could use the result as a napkin. The more napkins, the greater a soldier's respectability among his peers and presumably the cleaner his habits, and you know what they say about cleanliness being next to godliness. So what could be worse: being a prized bib for an ancient warrior of Eurasia, or a pile of grey ash in an urn stuck forgotten on a dusty shelf? I suppose the answer to that is in the manner of the dying. Better to go in one's sleep than be taken and topped by a wild redskin seeking to add to his collection. Although not all of you seem to want to go with quietude.

How fish got there

Some cause gravitational waves. Here comes a ditty!
When Einstein left, waved us goodbye,
his simple gesture left its mark;
down the years and through the sky,
the murmurs shudder through the dark.
Men shout at us from sullen graves
and Jesus breaks a piece of bread;
detecting gravitational waves,
you'll have the proof of what was said!

Take two big breaths, I said breaths, and there's plenty more fish in the sea is a statement often used after dissatisfaction over a loss has occurred which is, if you think about it, a strange way to try and encourage renewed effort or interest because to try and catch a fish from the sea to go out on the ocean to tackle up with the appropriate gear to dangle your line or net or whatever over the side and at the right time and tide with the correct and most appetising bait to attract that passing fish in the hope that it will grab what you are offering so that the hook or whatever will stick firmly into the mouth of the underwater piscatorial grazer and thus put you and what you have caught in touch with each other so that you can try and land the catch or the caught can try and become uncaught by wriggling and fighting to get free from the barbs or whatever that seem to have struck without warning and all because of being in the wrong place at the wrong time or from the other perspective the right plaice at the right time it does seem that the expression therefore that there's plenty more fish in the sea should not be used so blatantly when a phrase like 'Listen, old chum, you fucked up this time big time so don't fuck it up again,' would be far more apposite. Do you get my drift?

áɕ̀-àã ŋ̥ṕ: **Fly fishing**

Wimbleball Lake in Somerset nestles like an E-shaped ink spill in a green fold marked on Exmoor. It's an out of the way spot for trout fishermen and fair-weather sailors. On a misty Wednesday morning in mid-September the party of anglers arrived to catch trout. The men, eight of them, had motored down from Bristol in three different vehicles and rendezvoused at the water's edge. The paraphernalia needed to catch fish was unloaded from the cars and put into the four boats that each pair of fishermen would be taking out onto the water. Electric motors and their heavy batteries were vital if they didn't want to row and none of the men did. Soft seats that clamped onto the hard, wooden ones provided more comfort, as several hours would be spent just sitting, waiting. The rods, reels, boxes of flies and spools of line; the priest for whacking the caught fish on the head, were all stored in canvas and leather fishing bags. The landing net, a bass and drogue, a cold box with drink, flasks filled with coffee, extra clothes and wet-weather gear just in case of rain, were all stowed into each boat. It looked as though the team had come prepared for anything that the lake might yield.

"What's catching, do you think?" said Tim.

"I'm going to start with a small stick fly and something with a bit of orange in it. See how I get on." Ned was tackling up, threading two, the point fly onto the thin leader line and the other onto the dropper. He held up the orange-coloured fly which he'd unhooked from his fishing waistcoat where he kept his favourites. It didn't look like a fly you'd find in Somerset, but rather an exotic insect from the jungles of South America. It was a made-up fly of course, the figment of the fly tier's mind. Ned had caught with ones like it before. It was all guesswork to start with, though. They'd have to wait and see what the fish thought, what they were going for. The flamboyance of the fly seemed to match Ned's mood. He squinted at the job in hand. His big hands and sausage fingers didn't look as though they could handle the precision of attaching it to the thin leader, but they did.

The team had booked and paid for the four boats and had the whole lake to themselves. It was too early for the sailing fraternity. Competition was going to be fierce but friendly.

"We'll have caught our limit by lunch!" Tim shouted and laughed at the others as he and Ned pushed off from the floating quay where the boats had been moored. They were the first two out on the water, ready before the others and their electric motor purred into action.

"We'll head for the far end. The bloke in the hut said they were catching there yesterday." Tim swung the bow around and pointed it towards a concrete road bridge that crossed the lake at its northern point a quarter of a mile away.

It was grand to be out on the water again. Tim and Ned were good pals. They liked to fish together and, although Tim was more experienced, Ned was perfectly competent. He could cast a good line without catching Tim in the back of the head with his hook. He wouldn't get too many wind knots. Neither man would talk the hind leg off a donkey either. It wasn't much fun sharing a boat with someone who couldn't stop talking. With any luck they'd both be into some fish before too long.

The boat slapped its way through the clean, dark water. The fishermen were pleased that, as the mist cleared, the conditions were overcast and the wind only light. Canada geese loitered on the bank, picked over things in the mud where the water level had dropped, and squabbled among themselves in ungainly fashion; hooted at each other like a traffic jam. Two teal bobbed on the water then shot like skyrockets into the air, their wings working overtime. Cormorants trawled, their long necks like periscopes riding the lake's swell. From the boat they appeared not to have bodies, only necks and their wicked bills. The mew of a buzzard as it circled somewhere over the surrounding woodland made the men realise that they were not alone as the hunters or the hunted.

Ned dropped the anchor over the side and soon the boat took hold. The fishermen checked their tackle before making the first casts of the day. The reels gave out their line with a high-pitched whirr and both men swung into practised action from either end of the boat. It was always satisfying to get the line straight onto the water, to watch it shoot out, fed by the power of the rod and human timing. Feather-light, the extended line rolled onto the lake. The flies fastened to the invisible leader line plopped then swam for a moment. They slowly submerged and, weighted, gently dragged the line beneath the surface after them. Sinking and waterlogged and beautiful, their dreadful barbs were concealed beneath their man-made bodies, tucked up like tails; tails with a deadly sting. They descended slowly, joined the lake, became a part of that watery world, nearly down with the weed, held in touch to the outside by a simple knot, just a twist and turn in the nylon. Inch by inch the lines were pulled back into the boat. The flies were darting through the water, sinking and swimming below the surface, tempting the trout to strike. What arrogance it was to think the fish would take that fly! An absurd creation, a trollop on a hook, a real hooker, done up like a dog's dinner to lure the snappy trout.

The two men sat and cast. Time and time again, the lift and swish, the line peeling off the water, the flies airborne and dripping, the rod just lifted and flicked several times between ten and two on the imaginary clock face where twelve was directly overhead. Ten o'clock, two o'clock, backwards and forwards again throwing its line out, yards away, onto the lake.

"Was that a rise?" Tim thought he'd seen something, a fish breaking the surface perhaps.
"Could be." Ned cast again, threw out a line with ease.

The take was like any other. The sudden excitement was like an electric shock. It took experience to master the reaction. The line between the catcher and the caught had to be under just the right tension. Too much and the leader would snap, too little and the fish could get off the hook. Ned's rod bent over so that it nearly dipped into the water. Ned stood up in the boat and let out the line as quickly as he could, his reel shouting at him at the same time as Tim did.

"You're on, boy!"

Ned couldn't keep control. His line ran out for some yards through the tip of his bent rod. Then everything went slack. The moment had gone.

"Bugger," said Ned. "I've lost it."

At the end of Ned's line, the orange fly leapt and lunged. It had broken free without much effort and rapidly rose to the surface. Like the springing teal, it burst into the air, shaking the wet droplets off its vile, hairy body as it took vigorous flight. Somehow the water had given it life, had turned the fingernail-sized nymph into a monster the size of the boat the men were in. The orange beast burst forth. The water boiled and both men became terrified. Their boat rocked violently but it was Ned who caught the full force of the flying insect as it came at him. He might have seen the bright orange flash of colour as the brute dived towards him. He might have felt the awful barb as it hit him in the face, splitting his nose like a pat of blood-red butter, and ripping through the roof of his mouth up into his brain. He wouldn't have known anything about being lifted off his feet and swept up into the air to be carried off over Wimbleball Lake.

Ted's boat hit the floating quay and he leapt ashore without tying up. He ran up the path to his car, abandoned everything, his face as white as the cloud in the sky behind him, his eyes as dark as the waters he'd just left. He gunned the the four-by-four into life and, stark raving mad, took off for Bristol.

You might call it coincidence. We'd call it planned procedure. It's when just before the telephone rings you know it's going to. Coincidence? Not a bit of it. If the telephone was going to ring we'd know exactly when and we'd also know who the caller was and what they were going to say, what they were going to bend your ear about, and we'd know what your answer was going to be, how you are going to react, what you are going to do next. We are know-it-all's. Even though we can see you destroying yourself, tearing yourself to little pieces, emotionally sieving your residues, there is nothing we can do about it because you have been given the freedom of choice and, although you might think that you are wrapped up in emotional chains, tied down, stuck fast like a boot in the mud, it is entirely of your own doing. If you believe the Persian poem, you're left in the dust, not knowing what you are there for, believing in the gospel according to despair: life, death, decay, with wilderness paradise enough. So why were you made thus and what, then, did the hand of the potter shake?

ά♂άᾶ ηP: **Trick or treat?**

The Halloween rain blew, blasted, blustered at the window pane of number 13 and little Esme peered out with her face painted, mock-horror, silly scars and blood. God had tricked her. No treats for her that wet, wettest, cold, coldest end of October night. Esme's mother tried to console, comfort her, but Esme was in no mood for excuses. She wanted what she wanted, needed, pleaded for her Halloween.

"But be reasonable, darling," her mother implored, implied, demanded in her way.

"I want to go trick or treating," said the little girl with a wave, shake, prod of her satanic trident; the black plastic, made in China, bought in Asda, three-pronged toy fork with stuck-on scary spider.

Another bucketful of rain hit, smacked, splashed the window and really answered the question for the two, both of them.

"Well, if we can't go out I'll just have to do it here," Esme's painted face cracked a hopeful, furtive smile.

"Of course, darling," said her mother. "Let's do it at home."

And so it was that little Esme took herself off to the kitchen to find the very sharp Japanese carving knife. She knew that she had to be careful with it. It was so sharp that it wasn't kept in the cutlery drawer alongside all the other knives and spoons and forks. It was kept on its own in a narrow, wooden box and Esme got it out and held it in her tiny hand. It felt much more real than the black plastic, made in China, bought in Asda, three-pronged toy fork with stuck-on scary spider.

Esme knocked on the closed door of the front room.

"Who's there?" sang, rang her mother in playful, sing-song surprise.

"Trick or treat?" said Esme as she squeezed the comfortable handle of the sharp Japanese carving knife.

There's more; always there's more. Less or more, treat or trick? The haves and the have-nots. It was ever thus. I was witness to the prophecy of Neferti and his words composed in the early 12th Dynasty. "Every mouth is full of 'I want', all goodness has fled. The land perishes, though laws are decreed against it, for destruction is what is done, and loss is what is found, and what is done is what should be undone: a man's goods have been taken from him, and given to the outsider." What has changed? In thousands and thousands and thousands of years since Man first grew legs and discovered how to use them, what the fuck has changed? I'll tell you what I think. Your respect for the wise, old man with the white beard has gone out of the window. Your so-called sophistication has made you less respectful. You no longer believe what you are told but seek to have it proved. Belief is something that has slipped a cog or two. You doubt the illusionist or magician. You hound the faith healer or witch doctor. Your education has emboldened you. The priest takes a back seat along with the bank manager and doctor, too. You question your leaders, you doubt your teachers, you laugh at those that you do and don't bother to vote for and you bend your rules. Your role model is a footballer or a singer or both. Your praise and attention, your loyalty only given as a passing fad for a one-hit wonder. Money and that latest piece of advertised schmutter push their way to the front of the queue. You worship in the supermarket and you attend those places set aside for contemplation and communion with your god only when it is convenient for you or you have to when wedding or funeral demands your attendance. If Jesus or Mohammad or the Dalai Lama auditioned for the X Factor they'd be buzzed off the stage because those that judge them on your behalf prefer to watch a scantily clad buxom girl with some dancing dogs jumping through musical hoops. You require instant gratification. You want it and you want it now. But, as I say; the haves and the have-nots. The haves have the transport that bring them the things they must have. The have-nots hurl themselves like desperate, childish shadows against the transport; not to get at the things but just to get a lift to a better life. It was ever thus. How you have changed. How you have come down or gone up. Ascent or descent depends upon from where it is viewed. But, either way, you have changed; are constantly changing and I'm left to make the initial judgement which, I'm bound to say, like death itself, has never, ever changed.

áǝ-àã ŋQ́: **Being critical**

It was, when all is said and done, a very selfish process. The writers met every two months or so. They'd take it in turns to host the sessions and before each meeting, e-mails or posted photocopies criss-crossed between the five participants. The rule was that no one could submit a piece of work longer than 2,500 words. Each creative member wanted a fair crack of the whip at every meeting. Each wanted their own work appraised by the others which is why length of the piece was agreed upon. Most had work in hand. Two of the group were progressing their novels and so a chapter or part of a chapter was presented for criticism. One was into short stories. One was a poet and one, struggling with a film script. So each member was given four pieces of writing to "crit" at least a week before the meeting. There were no real excuses for not having read and thought about their colleague's work before the gathering.

Just before Christmas it was the turn of Penelope to hold the meeting at her flat. When she got home from her work, she tidied up the sitting room, cleared the table of all evidence of her writing. She did everything in longhand, didn't have a computer like the others, and was as pleased as Punch with her Conway Stewart fountain pen with its fat, golden nib. It was, to her, a magic writing wand. She tipped a jumbo bag of Kettle crisps into a bowl and unscrewed a glass jar of chilli dip. She found five glasses and a bottle of Lambrusco. She hoped that some of the others might bring a bottle. Not all of them would. Justine was penniless, poorer even than Penelope. Maybe Kirsty would bring something home-made. Kirsty was like that. When she wasn't writing, she'd be turning the hedgerows into something wholesome to eat or drink. Gregory would certainly bring a bottle. It would be a half-decent red. He'd present it to Penelope with a flourish and then proceed to drink most of it himself. Duncan would be on water.

She turned on the lights to the artificial Christmas tree. The little white bulbs burst into seasonal action and Penelope briefly marvelled at the Argos creation. She wasn't feeling Christmassy, but no doubt she would nearer the time. Seven o'clock arrived and so did Kirsty. She bustled into the flat wrapped up like Mother Nature. From an old wicker hen basket she produced a blackberry and apple pie and a bottle of elderflower wine and a sheath of paper with the typed and written submissions from the group.

"How's it going, darling?" Kirsty kissed Penelope lightly on the lips and started to unwrap the layers that protected her from the weather and other unwanted approaches.

"Alright, I suppose," said Penelope taking the pie and the bottle off to the kitchen as though they ought to be put into quarantine. "How's it with you?" she asked over her shoulder.

"Oh you know." Kirsty and Penelope had been in the same group for the MA in creative writing at the university college. They'd both chosen Love Story as a context module.

"Who are we expecting this evening!?" Kirsty shouted to the kitchen.

"The usual suspects, I think. Justine should be here if she can cadge a lift. Duncan's on, and Gregory will be late. As always."

"As always," sang Kirsty in agreement as her friend reappeared.

"Would you like some of this?" Penelope brandished the Lambrusco.

"Half a glass, darling. I've got to drive."

Half a glass later, the others had arrived.

Justine looked like she always did; as though she didn't have two bob to rub together. Her hair was lank and lacklustre. It hadn't seen shampoo for a week or more.

"I didn't know what to bring," Justine's pathetic apology bounced off the others. Penelope and Kirsty exchanged knowing glances. Justine might be a very talented writer, but oh dear, was she ever a leech. She took off her brown parka jacket with its moulting fur collar and slung it over the back of the chair that she was going to occupy for the session. She unpacked her satchel and claimed her space on the table.

Duncan had a cold. Duncan always seemed to have a cold.

"I'm afraid I'm all bunged up. Don't think it's infectious, though." Penelope decided to sit as far away from him as possible just in case. Duncan took a seat at the table and from his plastic carrier bag produced his own sheath of paper and a biro, a net bag of satsumas and a Vicks nasal stick.

"Anyone want one of these?" he asked, waving at the things around him.

"Not overkeen on the thing you've been sticking up your nose, but I might have a go at one of those for the vitamin C a bit later on," said Gregory who'd arrived while Duncan had been unpacking.

Gregory produced a bottle of French claret from his floppy, leather briefcase and handed it reluctantly to Penelope.

"Quite a good year for a Saint-Emilion and rather a good Saint-Emilion at that." Gregory couldn't wait to try it, but would probably have to suffer a glass of Lambrusco before the red treat.

"So how are we all?" he asked, pretty much knowing the answer.

How fish got there

"I've got a stinking cold," said Duncan.

"Lots of it about," said Gregory.

"And how's the Good Life and how are the bees?" Gregory addressed Kirsty, as he always did.

"The allotment is fine, thanks, Gregory," replied Kirsty, as she always did.

"And the writing, Justine?" said Gregory.

"No one wants poetry." Justine sounded gloomy.

"Nor short stories," said Duncan with his Vicks applicator stuffed up one nostril.

"Shall we crack on, then?" suggested Penelope, taking her place at the table and spreading her paperwork in front of her. "Who shall we do first?" she said, looking around the table at the writers.

They chose Duncan's short story because Duncan wasn't sure if he'd be able to last the whole session. It wasn't one of his best. Obscure to the point of becoming muddling, everyone agreed that they all had to read through it at least twice before things became sort of clearer.

"I didn't understand the bit about the eating disorder," said Kirsty. "What was the point you were trying to make?"

"I agree," said Gregory. "Doesn't ring true having a top-class chef with bulimia."

"I thought the idea was funny," said Justine.

"Wasn't supposed to be," said Duncan. "The chef was revolted by what he had become. He could no longer stand to prepare the food for his dreadful clients so he spewed up what he tasted and added that to his dish of the day."

"Charming," said Penelope.

"I think it should be longer." Justine thought out loud. "I'd like to see the character developed more. What drove him to do what he did? Why did he resort to the meat cleaver on the head waiter? We need more background story, I feel. What does anybody else think?"

"It doesn't matter a toss what anybody else thinks," said Duncan nasally. "It's my story and I think it's fine just as it is."

There was an abrupt pause.

"Right," said Penelope, gathering up the situation. "Let's move on."

Justine's poem was, thought Gregory, something like Leonard Cohen might have written. He'd meant it as a compliment but Justine didn't take it as one.

"What the fuck do you mean?" Justine scowled across the table and made Gregory feel very anxious as he took another large gulp of the fizzy, warm wine.

"I like Leonard Cohen. Used to get very pissed listening to his stuff," Gregory wasn't helping himself other than to another refill.

"I used to cry a lot, too," said Duncan nasally, instantly making Justine hate him as well. He caught her awful gaze and rammed the Vicks stick a little too firmly up his nose.

"Well, I thought your poem was full of beautiful imagery and creative cunning," Penelope attempted to pick up the pieces. "I particularly liked 'oft to dance in the dragons' den where fearful smoke choked puffed-up men'. That socked it to me, struck a chord in my psyche."

"Yes," piped up Kirsty, eager to keep things positive. "I really liked the way you have a go at the dominant male pomposity."

"I don't," Justine looked horrified.

"Oh," said Kirsty. "I thought you did."

"Well, you thought wrong. I didn't."

"Well, I'm pleased about that," Gregory laughed. The Lambrusco and the recently opened potent elderflower wine was making him feel light-headed.

"Leonard pissing Cohen," was all that Justine said as she shuffled up the papers like a newsreader at the end of the news.

Duncan peeled a satsuma.

Gregory's film script was riddled with mistakes. Grammatical as well as factual.

"You can't have a mobile phone going off, can you? I thought the scene was supposed to be set in nineteen bloody sixty-eight." As he spoke Duncan peeled the white stringy bits from the orange segments before he slipped them into his mouth one by one.

"Yes, I know. Bit of a cock-up, that bit. I'll have him using a coin box. Or change the date," Gregory had meant to edit that bit before sending it out to the others.

"I'm just not convinced by your two main characters," Kirsty wasn't convinced. She continued. "Never have been. Your writing is a bit like you really. Not one bit convincing."

If a pin had dropped, it would have been a sudden, crashing

interruption to the explicit silence, but as it was, Gregory's robust slurp from his glass of elderflower created the epicentre for the resonant crescendo.

"I'm convinced you're a dyke," Gregory mumbled into his glass, under his breath, a little too loudly.

"What did you say?" said Kirsty.

"I said, I'm convinced you're a bean flicker," Gregory threw caution to the wind; uninhibited and greatly egged on by cheap, warm, Italian fizz and homemade plonk, he let rip.

"I think you better apologise for that," said Penelope.

"Why? It's true."

"You're a pompous prick!" said Justine. "But we don't go round telling you."

"At least pricks are useful," said Gregory, throwing down his empty glass, gathering up his papers and pen and stuffing them into his battered briefcase. "I'm out of here. I'll take my bottle of wine with me. You lot haven't got an ounce of taste between you." Gregory got up and headed into the kitchen where he retrieved his unopened bottle.

"Goodnight and fuck the lot of you." Gregory slammed the

frail front door as he left and the Christmas tree lights shook with the excitement.

"Well!" exclaimed Penelope. "Who shall we consider next?"

Kirsty's novel was about a promiscuous love affair between an older woman and her niece and a pet Tamworth sow. The passage from a chapter that the group had been asked to 'crit' involved a scene where the older woman was introducing her niece to artificial insemination techniques with the pig.

Duncan was obviously extremely uncomfortable with the writing and said so.

"Who the hell's going to read this sort of porn?" he asked.

"It's not pornographic. It's colourful creative prose with a hint of erotica." Kirsty was being defensive.

"I agree," said Penelope.

"You'd agree with anything she said," said Justine.

"No I wouldn't."

"Yes you would."

"No I wouldn't."

"I think Gregory was right," Justine brought the silly banter to an end.

"Well, you better follow him out, then," said Kirsty.

"I think I fucking will," said Justine, scooping up her belongings and grabbing her parka. She headed for the front door, turned and shouted at the thinning group. "Do you know what? You can stuff that Christmas tree right up your arses and spin on top of it like fucking fairies until the next millennium. Good fucking night."

For the second time the thin front door took a battering.

"I think I ought to be off," said Duncan. "Shall I leave the satsumas?"

Penelope and Kirsty sat and looked at each other once Duncan had seen himself out.

"Well," said Penelope at last. "Not the most successful session we've had."

Kirsty burst into laughter. Penelope joined in. The two women rocked with mirth until the idea faded. The Christmas tree regained its ground as the most amusing thing in the room once again.

"Why don't I fetch that pie you bought?"

"Good idea."

The pie was brought to the table with a bread knife and Penelope cut into it with precision.

"Yummy," she said after the first bite.

"What about your work? Let's look at that, shall we?"

Kirsty found the relevant handwritten sheets of paper on which she'd made her notes about Penelope's writing.

"Apart from one or two minor points of poor punctuation and a couple of places where your spell-check seems to have gone on the blink, I basically liked your writing, Penelope."

"You know I don't have a spell-check, but thanks anyway," said Penelope with the powdery crumbs of Kirsty's pastry sparkling on her lips.

"There is, however, a problem I have." Kirsty hadn't finished.

"Oh. What's that?"

"You've stolen the plot."

"What on earth do you mean?" said Penelope, almost choking on Kirsty's fruit pie.

"You've taken the story I was writing, the one I told you about on the course, and you've used it. Stolen it from me." Kirsty was being serious.

"Don't be so dramatic. Don't be so precious. You were never going to do anything with it. Besides, you've always said that I'm a far better writer than you'll ever be," Penelope had gone too far, said too much.

"You're a cow," said Kirsty.

"Oh dear," said Penelope.

"And a copy cunt!" said Kirsty which she knew was probably the worst insult she could have issued to her fellow scribe.

"Please take that back!" yelled Penelope and, although she didn't mean to, something inside her snapped and she threw the rest of the blackberry and apple pie at Kirsty. It narrowly missed its intended target and stuck to the wall behind, ever so briefly, before crumbling to the floor.

Quick as a flash, Kirsty grabbed the heavy serrated bread knife and whacked it down on the table with a frightening bang. Her sudden guillotine action caught the end of Penelope's index finger, the one on her right hand. The amputated tip shot across the table as though it was under its own steam and flew off the edge, landing under the Christmas tree like some vile, useless and unwanted bloody present.

Penelope had enough adrenaline to return the favour to the enraged and shocked Kirsty. Her Conway Stewart found itself embedded rather too deeply in Kirsty's left eye; its broad nib had entered her brain with the result that her unusual novel, her allotment days and the Good Life were untimely taken from her before the ambulance arrived.

The blue flashing lights from the street outside eclipsed those from Argos strung on the tree. They had a more dramatic urgency, a critical purpose. They weren't hanging around like decorations, a festive flash in the pan for a few weeks. The blue and white light glistened off the blood-red graffiti, dribbled and smeared across the sheets of paper scattered over the table and on the floor of the empty flat. Under the red trail, almost running through it, the ironic handwritten words on one of Penelope's pages: 'the finger writes and having written, moves on.'

Penelope's New Year's resolution while at Her Majesty's pleasure was to learn to type. She decided she didn't need 'crit' sessions anymore. She'd get on just fine without them.

What is it that makes a good writer? Is it the ability to use words in an order that others will find interesting? Is it understanding one's audience and then pampering to their needs? Is it telling a damn good story? However badly relayed, a good story has legs. Is it, do you think, luck? Is X any better than Y? Both robust characters writing about robust characters, if you get my drift. X more relevant, I suppose, more up to date, although Y will last for a dickens of a long time. I'll tell you what I think makes a good writer. I'll tell you 'cause I'm allowed to. Can think for myself, well, I could always do that. So my idea about a good writer is somebody who can create an ache halfway between love and fever. Penelope may become one such thanks to critical influence and the way she slung that pie. Perfect timing. That's always important at any time of the calendar.

άɔ̃-ɑ̃ã ŋɑ́ : **Christmas message**

Doesn't it come round quick? It seems like only yesterday I was telling you all about Sissy and her troubles and now we've buried her next to Arthur and it hardly seems possible that her Bert (her second husband) will soon be joining them both. It's a good job that my Henry is still on the PCC and still has the vicar's ear, as it were. Getting space at St Andrew and the Virgin's graveyard is worse than trying to get tickets for Glastonbury! Talking of which, the girls had a lovely time there last June. It rained of course (when hasn't it?) and it was their first year. They got on rather well and met a nice crowd of other youngsters, it seems. Penny is still seeing Bonzo the nice boy with his own business in Birmingham. He drives a big, black BMW which Penny says he needs for his job. He's into sales; pharmaceuticals, I think, and is doing rather well. Apparently he sells them at all the festivals according to Penny, which shows an entrepreneurial streak and a work ethic above and beyond the call of duty. Penny is very keen on him, although my Henry isn't that sure. He's never liked tattoos much, although the spider's web on the side of his neck looks very artistic. Gillian is growing up fast and she, too, had a ball this summer. Probably rather too much fun and not enough study! Her baby is due in March which is as much of a surprise to her as it was to us.

But children will be children and it'll be nice to have our first grandchild, even though none of us know who the father is as yet. My Henry hasn't taken the news that well. He blames the government and has decided when the time comes to vote UKIP. Actually I quite like that nice Mr Farage. He seems like the sort of bloke you could get to know down the pub; chat to, share a laugh and a joke and then set about putting Mr Putin and those awful hooded Isis people back in their place. The world is in a funny state, no doubt about it, and it needs men like Mr Farage to get to grips with it. We stopped shopping at Tesco since Lidl moved in. We eased up after the horse meat scare. My Henry said we were becoming like the bloody French, eating horses. I liked the other foreign one but my Henry says that Lidl is a Lidl bit better than Aldi. We had to have Danny put down after he started leaving messages in the kitchen every morning. He had lost all control in the end so that was that I'm afraid. My Henry says I'll have to do the same for him one day. We're still watching 'Strictly' and my Henry likes the way the girls move around the floor. I'm only sorry that that nice Steve Backshall has been knocked off. Such a pity but I expect he'll be pleased to be back with his monkeys. Apart from the occasional twinge, my back is holding up well. I've got a new chiropractor with fantastic hands. My Henry says he has me around his little finger. It's not his little finger I'm interested in and I see him once a fortnight for a good going-over and he seems to be manipulating me just fine. Wasn't it dry in the summer? My Henry thought there'd be a hosepipe ban so he made some water butts and kept the bathwater for the garden which made everything smell of Yardley bath salts. We're saving up for a new car and my Henry has been reading up on what Jeremy Clarkson says but I think he's one stroke short of two if that makes sense. I like the old Toyota and a bit of rust never hurt anybody. We didn't go away this year as Uncle Simon was using his static van at Haven and besides, it was nice just being in the garden, even though it did smell of my bathwater. Hey ho, that's all our news. So we hope that you have a lovely time at this festive bit of the year and we'll look forward to hearing all your news as and when.

All love from Brenda, Henry, Penny and Gillian.

P.S. If you're ever this way, do pop in.

Communication has always been important. Even those colourful cards you send and receive that try to put into words what you are not capable of doing yourself. Often at that annual event of Christ's birthday, a brief essay tucked inside might reveal more or, like Code á$-ðã ꬺꝗ , it might turn out to be the last message from a family taken violently in a head-on collision, near Basingstoke, with a drunk driver on Boxing Day. Boxing Day for that unfortunate family was well named, it would seem, making that P.S. invitation a hollow offer until the life hereafter; if you believe that it exists. But you see, there is a thin strand that can connect. Like the spider's web that's created by design, those that infrequently discover it by accident, get snared by its sticky influence, struggle to understand why; most will fight it until they are overcome but some, the very, very few will tune into it and begin to understand *a little of what is happening on the other side. It is that rarest of murmurs, that faintest of sensations, beyond taste, sound, sight, touch or smell; beyond intuition, beyond even telepathy. Much like ley lines, the receiver has to be in the right place and the right state at exactly the right time. The transmitter is always perfectly poised, correctly set up for sending out the vibes. So we can make connections but they are rarely believed. If you have ears let him hear, as someone said. Ears are not enough. It takes special perception, special knowledge. Some call it the Knowing but you know what they say, too much knowledge can be a dangerous thing or sometimes, once in a very blue moon, a beautiful gift, but vengeance is often more satisfying if it is not exacted immediately.*

áéàā ŋȮ: **Looking a gift horse in the mouth**

She loved her horses and had grown up with them right from the first 'My Little Pony' to the hunter she now clung to as often as she could, a birthday present from her daddy. Running the company, as she tried to, the one her daddy had started almost twenty years ago, meant that she didn't have all the time to herself and her horse that she would have liked. Nonetheless, there were the odd days or half-days when she could skive off on the pretext of seeing somebody about something to do with work. No one really asked what the MD was doing. Nobody questioned her ability, or at least not to her face. There were some, senior management and co-directors but not shareholders, who muttered behind their hands about the MD's commitment to the job.

"Where's Miranda today?" the question would be asked, even though the answer was a foregone conclusion. Miranda was most likely out with her horse.

The company had been successful. Certainly in her daddy's day the firm had prospered. Making profits was getting harder and harder and Miranda didn't have the business acumen that her daddy had once shown. She didn't have the drive or the hunger that her daddy had used to grow the turnover every year. Basically Miranda wanted the perks of her position without the pain of office. She had grown up spoilt and, as one ex-employee once said, "The first generation makes it. The second spends it."

Ex-employees under Miranda's watch were getting to be more plentiful than current employees. Her record at HR (human resources) and hiring and keeping good people was abysmal but, like the days off, no one said much. Like an overindulged child with a new toy, she soon got fed up and wanted to move on to something new, something different. Being MD and a major shareholder gave her the power, that obnoxious inherited strength, to meddle with other people's working lives. If your face didn't fit then you were in and out of the job before you could say, "Where's my desk?"

Miranda didn't like doing the dirty work herself and always got her long-suffering FD (financial director) to clean up after her. He was a well-meaning accountant that her daddy had taken on years previously and who'd become the typical 'Yes' man that didn't always suit the business as much as it suited Miranda. He was the FD who had on countless occasions asked hapless candidates to meet him upstairs in the boardroom to face the process of redundancy or similar. The boardroom actually became known as the Departure Lounge amongst that part of the chattering workforce.

Unfair dismissal usually followed unfair dismissal, and always Miranda's daddy would dig deep to settle Miranda's whim; paper over the cracks of her poor decision-making. Most victims would disappear without a fight, some happy to be let free from a job they didn't much enjoy and some, the more senior, with a little tax-free pay in their pocket and a few weeks' gardening leave because Miranda didn't want them reappearing in the competition's camp straight away.

One day in January, just when everyone had started back after the Christmas break, Miranda asked her FD to get rid of Billy. Billy, she had decided, was no good at his job in the warehouse and his position could easily be made redundant, saving a few grand a year and helping to cut the overheads in an effort to shore up the business against increasing losses.

"Billy is surplus to current requirements," she told the FD, "so please get rid of him."

Now, even though Billy appeared a bit simple and was the sort who'd never look at you when being spoken to, he didn't take as obvious what the FD told him about his job being made redundant.

"Who's going to drive the forklift, then?" he asked the FD who in truth couldn't answer.

What Miranda had failed to tell her FD was that she had

promised a friend of hers, someone from the riding stables, that her son could have a job in the warehouse for less than Billy was being paid. What she didn't know was that Billy and the new boy drank in the same pub and that the night before Billy was invited by the FD to the Departure Lounge, he and the new employee had been toasting their new working relationship together.

"That's a bit of a cock-up," said the FD when the truth came out. "You can't make a role redundant and then take someone on for the same job."

"I know that. I'm not thick." Miranda knew that she had made another mistake. She also worked on the premise that the best form of defence is attack.

"Billy won't do anything about it," she said to her FD dismissively.

But she was once again wrong. A letter came in from Billy's solicitor, the one he went to see and the one who was happy to take on his case.

"We'll sack him, then," said Miranda annoyed that this hiccup was anywhere near her desk. "Let's do him for gross misconduct or anything. There must be something on him we can get him for."

The FD's task was to find something on Billy and the witch-hunt began. There was a verbal warning on his personnel file when he'd parked his red van in one of the Director's car parking spaces that time he was late and couldn't find another space anywhere. He'd meant to move it, but had forgotten, and by mid-morning the question had been asked, "Why is that tatty red van parked in the Director's car parking space?"

He had too been told not to drive the forklift so fast and without a hard hat on. There wasn't a paper trail on this but the warehouse manager, who hadn't been in the job that long, remembered that Billy had been told.

"Put everything in writing," said the frustrated FD who always put everything in writing.

What got him in the end was the misuse of company e-mails. Billy had sent a communication from the company e-mail address to a mail order firm asking for some pills for enhancing sexual performance to be sent to him at his place of work so that his mother, whom he lived at home with, didn't get to see the packet that the postman eventually delivered. She would have opened it as she did with most of Billy's post. It was, so the FD told him, a serious breach of his service agreement to use the company e-mail system for unauthorised personal use and as such Billy was going to be suspended.

Sadly, Billy's case never went to the tribunal that considers such things. Billy couldn't afford the fees that his solicitor needed to fight his corner.

"You might have a good case for unfair dismissal," said the lawyer, "but I'm afraid that it's a case I cannot take on if you're not insured." Sadly for Billy he wasn't.

Miranda brushed aside the affair and Billy's departure made way for her friend's son, the one she'd promised the job to. She met her at the riding stables and her friend thanked her for giving her son the job.

"I'm not the managing director for nothing," said Miranda as she set off on her high horse; set off for her usual Monday afternoon's hack in the countryside.

Miranda didn't see the thin wire stretched tightly between the two gateposts, like a giant spider's thread, at about hock height. Her horse, who'd been encouraged into a decent canter, didn't either and as the wire sliced neatly into its flesh, the animal crashed to the ground with an ungainly lurch that put its rider clean over its head so that when the two had finished sliding along the firm ground, both had broken their necks. They lay together, face to stunned face, head to bleeding head, in grotesque close proximity.

No one saw the tatty red van as it pulled away from the lay-by not far from where Miranda was looking her gift horse in the mouth.

Just deserts as the old French would have it. What comes round goes round, as more common man might guffaw. Each to their own, and as some soon find, it's their own they reach out to magnetically and you do show your emotions from time to time. Tears roll when the triggers for pain, sadness or happiness are clicked. The response to pain is the most easily understood. It hurts, you cry out. It's almost a mechanical process learnt from childhood, from when you first emerged from your screaming mothers. The reaction to joy or sorrow is more complicated. A child dies of cancer. Why you ask yourselves? What sort of loving creator allows a child to travel such a terrible journey? Why should a child be taken, cut down in such a dreadful and random way? You understand or become immune, deadened to a child's death in a war-torn Syrian city, but a ten-year-old daughter/granddaughter/sister/cousin/school friend from leafy, peaceful suburbs who suddenly develops a brain tumour: you will shake your fists and curse those you feel are responsible and you'll enter that bleak and lachrymose landscape where the well of misery will never run dry. You have a capacity to mourn and the act itself watched by fellow beings from afar will prompt sympathetic grief from those observers. It's infectious or hereditary or genetic or simply a message of solidarity from one living animal to another. A statement of 'I cannot imagine what you're going through but I will share a bit of it before moving on to the other things I have to do.' Happiness is more communal, more public than grief. You will sit in a hall together and laugh at the person you pay to perform and if he or she makes you cry, then it's been money well spent. From where I sit in this Chamber, more souls will cry on their own than they will laugh and often, too, those that do laugh, will laugh all the way to damnation.

áᵭ-àā Ǹí: **Palm print**

I can see the sea, chanted one of the children from the back of the car. No you can't, said the other. Yes, I can, insisted the first. I think it's the sand dunes, said their mother, turning around to quell the outburst. The sea won't be far away, she added, will it, Daddy? She sang to her husband on behalf of her and the children in that way parents often address each other once children become a fixture in their everyday lives. No, it won't, he said. Probably just over that sandbank. Both children sat up like bobbing meerkats on the back seat and peered into the bright distance for that glimpse of blue. The VW hire car pushed on towards the line of sand almost as though it knew the route by heart. The tropical evening sun was sinking away to the other side of the world and the family's all-inclusive fortnight was just a few hours old.

Before I got sick, I was waitressing there for my summer holidays. It was a reasonable job with little pay, but looking good in very little gave me the poolside roster most days and after restaurant duties, all day Monday and every night were my own. The local boys were too local. There was another waiter, a Serb, who was so shy that he didn't speak to anyone and so I made do with the flirtatious attentions of the guests. It started with, "What's a nice girl like you doing in a place like this?" and ended with a stroll in the surf and, if I was lucky, a decent tip.

Look at our room, Daddy! the children shouted as they scampered across the tiled floor and exploded into their own space like ping-pong balls. You've got a big bed and we've got bunks...bagsy me on top, and then the squabble echoed around the family room until their mother intervened with a sensible solution. She was full of sense. Hadn't always been, but motherhood and mortgages had made her so. She'd lost that reckless streak. She was no longer the woman who'd take it from behind while pottering in the kitchen, spun around, knickers on the floor and slapped bare-bottomed onto the granite worktop for a good seeing-to, an uninterrupted giggle, coming in front of the bread bin, giving the toaster a different reason to pop up. Those were the lovey-dovey days of before the children, and don't stop, please don't stop. The kitchen these days was a place for serious taps and vitals. No frivolous slaps and tickles. He was just the same, less interested, less attentive, less romantic; fewer flowers and fewer gentle remarks about how pretty she looked, how good it was to be with her. He liked his headlines, his first drink of the day, that G and T that soothed the dullness away and as she prepared the evening meal, his thoughts were more about decanting the wine than getting his end away or making love to the woman he'd married. There was a time not long ago when he'd raced home early, if he could, to find her waiting and willing, more pleased to see him than a laugh on a clown. Spreadsheets, not bedsheets anymore. Now like individual furniture more used to its place, each of them sat apart, were there for the children, for the family gatherings, for friends to visit but, like a pair of armchairs, on their own just inanimate objects, each a comfortable place to rest a while rather than a great, big, friendly sofa. Some married couples were straight out of the sofa showroom, stayed like that for ages, joined at the hip, plumped up together all comfy and relaxed, entwined; snug and smug like two bugs in a rug, curled up watching the TV blinking back. Yes, dear. No, dear. Three bags full, dear.

I finished clearing the tables. Putting the grimy lids back onto the ketchup bottles was a dreary chore. Why couldn't they do it themselves? Why did they ask for the bloody stuff anyhow? Brits and their kids on holiday. The worst. They want it just like it is back home. Sky TV and Cartoon Network, burgers, fish fingers and nuggets and the bloody Daily Mail. That and the sun. They must have the sun and any cloud in the foreign sky was as welcome as a morsel of dead horse in a Findus cottage pie. I loved the beach, though. It was compensation for dealing with crap. It was the feel of the warm sand between my toes, the pull and push of the surf that made all those sticky ketchup bottle tops a minor irritation. I walked along the shore away from the hotel complex most evenings and loved to watch the sun going down. I got a buzz going down myself and his hands outstretched by his sides pushed deep into the sand as he sat, quivering, with his back to the palm tree. With my eloquent mouth, I went to work on the holidaymaker who'd left his wife to read the children their bedtime story with her own brand of grandiloquence.

You can put them to bed tomorrow night; his wife greeted him over her paperback as he went off to the shower. He needed to clean his conscience.

Monday on holiday was just like any other day. A day off for me and another day off for the holidaymakers. We two women met by the beach kiosk and nodded, each knowing the other. Day off, she enquired. Yep, I said with my warm smile. And almost at once we knew that we could be friends. Not many years between us, maybe ten but not fifteen. We walked and talked.

Nervously he watched from his sunbed. The children splashed in the pool. Shouted, Come on Dad, but he was looking at the beach. The two of us parted and she returned to his side, back to her sunbed, her towel and bottle of sun oil. Do my back, will you? He did as he was told and poured the oil over her red skin and watched as I walked off along the beach towards the palm trees in the distance, my beach bag slung over my bare shoulder and my golden legs like two beautiful snakes gliding over the sand. Later that afternoon she left him and went for a walk. She took the camera. Was going to get some shots. The hotel from the beach, the sea, the dunes. He watched her go, her all-in-one swimming costume mostly covered with a white cotton shirt that flapped gently in the sea breeze. Her legs, different from mine, more stout, more used to being covered up. Within a few minutes she was just a distant speck shimmering as she approached the trees, a white blur in front of the palms.

How fish got there

The holiday photograph was very clear; explicit in every detail. She would have kept it hidden away from her husband and the children, of course. I kept my copy in the hospital bedside drawer and liked to look at it as a reminder of when I was fit. There was a neat crop of my pubic hair and below it, in that pert thigh gap of daylight between the top of my closed legs, you could see in the distance that palm tree; the place I liked to visit in my free time.

You used to treat your young and your old alike. You had respect for them. The newborn had no track record, only the lineage, the substance of the egg from which they were formed. You made much of them. Your arrogance at creating something with your own likeness, someone you could mould into something you approved of. The young were rarely a threat; only to each other and once they had survived the rigours of birth, the trial of a night out on the hill or other ritual baptism, then they became your shadow, a second skin, something real on which you could build your reputation, brand your legacy. The old had form. They had lived, breathed, eaten, laughed, cried, argued, fornicated, loved, lied, cheated, stolen, given, taken, bad-mouthed, kissed, prayed, cursed, slept, worked, talked (oh how they had talked!), walked, shouted, whispered, patted, punched, killed, stroked, healed, mended, bended and bruised; cured, revelled, danced, sung, praised, worshipped even, clapped, fought, pontificated, schemed, spent and saved; they had ignored and been ignored. You yourself were young and old (if you were lucky enough) but how you forgot and how the generations slipped by and each treated the other with a little less respect, a little less fear, a little less attention, a little less love, a little less time…has it really become more precious or just a little less?

áếàā ÌŃ: **Armistice**

At eleven o'clock there came the peace but fighting men weren't at their ease;

And, even though the guns went dumb and men sprang up to stand as one,

with heads held high not cowed or bent or fearful for the bullet sent,

was this really the end to war or just a pause in men's furore?

Eleven strikes herald brief pause before commanding lethal force;

in God we trust and souls are slain; no armistice will save their name.

The Glorious Dead who march in line, an endless column to death sublime;

of noble ignorance and loyalty, of doing what's right for my country, for taking orders, sacrifice: Let's have a brew and damn the lice.

If Kitchener's finger pokes at me, will I be back in time for tea?

Or will I find some foreign place to bury my forgotten face

So that for many years to come those that want to sing their song,

oh valiant hearts, who to your glory came...

You have always had a relationship with the Devil. Call him what you will, the serpent, the dragon, the tempter, Iblis, the Shaytan, the adversary, the prosecutor, Baal Davar, the Evil One, the horned beast, Lucifer, Lord of the flies, Shaitan, Kroni, Mara, Set, Azazel or Asael, Baphomet, Beliai or Beliar or Bheliar, certainly some sort of liar; Mastema, Sammael or Samiel or Sammael, certainly some sort of poison of God; Lilith, the female beast; Mephistopheles, the Dark Lord, the Antichrist, Angra Mainyu, Ahriman, Kolski in colder climes, Voland in old Gaul, Abaddon, the fallen angel, which sounds like one of your hostelries, chief of demons, which sounds like its owner; deceiver, devourer or father of contention, Old Nick if you're frivolous, Satan or the Devil and all his works if you're not. You have given a name to all that is bad, all that smells of evil. You have passed that buck. You have labelled your weakness, your own downfalls, your dreadful misdeeds, your pathetic sins, your demons and you have fastened that tag onto your scapegoat; the one you call the Devil. It's his fault you cry and how many through the ages have donned the sackcloth and ashes and wailed and gnashed their teeth because they could not, would not face the blame? La plus belle des ruses du diable est de vous persuader qu'il n'existe pas, if you get my drift. But he does exist. He's embedded in every one of you and, although it's not my job to persuade you one way or another, I could, given the nod, the approval from my superiors, take on the challenge of trying to guide you, point you in a direction that is deemed as right. But you know what they say. You can take a horse to water but never pat a burning dog!

áɕ̀-àã Ǹɱ: **How fish got there**

After something like a three hour climb through the woods out
into the boulder strewn rough terrain, then scrambling higher
between the serious rocks themselves, the Lac Bleu is reached
with a final assault that leaves the veins gasping for more blood
and the lungs bellowing their hardest. The lake is deep and the
water in it is unnaturally blue. Formed by the erosion of long
gone glacial cut and thrust in the Hautes-Pyrénées, the expanse
of ice cold blue water is imprisoned at over two-thousand metres
up the mountain. If you walked right around the edge of the
lake you'd travel for maybe a mile or more. The water is freezing
and even on the hottest midsummer day the temptation to dive
in must be resisted as a heart attack could result from the shock.
Death could be fairly instant.

Graham did dive in. He ignored the warnings we gave him and
stripped off and went in head first. If he died up there it would
have to be a helicopter job to get the body down again. We
weren't going to carry a stiff down. It was a hard enough job
managing oneself. Anyhow, Graham didn't die then. He came
out less than a minute later looking as blue as the water he had
foolishly dived into. His teeth didn't stop chattering for an hour

and we just looked at him and said we told you so, you chump. His girlfriend was a bit more sympathetic and tried to rub some warmth into him. It was a good job that they didn't want to go off behind a rock somewhere for a celebratory summit shag, like some mountain climbing consenting couples do. Graham's lively girlfriend, Aranea, wouldn't have found anything worth getting hold of between the guy's frozen legs.

"There's fish in there," said Graham when he'd got some of his senses back. "I saw one."

"You were hallucinating," said somebody. "There's never any fish in there."

"There is," Graham was sure he'd seen one.

"What sort was it?" someone asked.

"A fish," said Graham. "About that long." He held his cold, shivering hands about eighteen inches apart. "It was a...fish."

"Bollocks," said somebody.

"Pollocks," said somebody else rather wittily.

"How do they get there?" someone asked the question.

"I'll tell you," said someone else and the group settled down on the rocks in the warm afternoon sunshine to listen to the explanation.

"Once upon a time there was this shepherd, see. This shepherd looked after his sheep up here in the summer to stop the wolves from getting at them. There were wolves up here back then, see. Anyhow, the wolves would come up here at night and take three or four sheep and the shepherd couldn't do much about it, see. The wolves could smell the flock, see, and they knew there was a square meal waiting for them. The shepherd had other ideas and he heard that wolves don't like the smell of fish, see. So one day he bought up from the valley below a whole load of dead and rotten fish, see, and he covered his flock with them to hide the smell of sheep, see. The wolves didn't like the smell and didn't bother to come up after a rotten fish supper, see. Now some of the dead fish had eggs inside them and they washed off the sheep when they drank from the lake and that's how the fish got there, see."

"Bollocks," said somebody again. "I'll tell you how the fish got there, if they did."

"The shepherd you've heard about spent day after long day tending his flock and all he had to eat was mutton, mutton and mutton. He thought to himself, wouldn't it be wonderful to have something else? He began to hate the taste of sheep so much that it really was beginning to affect his job. Sod it, he thought to himself. If the wolves really want a go at the sheep, let them. This was a dangerous attitude for a shepherd. There was nobody else on earth at that altitude who could kill and prepare a sheep in so many different ways. Roasted, stewed, curried, charred, slowly done on hot rocks, flash-fried, deep-fried, boiled and cold. There wasn't a way that the shepherd hadn't cooked or eaten bits of his flock and there wasn't a bit of the sheep he hadn't tried either. There was, he found, a rather distasteful film of sheep fat developing as a permanent feature on the roof of his mouth. He smelt of sheep, kept warm in their fleece, had intercourse with them, ate them, counted them when he was awake, dreamed of them when he was asleep. He could hear sheep, he could smell sheep, but above all he could taste sheep. And that's when it dawned on him that if he bought some live fish up from the river that ran through the valley bottom, he could enjoy the occasional fresh fish to eat. So that's what he did. The very next time he went down the mountain, when he returned, he brought with him on his back in a milk churn filled with river water, fourteen trout he'd tickled from the river. He built a sort of keep net of sticks and stones right on the edge of the lake to stop the fish from escaping out into the lake. He fed them scraps of bread and mutton and watched as they put on weight. One morning he found four floating on the top of his makeshift dam and he didn't know if they died because of the altitude, diet, disease or some unseen predator, although he couldn't find any out-of-the-ordinary marks on them. The remaining ten thrived and the shepherd enjoyed several gastronomic experiences with the fish. The last three mysteriously disappeared from their holding pool one night.

Whether they leapt to freedom or more likely forced their way through the protective but weakened containment structure wasn't certain. What was, however, was that three big trout had escaped into the lake and that was how the fish got there."

There was a minor ripple of applause from some of the group.

"My turn," said someone keen to have a go.

"The fish have always been there. You see when the lake was formed all those hundreds of thousands, millions even, of years ago it wasn't up here. No, my friends, it was down there. What happened was that the fish were already in the water when the lake - it was probably only a pond then, a puddle, even - found itself pushed up with the emerging mountains. Bang went the earth's plates and up popped the Pyrenees with the fish trapped in the rock pools that were thrust upwards. It's as simple as that and that's how the fish got there."

"Yeah, right," said somebody obviously not impressed.

"It was the birds," somebody else spoke up.

"When the birds, the osprey and the like, used to catch fish for their young from the river below, they'd fly over the lake and some of the fish would wriggle free from the bird's talons and drop into the water. Some would die but the strong ones, the survivors, spawned the shoal. That's how the fish got there."

"Actually they came in from the rain." It was one of the girls, the one from Tunbridge Wells who did lots of climbing.

"You know when it rains sometimes and you can almost smell the camels, see the red dust that the winds have blown over from North Africa? Well, it's the same here. The strong winds howl around these mountain peaks. They carry with them the detritus they pick up on the way. Tiny fish are scooped up and dumped here in the lake and that's how the fish got there."

"Right. I think it was in the stomachs of animals that ate the fish, right," said a lad who was convinced that it was in the stomachs of animals that ate the fish and was trying to impress the girl from Tunbridge Wells.

"Imagine the animals and birds that eat fish, right. Well, they eat fish and some of the fish doesn't die, right. So the fish that doesn't die is alive in the gut of the animal or bird that's eaten it, right. Some hunter shoots the animal or bird that's eaten the fish and out pops the dazed but distinctly alive fish, right. If the animal or bird that's eaten the fish has been killed near the lake, right, then the released but confused fish could end up in the water. It could get revived, right, find a mate, right, and that's how the fish got there."

The girl from Tunbridge Wells wasn't that impressed.

"They got there like they got into the sea." It was the girl from Tunbridge Wells's mate.

"How did the fish get into the sea? Well, they got up here into the lake in the same way. Except of course that they are not saltwater fish. Freshwater, more like. But they got here just the same. And how did they get here? It was God that put them here on the fifth day if I'm not mistaken. He put all the creatures on the earth and all the fish into the sea. I remember how. 'Let the waters bring forth abundantly the moving creatures that hath life, and fowl that may fly above the earth in the open firmament of Heaven. He created great whales and every living creature that moveth which the waters brought forth abundantly.' Abundantly seems to be the word to sum up the activities of the fifth day. So that's how the fish got there."

"You've got a bloody good memory," said the bloke who pitched a flat stone onto the lake's surface so that, as most looked on, it skimmed off into oblivion and, like the Messiah walking on the water, left only the rippled marks of its progress.

Graham coughed. He was feeling warmer and the sun and his girlfriend's embrace had helped to restore him.

"Actually they didn't fly down from the sun or walk there or were somehow dropped off and, although I like the idea, I don't think the shepherd stories carry much weight. The fish I saw was probably a reflection of my own indulgence. Each time we think that something cannot possibly be there, it is. What we thought couldn't happen, has. Man becomes fish, fish becomes man. We're interchangeable, connected, convergent, complicit and compliant; like a spider's web."

Graham slipped out of Aranea's desperate grip and, while she screamed uncontrollably and her terrible echoes swirled around that lofty amphitheatre, he dived back into the lake and this time none of the party ever saw him again.

Years later I did. Well, I don't know if it was Graham, but it was the remains of a fish in which a lively black spider had taken refuge. On the dry edge of the lake, tucked into a little rocky inlet in the warm sunshine, the dead fish and living spider seemed to give reassuring comfort to each other; right next to the pyramid of loose stones that had grown-up there marking the place where Graham and, sometime later, his distraught girlfriend disappeared. It remains a mystery how fish got there.

The fault is not in your stars but in yourselves, that you are underlings. If you know your Latin, you'll understand that spider is aranea and that Aranea was that spider; perhaps. But, please; I'm not part of some dystopian society. I hope I don't reflect all the bad and I do see plenty of it as it passes through the Chamber. There is good, you know; lots of good and when you catch me on a good day, well, I'm as happy as a pig in shit, a fish in water or a poetic businessman indulging his expense account to the full, dipping more than his toe into the scummy washbasin water that is impermissible intrigue, if you get my drift.

áɕ-àā ǸǸ: **Novotel nooky**

It was a normal sort of a day
(routine)
when we bunked off to go and play
(spontaneous)
and spoiled laundered fine, white sheets
(selfish)
in leaps and bounds of passionate feats.
(uninhibited)
She was in sales, sailed with the breeze;
(intriguing)
I was the boss she seemed eager to please.
(flirtatious)
Driving and not a moment too soon,
(eager)
"We'd better get ourselves a room."
(private)
Up above that fumed bypass,
(high-octane)
she let me stroke her perfect arse.
(intimate)

It was at the Hammersmith Novotel,

(urgent)

we had our fling on the company's bill.

(illicit)

Room sixty-nine, it said on the door

(fun)

and we did as instructed; then a lot more.

(sexy)

And oh, that afternoon's delight

(passionate)

with whispered pleas for every night

(wanting)

and lust's early grip on common sense

(headlong)

rushed up in the lift and descends intense.

(shameless)

The unquenchable quest, the brain's one desire

(lustful)

that rules the system, sets muscles on fire,

(satisfying)

so the mind plays a reckless game of its own

(foolhardy)

ignoring the rules that are well laid down.

(reckless)

It lasted an hour or maybe much more,

(vigorous)

then we headed west back down the M4;

(triumphant)

back to our respective spouses for tea,

(brazen)

wrapped up in our smug infidelity.

(routine)

As accidents go it was quite a clam,

(shellfish)

head-on into the DHL van,

(spontaneous)

fired through the windscreen just like a shell

(uninhibited)

an end to our dalliance at that Novotel.

(intriguing)

Once bitten, twice shy is a waste of words to the widow of the deep sea fisherman taken by the great white. More pertinent to the vulnerable girl who gave her love to the serial heartbreaker, but even then well meant words are too late to save infidelity. Once bitten is often a bite too deep and too damaging to worry about the next time. But you do. You do worry and you always give yourselves a second chance! In the Chamber you've only got one. Life is not a dress rehearsal for death. Life is Act 1 and death Act 2. If you capture the imagination of your audience in Act 1, then they might stay for Act 2. If you don't, they won't and the curtain will fall accordingly. Just sixty ticks of the clock and another performance slips away; like a child every minute brought down by the mosquito, the world's biggest mass murderer. But do we condemn all Culicidae? It's the female that is more deadly than the male. She is the one equipped to pierce the skin and suck the blood. She is the beast with the taste for it. She is the Lady Macbeth and some. Steeped in gore and frequently laden with disease, she has millions of deaths on her labium; she is the one we have to post R>E>D. Can you blame the male for procreation? The poor weak thing doesn't stand a chance!Dear me, no! The females stream into his cloud and have it away dropping their ripe eggs into the wet somewhere so that the larva and then the pupa will wriggle and burst and spew forth another adult within a matter of days so that the whole cycle can be started all over again. It's a merciless process but then we females subscribe to that, if you get my drift. We have to be; taken from the rib of Adam and tempted by a snake, for God's sake, and if you believe what was written. Here, lovey. Take a bite. Forbidden fruit or what?! It bleeds just like we do. Not blood like ours, but nonetheless the juice of life.We bleed because we have to.That's the way we're made; we're all of us created from stardust and like the female mosquito, we revel in our own malfeasance.

áɕ̀-àã ǸṔ: **Stealing a kiss**

Pudding proposes to her. She hasn't been expecting it, although they have been an item for over a year. He goes down on one knee and like a Prince Charming squeezes a silly tin ring over the finger she offers. They laugh and their merriment is made more with the frivolous French bubbles. He thinks that he loves her and she hasn't really known anybody else, so he is probably the man for her.

Her own Pudding. As they fool around, he once again discovers that place, the delicious dark secret, her 'Incy Wincy' as he calls it. It's a pet name for that crop of short, dark hair, the friendly female spider that sits between her legs, the one he first caught sight of through her transparent white underwear that time he gently pulled her up the riverbank after they had been swimming. Now engaged, they make love. It's just the same. Afterwards she isn't sure and tells him to go home. So he does, back to his country cottage. He shouldn't be driving. Before crashing to bed he plays loud music and sings along with another bottle and The Stones. His emotions are confused and he is not sure of anything other than the lyrics ringing in his head.

Way off, perhaps the sound of a bell. The cobweb at the back of his mind trembles with the sound. It is as if a trapped mite is struggling to escape from the eight-legged marauder, causing the silver lines to quiver. But each frantic movement is sending a message back to the grim captor. Stillness would be a safer option. The alarm wails in urgency and gets louder. Ring ring. RING RING. The noise won't go away. It mixes with the heavy echoes from that nightcap rock and roll band. In a trick played on the half-witted, semi-conscious; maybe it's the church bells from across the wooded parkland being hammered in sympathy for the Devil. Perhaps it's a call to the front door by a midnight rambler's crooked finger pressing firm to the bell push. Or is it time for assembly somewhere; a stampede of wild horses? You can't always get what you want but if you try sometimes, you just might find you get what you need. The familiar sounds turn sleep to drowsiness which then becomes an urgency to take note and the alarm, the ring, is really a phone.

At early doors, say two or three in the morning, when the phone rings everyone knows, suspects at least, that the news is not good. Good news can wait. Bad news can't. Such is the way we've given emphasis to it.

At last.

"Hello."

"What d'you mean?"

How fish got there

"Let me get dressed. I'll be there in, say, forty minutes."

There is a scramble to put on the clothes that have barely had time to crease, and a quick rinse with a glug from the fat Listerine bottle. Spit and go. Slotted in the fridge door next to the half bottle of, tart white, the semi-skimmed straight from the soft, plastic milk bottle suddenly tastes of mint: so just a token swig is forced to try and coat the film of alcohol from a few hours ago. Swig and go.

Driving in the early hours won't take anything like forty minutes. Wombling badgers are the other traffic, two of them in a huff. There's the wily fox who pauses perilously in the headlights just to try and stare them out. The vixen's tongue licks her lips at the thought of all the insect life collected on the windscreen. Easy prey, but what a messy waste. The racing car slices through the million silky cords stretched out across the night-time lanes, from hedge to hedge, nearly more violent, more destructive than anything on earth. All those spiders work in vain. Forty minutes. It could be done in thirty at the most. Rushing towards distress. Her bedtime cheeks are streaked with salty tears and useless make-up. She sobs, cries real drops and wants her lover to be there with her.

"Please come, Pudding," she implores.

"What d'you mean?"

"I need you to be here now. It's not safe."

"Let me get dressed. I'll be there in, say, forty minutes." Thirty more like, as long as the warning red fuel light is only joking.

"Bollocks." Now of all times. On a cross-country mission and low on diesel. Old Proctor's farm would have some in the yard in the green tank stuck up on bricks. If that was locked, one of his tractors could be siphoned. There might be a chance of just driving in and helping oneself. Old Proctor's farmhouse stands like a sentry box overlooking the scruffy yard. Stop in the gateway. Leg it. Find a can or plastic container and just nick a gallon or two. Come back and pay Proctor in the morning. Or not. The green tank stinks of heavy fuel and the nozzle isn't locked in place. Typical of old Proctor. He is a slack sod, thank God. Rinse out the spray can with the red fuel, fumble in the semi-darkness brushing off the cobwebs that cling to everything and appear like very fine, dusty net curtains to the low harvest moon. Spiders were here before the dinosaurs and their webs will hang around long after all of us have gone.

There is no warning as such. Just the sudden blast from a twelve-bore that cuts Pudding in half. Old Proctor didn't miss at close quarters.

So he never did arrive, never did discover the reason for her upset. It might have been so different.

How fish got there

"What d'you mean?"

"I need you to be here now. It's not safe."

"Let me get dressed. I'll be there in, say, forty minutes. What's up, honey?" he might have asked, to be told hysterically that a large spider had just woken her in nightmare, terrifying her with the softest touch of one of its eight hair-covered legs. What she didn't know was that it had dropped onto her pillow, crawled through her flowing hair and across her right cheek to find her lips, on purpose, stealing a kiss. Something Pudding would never ever do again.

You have always worshipped Mammon. Call it what you will: a grand, the folding stuff, smackers, filthy lucre, loot, dough, a stack, money, wonga, swag, bucks, teuro, sen, lolly, kupang, greenbacks, duckets, fogskins, spondulicks, a monkey, ringgit, panji, quids, dassi, bissi, a score, moola, icker, peti, coin, khokha, dosh, grivennik, silver, chervonets, reddies, limon, wampum, arbuz, shillings, klover, pennies, riksdaler, selma, a bag, simoleons, currency, wads, sterling, shekels, chremata, bezants, gold bars and not forgetting bread on which of course you know that man cannot live alone. Cash is king and the acquiring of it seems to concentrate your mind to an unhealthy degree. It's vulgar to talk about it because it's vulgar. Royalty doesn't bother with it or so it's said. Bankers and their like talk about it behind closed doors and in a jargon that no one else could possibly interpret. Those who haven't got it talk about it and then only in terms of, "Got any loose change gov?" You might not be able to take it with you, but it probably helps you to get there and once in the

Chamber it doesn't matter a tinker's cuss how much you accumulated, invested, squandered, spent, saved or simply pissed up that wall. I don't accept tips of a pecuniary nature!

áǵàã Ǹṕ: Penny's for Guy

The annual village bonfire party usually provided a colourful interlude in an otherwise dull November. The schoolchildren in particular looked forward to the evening. A working party of dads built a giant bonfire in farmer Padgett's field, the one that was next to the pub and had been kept as grass for as long as anyone could remember. This year's effort was particularly grand because someone on the organising committee knew someone who had a furniture factory on the trading estate, and a very large wagon of wooden bits and pieces of surplus and broken furniture turned up in Padgett's field.

"Looks like a chair mountain," somebody said when they had finished building the pile which was higher than the pub itself. Padgett always had the job of fixing the guy to the top, and this year he was going to have to use one of his tractors and a front-end loader with its hydraulic extension in order to reach the dizzy height. The schoolchildren were encouraged to make a guy and on the two Saturdays before the 5th, a few of the bigger children would take the creation into the local market town to raise money. All the proceeds went to the school and 'the penny for the Guy' collection normally yielded welcome funds.

The headmaster, Guy Watson, was delighted with the efforts made by his parents and their children and the money - last year it was one-hundred-and-sixty pounds- was used to purchase some materials for the art classes. Running a C of E village school wasn't easy and all contributions were gratefully received. Mr Watson was into his art and a firm believer that his children should be encouraged to express themselves right from the start.

"They must be allowed to find their inner creativity," he would tell all new parents.

The headmaster had found his own inner creativity with Miss Penny Dugworth. Miss Dugworth had joined the staff of three to take charge of the infants. Miss Dugworth was fresh out of teacher training college and the village school was her first hands-on job. Mr Watson wasn't.

The two of them had been attracted to one another from day one. From the interview really. Mr Watson had never liked redheads. He always thought that people with red hair had short tempers; too much Celtic blood in their veins. He didn't know why he'd carried the impression with him, but he had. He'd never been with a girl with red hair, nor ever kissed one. The first thing he noticed about her, after the shock of red hair, was her smile; a big mouth full of even, tombstone-sized white teeth. It was the sort of mouth that dominated the face. It took complete control of the lower half and when it broke out into a smile, became the focal point for the whole thing. It was like a big smile from a little girl; an innocent smile that drummed up mischievous thoughts. Her big green eyes twinkled when she smiled, danced with fun and expelled her sense of humour. She wasn't a beautiful girl but she did have an attraction, a youthful liveliness and intelligence that popped and bubbled around her. It wasn't, though, precocious in any way. She'd flirt without perhaps meaning to. She was one of those people who would look directly into your eyes when talking to you; would give undivided attention. She was one of those people who made you feel flattered, important. She almost had an aura, a static charge, about her, not a halo, but something that distinguished her from those around, those other pretty girls that Mr Watson would fantasise about, pore over from the pages of 'Men Only'. She was short and slim and looked as though she had been a gymnast. When she wore a skirt, which wasn't that often, her legs looked fantastic and whatever she wore, her bottom looked perfect. She was twenty-something and therefore nearly twenty years younger than he was. From the first time he met her, he fancied her, couldn't wait to get to know her, hoped she wanted to get to know him. Probably in his dreams.

They'd been working together for some months. Mr Watson was enjoying flirting with her more and more, and found himself thinking about her on those occasions when his mind should have been focusing on more important issues. One evening during a half-term, she invited him to her flat at the top of a Georgian building in the market town. She cooked seafood pasta and they sat together at a little round table in the flat enjoying the meal and each other's company. When she came to clear the empty plates, smeared with the juice of her cooking, he grabbed her hand and pulled her towards him firmly but not in any way threateningly; it was rather, a tug of encouragement. Their lips met and they kissed, his thin ones beautifully engulfed by her big mouth, swallowed up, with their pasta tongues circling each other. Soon pushing his chair back from the table, he manoeuvred her to his lap where she sat with her back to him. He started to kiss her nape, the vulnerable flesh covering the spine just before it reaches the brain. Her red hair was piled up somehow so that her slender neck presented itself as a new thrill. Before long the two of them were standing by the open window in the dark with only the outside street lights to guide them. They behaved recklessly, without worrying about the consequences.

Mr Watson certainly didn't want his wife to find out. They had to be careful. The headmaster didn't want any accusing fingers pointing at him. In such a small community, scandal was only a slip away. Miss Dugworth, on the other hand, had less to lose. She didn't seem to care about her lover's position. Not strictly true. She cared about it over her desk after school hours or in Mr Watson's big four-by-four, or in the little bed in her flat, but she didn't care about keeping the affair a dark secret forever.

"Why can't we just come out of the closet, Guy?" she asked him one evening.

"I've got my reputation to think about, Penny darling. And my wife and brother-in-law. God, what would they do?"

Mrs Watson was a very wealthy woman. She'd been a Padgett before she'd married. Her father had left her half of his estate when he died. While she had inherited the money, her brother had kept the family farm. The Padgett siblings had also assumed that close family bond that kept their position in society as the most important ingredient for their family's legacy. When Marjory met Guy and then married him, it was to all intents and purposes, something she need not have done. But it was, apparently, doing the right thing at the right time, and she did love him. He was, so some said, a lucky man. It wasn't many village school headmasters that could afford to drive around in the latest Range Rover. Guy Watson knew on which side his bread was buttered and, although he had no intention of falling out with his wife or her brother, infatuation became a tantalizing and compelling bedfellow.

So the secret relationship soldiered on behind closed doors with the headmaster and his junior member of staff getting deeper and deeper into each other's emotions, each other's inner creativity. There was gossip, ugly rumour, but no actual proof. Someone on the parents' committee thought that the headmaster was being overfriendly to Miss Dugworth. The two other members of staff thought so, too. They called her "teacher's pet" behind her back. But no one had any actual proof that the two had been carrying on.

"Where there's smoke there's fire," said one of the parents not long before the November celebration and the headmaster found himself under more scrutiny than ever before.

It was the vicar who approached him first.

"Everything, er, all right, headmaster?" he asked after morning prayers on the Monday.

"Yes thank you, vicar," replied Mr Watson.

"How is Marjory? Haven't seen her for months."

"Oh my wife's fine, thanks, vicar. Just fine."

"Good. Pleased to hear it. You're so lucky to have the love of a good woman."

"Yes. I am, aren't I?" the headmaster said, realising that he had the love of one and the lust of another.

Like all such 'chats', the vicar's words fell mostly on stony ground. Mr Watson's affair with Miss Dugworth had blunted the edge of his conscience so that he found himself justifying his infatuation with the younger woman. Marjory no longer really loves me, he thought. But she did, perhaps not as much as on the day, thirty years before, when they married, but nevertheless, she still loved her husband. Like an accident waiting to happen, the unequal triangle would turn pear-shaped. Marjory would get to hear about Penny ("the Penny would drop," he joked to himself in a macabre way) and then all hell would be let loose. Guy Watson just couldn't take the risk. He couldn't afford to upset his wife, lose her and the school, his comfortable slot and respect in the community. By playing with the redhead, he was playing with fire.

"I think that we ought to stop seeing each other." He spoke the words just like a headmaster would.

"What the fuck do you mean?" shrieked Penny Dugworth, unlike an infant's teacher.

"It's just that I cannot go on seeing you and lying to my wife."

"Does she know about me?"

"No. But she will. Someone will spill the beans."

"I'll spill the fucking beans, as you so put it." Miss Dugworth had never talked to her boss like that before.

"What on earth do you mean?" said the suddenly trembling headmaster.

"I mean that if you are trying to dump me, and I think that's what you're trying to do, then I'll go and see your wife and tell her just what sort of extra-curricular activities you've been getting up to."

"You wouldn't do that, Penny darling?" The headmaster looked even more frightened.

"I fucking well would, Guy darling."

"Then let's not rock the boat. Let's leave things just as they are. Aye?" The headmaster couldn't think what else to do. This was a situation he hadn't expected. As he pulled up his trousers and tucked in his shirt and watched as Penny Dugworth slid back into her underwear and jeans, he knew for the first time that the affair had become sordid. He felt trapped in the classroom, boxed into a corner with the dunce's hat on; a dark, messy, grubby place out of which he didn't know how to crawl.

As often happens, when the dam breaks, you either sink or swim. Guy Watson swam; doggy-paddled his clumsy way back to safety.

"I'm told that you and Miss Dugwold are, what shall we say, fairly pally." Marjory Watson came up with the unexploded bombshell over a Sunday breakfast on the morning when the clocks had gone back.

"Miss Dugworth?" replied her husband.

"What?" said Marjory.

"Her name is Penny Dugworth."

"Well, Guy. Whatever her name, are you being overfriendly with her?"

It all came out. The dam did burst and Guy told his wife the whole truth and nothing but the truth. He spared her the gory detail but explained that he was now trapped in a dreadful relationship with her, and that he was being virtually blackmailed by her. It was, he confessed, a dreadful decision to have taken on the Jezebel in the first place. He said he was sorry, really very sorry, and he begged his wife for forgiveness. Absolution was not as high on Marjory's agenda as retribution.

"Well, Guy," said Marjory seriously, as she sliced the top off her boiled egg with more conviction than usual. "You've been a bloody fool. I'll have to have a word with the woman and you can stop seeing her. She'll have to leave the school of course."

"Of course, dear," said Guy with so much relief that it gave him a headache to go with his dry mouth.

True to her word, Marjory Watson spoke to Penny Dugworth who left the school immediately. She didn't stop to say goodbye, didn't leave a note for her lover, and no one ever heard from her again.

The evening of the bonfire party arrived and the giant bonfire was set alight by the vicar. Right at the top, seated in one of the less broken chairs was the life-sized Guy. Marjory's brother had fixed it up there as was agreed. It looked grotesque sitting on top of the flaming pile. Its clothes, one of the headmaster's old three-piece tweed suits, looked almost unused. The floppy felt hat that had come from Marjory Watson covered the straw hair on top of the rubber mask with its dreadful grin. Through the open slots for the eyeholes, a pair of green pupils looked out lifelessly. The flames licked higher and higher and the straw ignited just before the rest of the dummy.

"Look, Mummy!" said one of the excited children, waving a hot dog towards the disfigured flaming effigy. "The Guy's got red hair."

"Yes, dear, it's flaming red, isn't it?" said the mother lackadaisically.

Out to lunch. In its true sense with culinary connotations. Dining al fresco, perhaps in a country restaurant's garden with dappled sunshine and fine rosé from Provence chilled with beads of condensation rolling down, a clinging diamond sheen, and an à la carte menu to die for with food so light and full of class; an intense work of art on a big white plate; your keen palate and the crisp, white linen napkin the only beneficiaries of chef's exacting skill and your best friends' company running around the table with genuine affection and high, tinkling spirits, like ice floating, bouncing, jostling and colliding on the side of fine cut glass. I can imagine it, see it, taste it, smell it, hear it, feel it all just as I can appreciate the brown juice drizzled over the fingers from the newly dug fat, quilted witchetty grub that is eaten with relish under the shade of the Black Wattle tree from whose roots it was untimely ripped. Raw, it tastes like almonds. But you know what you like. You have standards. Reserved table on the terrace or patch of dust under the bough. But out to lunch. Also an unfortunate term for not all there. One brick short of a hod, when the lift doesn't go all the way to the top, one sandwich short of a picnic, two bob short of a pound, a few crumbs short of a biscuit, not the most useful tool in the box, nor the sharpest knife in the drawer, where the wheel is spinning but the hamster is dead, when the lights are on but there's no one at home, not playing with a full deck, wouldn't know if he was Arthur or Martha, bei ihr ist eine Schraube locker or a one-handed clap. Those out to lunch or out to lunch; there's room for them all in the Chamber where we'll make of them what they deserve.

áɔ́-àã ǸP̀ : **Histrionics**

"What time do you call this, then? Coming in here waking me up without any consideration whatsoever. I wouldn't dream of doing that to you. You're so selfish, only ever think of yourself and never ever think about how I would feel. Out with your mates no doubt till God knows what time in the morning and not a word. Not a call or a text or anything to say what time you'd be home and all I can do is sit here and wait for you to show up when it suits you, no question of letting me know what's going on. For all I know you could have been lying in a ditch somewhere but what would you care about that? And I'll bet you've been with that tart, what's her name, that so-called PA, the one who fusses around you like a bitch on heat. PA. Pathetic Arse, that's what she is. Can't think what she sees in you, sits on your lap does she, takes dicktation no doubt, I bet she does and I bet she goes home to her boyfriend and tells him all about just how limp her boss is. And don't think I don't know all about it. You and your so-called working late. If working late smells like strong drink and loose, fishy women then you're a bloody expert. Trying to creep in here, taking your clothes off, getting into my bed, pretending that nothing has happened; it's all such a bloody sham..."

"Good morning, darling. I'm sorry to have woken you up. I'm just getting up. Would you like a cup of tea or is it too early? We don't want to be late for the funeral, do we?"

Marital bedroom or a firefight in a grim Gaza tunnel? Twin Tower or drowning at sea? Hospital bed or stinking, rat-infested trench? Lethal injection or choking on a fish bone? Crucifixion or R. T.A? Abortion or by hanging in an orchard of cider apples? Ebola or asleep in your comfortable bed? How will you meet your maker? Even though the means of your departure is as yet unknown, the departure itself is one hundred per cent certain. Will you be ready for the Chamber? There's no room for ifs or buts. No, "Oh please hang on a minute. I wasn't ready. I'm not prepared." You arrive and you will be judged on your credentials as presented. Your coded details. One chance.

áɔ̃-àã ǸǪ: **Marking the territory**

When Dorothy bent over you could see that she wasn't wearing any knickers. It wasn't a pretty sight. It wasn't unattractive either. It was... well... a surprise. You didn't expect to see the secret kept undercover between grown girls' legs. Dorothy was over eighteen so she could do pretty much what she liked. 'Fan touché flashing', as she christened the act, became a sport for one hot summer. Dorothy and her friend Charlotte liked to play when they were bored and the mood took them.

It was while out shopping on warm Saturday mornings that the two girls set up the game. What had started out as a bit of fun became an art form and they took it in turns to photograph each other and their victims' reactions to create an album. Charlotte called it 'our bum album'. Their targets weren't random. They were, in that the girls chose them from the milling crowds, but each was picked in the same way a pickpocket might select his quarry. The girls wanted to create an impression; didn't want their efforts to go unnoticed, and so choosing the right subject was every bit as important as delivering the visual display. Dorothy favoured men of a certain age, those that probably hadn't seen a 'fan touché' for years. Charlotte didn't mind who saw hers. What both of them avoided was being exposed to anyone who knew them, the law or CCTV, and they never performed in the same place twice.

A 'bend over' that involved almost touching the toes was the easiest way to flash. It looked the most casual and innocent of the moves. It was most effective when performed inside and the simple act of bending over in a shop on the pretext of examining more closely the goods on offer, could reveal the goods not on offer. It looked to the observer like an accident and on more than one occasion the victim had approached the perpetrator with almost apologetic advice along the lines of someone's forgotten to put their underwear on. The sentence nearly always ended in 'dear' or maybe 'deary', a condescension that certainly wasn't applicable. The bending over display gave witness to a lot of naked bottom, but if it was done with gusto and athleticism, then something of the 'fan touché' came into view as well. The bare rear on its own was not deemed as having gone far enough by the sporting girls. It was important to show 'fan touché'. 'Fan touché' scored points and points were prizes in the All Bar One or White Horse afterwards.

If the 'bend over' was a shotgun that could sometimes reach a larger than intended audience, the 'front flick' was a rifle with 'in your face' precision. The more purposeful flick of the skirt or dress at the front, left the onlooker with the impression that he or she had just seen something that he or she should not have. It often provoked the double take and was over in a flash, so that the recipient was never sure if what had happened had happened.

Points were scored according to reaction. Those exposed to the experience were always their own living scoreboard. The marks awarded were out of ten and to get top marks was very rare. Most were below five. Reactions ranged from nothing at all, as though the recipient hadn't seen anything or, more truthfully, was pretending not to have seen anything; to an over the top reaction that might result in yelling and the stopping of traffic. The marking process was conducted by the girl not 'flashing the gash', as Charlotte more crudely described it. So as Dorothy lifted her denim skirt (it was blue denim that day) in front of a guy who looked about fifty-five, wearing a waxed jacket and brown cords; so Charlotte observed and photographed with the long lens and gave marks. On this occasion the guy stopped dead in his tracks, while his head swivelled so violently following the passing of Dorothy, that his neck must have been stiff for a fortnight. The man stood gawping. Transfixed, but gawping, facing the way he'd just come from. Charlotte gave her friend a five for that. When Charlotte decided to bend over right in front of an older traffic warden, the reaction was less interesting than if the uniformed guy had stumbled across an illegally parked car. Dorothy awarded one. in Currys, a 'bend over' to look at the base of a large, plasma-screen telly, caused a ripple from three other customers and a whole new meaning to the expression 'High Definition'. Dorothy got a six for that.

On some days the girls would do what they called 'Fanny dress'. They'd deck their naked lower regions in fancy dress. Dorothy's most elaborate was as a Mexican complete with mini-sombrero, and Charlotte got Dorothy to paint a giant, colourful target on her bare bottom which of course provoked comments about scoring and the bullseye. Painting a fish so that its mouth became lifelike was a favourite outing, along with the speech bubble drawn on the high thigh, the talking 'fan touché', with the message, 'Amazingly enough I don't give a shit'.

Dorothy and Charlotte had fun. They were 'good' girls from 'good' homes and all they were doing was just having a bit of harmless fun with added adrenaline rush. They never did it when they'd had too much to drink, and had they been asked to explain their actions, they would have said that they were performing street theatre or pavement art. Dorothy even thought about applying for a grant, but Charlotte said she wouldn't stand a chance and the next summer the weather was lousy and Charlotte went to the south of France anyway.

Dorothy married a barrister and became a JP and was buried alive in an Alpine avalanche. Charlotte got engaged to a land agent and had twins.

When Henry took his cock out, like a limp Conger eel, and waved it at the passing crowd before pissing into the fountain, someone told him to put it away and somebody else called the police. He told the court that he was only marking his territory, but the Chair of the Bench told him that he'd already upset public decency and he'd have to pay a fine and that if he did it again he'd be in real trouble, even though she remembered the time when she and her friend pranced the same streets on Saturday mornings that hot summer flashing at those that, mostly speaking, didn't want to see what they weren't supposed to. Henry hadn't done too much wrong. He'd just been caught doing it. Henry had hit the nail on the head. It was, she reflected, all about marking the territory.

Cults. They won't help you. They'll take your blood and sweat, your time and your money and spin you a good line. They suck you into their webs and confuse your thinking with their own credible doctrines. Do you know how many so-called religious cults there are? Of course you don't. Why should you when a new one springs up nearly every one of your Earth weeks. Like clothes, though, you're tempted to try them on perhaps. Nice Kabbalah jacket. Suits you, sir. Moonie pants and your bum doesn't look big in them at all. What about that nice little Scientology skirt? It's not that short and anyway you like showing off your welcome mat. Or slip on this colourful African Theological Archministry pullover. Voodoo look good in it, if you get my drift! An anthroposophy bra will round them up and point them in the right direction and a Bábism pair of Islam stockings complete with suspenders from the Bethel Ministerial Association will wow them in the aisles. And please don't forget your Wicca knickers. Cults or, if you'd rather not use the C word, new religious movements, sound like the sort of experience you go through most days on the lavatory. Have you had a movement today dearie? Yes thank you, nurse, I've had several ranging from those with loose affiliations based on novel approaches to spirituality to communitarian enterprises that command a considerable amount of group conformity and a social identity that separates their adherents from mainstream society. But then, nurse, I ran out of paper.

áɔ́-àā Ǹɑ̀: **Departure**

Downtown Manhattan and the early alarm call sounds like a road drill.

Brrrrrgh!

Brrrrrgh!

"Arrrgh," comes the groan from deep within as you turn in bed and fart with a vengeance. Indigestion's calling card. There's no one there to hear you so you let it rip. Actually even if there was someone next to you, you probably wouldn't try and silence it too much. Although that would depend on how well you knew them, but if they were sharing a bed with you then you probably knew them pretty well, so it wouldn't matter, would it? Let them see you as you are, that sort of thing. Thinking about it, maybe you would try and hold it in, clench the buttocks politely. No one likes sharing a bed with a farter. But men fart and are proud of it, whereas women don't or don't admit to it if they do. It's probably one of those urban myths found in the 'strange but true' column snippets you might read in The Daily Whatsit. You've never heard a woman drop a decent one, drunk or sober, and yet at boarding school Liversidge (or was it Kenning?) could fart 'God Save The Queen' after lights out every night. Come to think of it, he (Liversidge or Kenning) never changed his repertoire. It was always 'God Save The Queen' followed by a goodnight to each member of the dormitory, a fart after their name.

"Goodnight, Cavanaugh." Fart!

"Goodnight, Jones." Fart!

"Goodnight, Russell." Fart!

You wonder what he's doing now (Liversidge or Kenning)? Probably an investment banker, civil servant or, you smile, working at the Met Office.

No, men fart, women can't. That's what you think and you do two more just to prove the point and roll over to think about the day ahead.

Fart!

Fart!

It's too bloody early. Ten more minutes wouldn't hurt, so you get as comfortable as your body lets you, curl into the foetal position and close your eyes.

Did you have a dream last night? Yes, you did! Sometimes when you wake up you remember your dreams and sometimes you don't. Sometimes it's not until you're in the bath or munching your Kellogg's that you remember. But you remember last night's, or bits of it and you open your eyes to try and make it clearer. It was vague. Faces and places, undefined but not threatening, colourless somehow but not in a land of black and white. Surreal springs to mind but then so does Ulrika Jonsson. What the hell was she doing there? Percy Thrower, too, the last century's Alan Titchmarsh. How strange the brain becomes when the body sleeps. Wasn't Percy Thrower trying to force geraniums out of Ulrika's ear, or was it the other way round? You don't remember. What you do remember was the last bit of the dream. You were falling. In the last minutes before the early alarm, you were falling and they do say that falling, to dream of falling, means something, but you're not sure what. You can't remember what they said it was supposed to mean. Never mind.

Another night.

Another dream.

You stretch the length of the bed and turn and turn again. Acid indigestion runs up and down. Sleep has had enough of you and, even though you really don't want to, you've got to get up. You've got to burst out from beneath your cover, fix bayonets, blow the whistle, go over the top and charge at the day ahead.

Another day.

Another dollar.

Your meeting with First Commercial isn't until 8.30 and as you run the bath you sort of imagine your opening pitch. You see yourself, smart-suited, word-perfect, confident, proud and loud, not giving an inch, just going in and getting the business.

The bathroom fills with steam long before the bath itself is ready and you wipe your hand across the misted mirror to reveal your face. It's all there, pretty much the same one you went to bed with and, like scores of others in bathrooms across the city, you do your early morning acting. When Michael Caine gets up and goes to the bathroom and examines his face in the mirror, who does he think he is? My name is Albert Anthophila, he might say in his Michael Caine voice, which wouldn't be right at all. This morning, this September morning, you are Adolf Hitler. The bristles of the electric toothbrush, a mean Nazi moustache and your hair ordered to the front sweeping down to the right eyebrow, threatening to invade it.

"Seek hile," you say softly to the mirror, clicking your bare heels together on the bathroom floor.

"Seek hile," you say once more, creating a bad impression.

Seek

Hile

Baths are so much more than showers. You get intimate with them. A bath is more like making love, whereas a shower is at best a quickie. You settle in for your session, half man, half water.

You sink.

You think.

The First Commercial meeting could go one of three ways. You could come out with the deal. Unlikely. They could say thanks but no thanks, but that was not on the cards as they had called for this latest face-to-face. What they were probably going to do is say go away and sharpen your pencil, redo your sums and come up with a better offer. If that were the case you'd have to really cut the cloth and look long and hard at cost savings. To work on a margin of less than three per cent would not impress the board. You'd have to do some pretty smart talking to get around that one. Get your ducks in line, convincing Richard that it was a deal with a future worth having. Once Richard was on your side, the others, F.D. included, should all agree. Your rock-bottom line was two point two five per cent and if they wanted you to beat that, then you'd just have to turn and walk. You'd know one way or the other by ten. Fingers crossed and all that, it would be great to pull off another Afghan deal. Selling arms to the Third World is a tedious business but it pays the bills.

You pull the plug and the used bathwater starts to disappear to the Hudson, you suppose.

Gurgle.

Gurgle.

You wet shave in Hitler's old mirror and as always, you marvel just for a brief moment at how the can, the Gillette shaving can, can hold so much foam. How do they get it in there? Why don't you read about them blowing up with the pressure, covering bathrooms in crazy foam? Perhaps they do but you never hear about it. Crazy foam terrorists aren't newsworthy.

Pssssst!

Pssssst!

You dress in the uniform you chose last night. White Oxford cotton button-down shirt, pale pink silk tie and the Gieves double-breasted pinstripe. Polished black Church's for the feet: you remember your mother's words about how you can always tell the quality of a man by the quality of his footwear.

By 7.00 you're ready to leave. The driver is in the lobby at 7.20 and you take the elevator down to meet him. The raucous roar of the Upper West Side hits you as you slip from the air-conditioned building into the back of the air-conditioned limo and off to the World Trade Center.

Your driver is pleased to see you and yes, you are enjoying your visit to the Big Apple and yes, you will be going on up to New England and no, it isn't as beautiful as it will be next month in the fall. It's small talk in a big car.

Small.

Big.

You never discover which way First Commercial really wants to play it or who their clients are. The deal is never done. Something atrocious happens. You leave without a word and you're never seen alive again. They put your possessions in a Jiffy bag, the only sign that you were ever there, your things and the silver Cross fountain pen, the one I gave you last birthday with the initials on it, the one they took from your suit pocket when you arrived at the St James Infirmary, dead in the back of the limousine. Your heart must have known all along and kept you from the horror. They said that you had had a massive heart attack on your way to what they now call Ground Zero.

Nine.

eleven.

How fish got there

You know I like my lists. Eliza the list maker. Eliza's list. Rolls off the tongue like words from Coleridge. Like crackers and cheese or heart and attack or Bin and Laden. Comes with the job, I guess. I've got that sort of mind; one that thrives on lists. You set me off and I'll make a list. Shagging. The Devil. Ways of dying. Cults. P words. You name it and I'll make a list of it. But lists in themselves don't amount to much. Anyone with half an intellect can list a list. Lists are used as a means of defence. It was on my shopping list. You ring-fence yourself with them and expect their effectiveness at dispersing any critics. Like covered wagons and the Apaches. Lists are my chuck wagons. Make me look bright, with it, streetwise, up together, matter-of-fact, in the know, on the ball, tickety-boo, on the button, sharp as a knife, quick-witted, on the money, queen of the hill, top of the class, number one, numero uno, cunt of the walk, queen bee, crème de la crème, top of the list. See what I did there? Just like shelling peas, easy-peasy, peace of piss, a doddle, a cinch, a dead cert, simples; and there I go again. But you know what they say? Reductio ad absurdum or is it repetitio mater memoriae? Hint at it and post hoc ergo propter hoc. Quod erat demonstrandum, if you get my drift. Christians and lions, like chivalrous beings entering the lists. Make a list of the lists and list some more martyrs? Why with the greatest of pleasure. Martin Luther King Jnr, Maximilian Kolbe, Saint Stephen, Joan of Arc, Nathan Hale, St Putarinia, Archbishop Paulos Faraj Rahho, Manche Masemola, Patriarch Gregory V of Constantinople, Athanasios Diakos, Bhagat Singh, Socrates, Vladimir Bogoyavlensky, the Souliot Women, Jean François de la Barre and let's not forget the Tolpuddle Martyrs from 19th-century England, those hardy agricultural labourers who did their bit for history. Some movements feed off their martyrs. Judaism is itself a religion of martyrdom, and shahadat is a fundamental concept in Sikhism. Guru after guru gave themselves to that service as martyrs. For others martyrdom is the devotion of oneself to service to humanity, or so said Bahá'u'lláh, and I bet more than once you've been told not to be such a bloody martyr and how many followers have you accumulated thus far? So let him that is without sin cast the first stone or something like that. A good line if ever there was one. We could all be martyrs if we tried. Be the thrown at rather than the thrower, the beaten rather than the beater, the murdered rather than the murderer. Depends whose crowd you're in, which side you're on. It takes courage to stand up and out of the crowd. That's what makes a good martyr; to stand up and be counted and to meet a really gory end with the more blood and guts the better. But what comes around goes around. What monster is society that seems to have priority over me, a mere minority? For if my mere minority became a large majority we would have priority and thus become society, if you get my drift. Martyrs always spring from the weakest, most persecuted side but who can say that any martyr has a God given right to a G>R>E>E>N ticket. Might not a martyr to the cause be as misguided as an ancient chart to a space traveller? So the plea of 'Dear God, please let it be quick,' could be a selfish cry for help for a selfish god who does things in his own mysterious way and at his own leisure and, let's face it, whose answer you'll never understand anyhow.

áś-àā ŇỌ: Twisting the words and arguing to infinity or death, whichever comes first

"What can I say?"

"Nothing."

"What?"

"Nothing. Nothing at all."

"So that's an end to it, then?"

"Yes. I guess so."

"All over?"

"All over."

"What if I said I was sorry?"

"Are you?"

"Well, I could be."

"You could be?"

"Yep. I could be sorry."

"Well, are you or aren't you?"

"I could be."

"You could be?"

"Yep. I could be."

"Well, that really won't do."

"I could be sorry and that won't do?"

"Yes. Could be isn't good enough."

"We agreed we could be good for each other, didn't we?"

"That's just twisting the words."

"No it isn't."

How fish got there

"Yes it is."

"Well, it could be."

"There you go again."

"What?"

"Making light of the situation."

"The situation?"

"Yes."

"We're in a situation?"

"Yes. I think we are."

"Not a relationship, then?"

"Not anymore."

"A situation, then?"

"It's not a joke."

"Not a situation comedy?"

"Very funny."

"But not a joke."

"I'm not laughing."

"I can see that."

"Well, what do you expect?"

"I've said I could be sorry."

"Yes, well, I've said that could be isn't good enough."

"Could be isn't good enough?"

"Yes."

"I see."

"No. I don't think you do see."

"OK. I don't see, then."

"No, you don't."

"I agree."

How fish got there

"What can I say?"

"Nothing."

"What?"

"Nothing. Nothing at all."

"So that's an end to it, then?"

"Yes. I guess so."

"All over?"

"All over."

"What if I said I was sorry?"

"Are you?"

"Well, I could be."

"You could be?"

"Yep. I could be sorry."

"Well, are you or aren't you?"

"I could be a bee."

"You could be a bee?"

"Yep. I could be."

"Well, that really won't do."

"I could be sorry and that won't do?"

"Yes. Could be isn't good enough."

"We agreed we could be good for each other, didn't we?"

"That's just twisting the words."

"No it isn't."

"Yes it is."

"Well, it could be."

"There you go again."

"What?"

"Making light of the situation."

How fish got there

"The situation?"

"Yes."

"We're in a situation?"

"Yes. I think we are."

"Not a relationship, then?"

"Not anymore."

"A situation, then?"

"It's not a joke."

"Not a situation comedy?"

"Very funny."

"But not a joke."

"I'm not laughing."

"I can see that."

"Well, what do you expect?"

"I've said I could be sorry."

"Yes, well, I've said that could be isn't good enough."

"Could be isn't good enough?"

"Yes."

"I see."

"No. I don't think you do see."

"OK. I don't see, then."

"No, you don't."

"I agree."

"What can I say?"

"Oh! Why don't you just fuck off and die!?"

A tad abrupt, if you ask me, but I said you'd understand eventually. Infinity started with an abrupt Big Bang, so they say, and it could end with a similar ejaculation. But take comfort in what you will. Seek solace in crop circles or other homespun delights; marijuana, the lead in your pencil and the sandals on your feet, strong drink, the newly born, a tent, igloo or other shelter from the storm, anabolic steroids, country walks with an eager but obedient bitch, girly lunches, looking in the mirror and lingering a while, cheese, an adagio for rising and falling strings or drum and bass to give you wings, weeping, the weekend newspapers, a good gossip, a long weekend itself, stimulants, clothes that make you look thin and better still, those that empower you, make you feel you look fabulous, yoghurt, the fruit of your loins and your offspring's success, the very latest gadgets and moving pictures, circular breaths from the didgeridoo, discreet and punctual room service, snow with a full moon, brainwaves, a temperate climate, laughing and sighing, crying with a dildo and the digerati themselves, opioids, a limitless credit card and wads of cash, wasting time, clean underwear and a clean conscience with a clean bill of health, nicotine in patches or just taken straight from the packet, freshly laundered cotton sheets, a handy parking space, the right toothpaste and flossing without bleeding, art galleries or markings on the wall, libraries and cathedrals reeking of holy smoke or burnt candle wax, tasting things with your tongue and your eyes tight shut, tip-top interior design with fine soft furnishings, a circus without the wild animals, social interaction and win or lose football matches, fizz, comfortable beds and a good night's sleep if that's what you want, neat oxygen and the smell of fresh-cut grass and cocaine with lines on your lawns, hallucinogens, intellectual stimulation, affairs with other married or unmarried people, a really good wedding party, a satisfying job that pays over the odds, deserted islands with waving palms and hot sand creeping between your breasts like a rash of uninvited dates, sad goodbyes, life changing films, Cuban cigars and fat, productive goatherds clinging to thin mountain pastures, gin and mother's ruin, foie gras forced out of overfed geese or ducks as well; sugar, brown, white or invisible and a bulging net full to bursting with fish, hard work that brings on sweat, a good fist fight or cutting flesh with a knife, hot-air balloons, rice pudding with banana, the sea as she rolls up the surf with her spring tides, holidays, rabbit on its own and nothing but rabbit, kites, dykes, candyfloss and rampant copulation with a satisfactory orgasm or three from a youth with a cork-sized cock, angel dust, the caravan and paperback books with unsatisfactory short stories, aspirin, the snug fit of a gun in your hand, a vacuum cleaner that sucks and a lover that doesn't, swimming in salt water, burnt toast, expensive make-up, fine red wine and fast horses, antifreeze, family and friends, the song of an accurate flying arrow, occasional solitude, a hot cup of tea, foreign sports cars without seat belts or jelly babies without sex, a chained-up and barking dog alarmed by an angry approaching stranger, the roar of the crowd and of the bears, too, but don't be fooled by false prophets and never, ever admit to gross profit. The trappings, the gold, the silver, the diamonds and pearls, the comfortable (and uncomfortable) shoes and gaudy handbags; all the creature comforts will add to your own sense of achievement, your own well-being, but they will not make the slightest difference in the Chamber.

áś-àã Pí: **Novice Novotel nooky**

Stanley was a nice boy. Cheeky but charming. Such a shame he died so young without having the chance to put his stamp more deliberately on life. He was learning the ropes about lighting and living, and worked with David, the photographer, on some of the shoots I modelled for. One time we had a three-day job at Blenheim and I drove from town and picked up young Stan from Ladbroke Grove on the way. He was a good-looking and lively seventeen-year-old, without a surly, teenage attitude. He had a shock of surfer like blond hair, big, brown eyes and Mick Jagger lips. He was the type of lad you could talk to and he'd converse back without grunting. He was interested in life and obviously keen to get on. He'd been on location and in the studio with me before and we felt relaxed in each other's company. When you're strutting about in just your pants and bra you have to get used to guys looking at you. We got as far as Reading on the M4 when the mobile rang and told us that the shoot had been postponed because David had apparently hurt his wrist that morning. That would be the wanking, said Stan and we laughed. Something you don't need to worry about, I bet, I said to Stan as we turned off the motorway over the bridge and headed back to London. What d'you mean, said Stan. I mean that I bet you've got a lovely girlfriend or two who take care of all your needs. I have, said Stan rather coyly, but we don't do it as such. What do you mean, I said. We don't have sex, said Stan. Why on earth not, I asked. I've never done it, said Stan, and my girlfriend hasn't either, so we just snog a lot and fumble about a bit and that's that. God, I said. How frustrating for the two of you. Yep, said Stan. And you've never made love, I said. No, said Stan, want to but never had the chance. What about you, said Stan. What about me, I asked. Are you getting plenty, he said. What sort of question is that, I said. Well, you're fit and I certainly would if I had the chance. Oh come on, Stan, I said. I'm nearly ten years older than you. So, said Stan. I'd do you, he said, if you'd let me. Would you indeed, I said. Sure I would, he said, if you'd let me: and that's probably what made me swing the Range Rover off before the Hammersmith Flyover and under the Novotel into their car park. Come on, I said to Stan. He followed me sheepishly up the escalator and into the hotel's lobby. I want a bedroom for the afternoon please. We're on our way to Heathrow where our flight isn't until this evening and we need a place to freshen up and grab forty winks. Right, said the girl behind the reservations desk and she almost winked at me while glancing at Stan who was loitering some way off like a surfer without a wave. We took the lift to our floor and found the room with its double bed and bathroom and TV and minibar. Good-oh, said Stan as he opened the fridge door. Look, I said, we've come here to shag Stan, not to drink ourselves silly. What, said Stan and his eyes grew to the size of saucers. Get your kit off, I said, and get into bed. Stan paused for a second and then without any degree of ceremony he tore his clothes off, leaving his boxer shorts on and shot into the bed. I went into the bathroom and emerged undressed but wrapped in the hotel bath towel as pretence at modesty. As I came alongside the bed, I slipped off the white towelling and joined Stan between the sheets in one slick move. The daylight streamed through the big double-glazed window and we could hear the hum of traffic noise below us. Right, Stanley, I said, leaning up on one arm and looking down at the boy who was lying as flat and as straight as a ramrod next to me. If we do this thing, if we make love, then no one must know. I don't want to hear any fruity gossip or tales out of school about how you bedded me, so you don't say a word and I won't either. Is that understood. Stan just nodded. He did look a bit like a rabbit caught in headlights. Relax, I said, and let's have some sex; let's have some fun. First, I said, it would be a good idea if we took these off, and my right hand went down to his boxers and snapped the elastic waistband so it pinged against his firm tummy. He wriggled out of them. Now then, Stan, I said, feeling excited that what I was doing was very sexy. I'll lie where I am and you slide on top of me and we'll see what comes up. Stan did as he was told and sure enough something did come up. What a girl loves, Stan, is some foreplay. You shouldn't just go at it hammer and tongs. You need to encourage your woman, bring her up to the boil unless of course she's ready and rearing to go. With Stan's firm, youthful body on top of me, I was ready and rearing to go but I didn't want to rush Stan's progress or hurry the lesson. Will it be alright, said Stan. Will what be alright, I said.

Will we need some protection, he asked. That's all taken care of, Stan, but how nice of you to enquire. If you kiss me, Stan, you'll find that the act of a decent kiss will make everything else just follow on as nature intended. So he kissed me. He was, as it turned out, one of the best kissers in the business. I guess that all the practice he'd been having, kissing without sex, had turned him into something of an expert. Sadly some of my boyfriends thought that a good old-fashioned kiss on the lips was an unnecessary extra, like VAT. Stan's mouth was a real delight and pretty soon I was coaxing his erection into a special place it had never visited before. Dear Stan's erection was about the size of a champagne cork, which I must confess came as a surprise and a disappointment to me. I hope that my reaction and my squirming for more please, Stanley, more, didn't put him off. I think he really enjoyed himself and when, after a serious bout of trying to get the most out of what was on offer, I had a noisy orgasm. Stan propped up on his elbows and said, Was that OK. Yes, I said. It was great, thanks, Stan. Stan, I said. Have you finished. What, he said. Did you come. What, said Stan. Have you shot your load, Stan. Oh, he said. No, he said. I thought that if you'd finished then that was that, he said. Stan, I said, when two people make love it's perfectly normal for both of them to be satisfied. It's great if they can reach an orgasm at the same time, come together as the song would have you believe, but actually that rarely happens. More often than not the man comes and then the woman follows if she's lucky. Oh, said Stan. I see, he said. Do you want to go again, he said, smiling at me through a tousled mass of blond hair. This time, Stan lay flat on his back and I lowered myself onto his hard champagne cork and off we went. His youthful hands found my bosoms and he clung onto them as I rode him high above Hammersmith. With wild satisfaction, I came again with my eyes tight shut and my head thrown backwards, trying for all I was worth to push down onto the cork-sized cock so that my pupil might be given a lesson he would remember. How was that, said Stan, looking up at me from his pillow as I came to a halt after the galloping escapade. Great, I said, popping off my mount and slumping back beside Stan. What about you, I asked. How was it for you. OK, said Stan. But I wasn't excited, he said. Would you like a drink now, he said. Yes please, I said, and he got up and went to the minibar. Diet Coke, I said, and he found something fizzy with allegedly less sugar in it. Hey, he said as he sat back on the dishevelled Novotel bed with that enormous youthful grin of his. What is it, Stan, I said. Can we try it doggy fashion now please, he said. You feel such a nincompoop, like a fish out of water, when you've been conned.

My head will not be turned by the cut of your jib, the pop of your particular cork or come to that the cut of your suit either. It's what lies underneath all the bluster and show that concerns me and my masters. But I've told you that before. As with all learning, the more times we say it, the greater it will sink in. As to life after death that's for you to determine in your own way. Treat it like a hangover after a heavy night. Cause and effect. Good life before death equals good life after death. But what if you just get dead and are buried or turned to ash? That could be that; the end of it. It really is up to you to decide. I have filed away those as you have witnessed. I have cast my eye over the evidence. They will be judged accordingly but I won't be wrong. I, Eliza, the list maker, will work in ways that you'll again find difficult to comprehend. I am a being of heft and influence. I'll be there but you won't see me. I won't be there but you'll think you'll feel my presence. My mystery will be all-pervasive but invisible. I cannot prompt your conscience like a conductor steers his orchestra and you will play your heart out as you will. Whether you hit the right notes will depend upon your attention to detail, your understanding of the score, your ability at practice, the correct employment of your assets, your agility and dexterity with the instrument you have chosen and your willingness to believe. So please, I implore you, never forget, that when you die, it's never the end of things.

áǵ-àã PḾ: **Tangible assets**

Tanya was undoubtedly a big girl. Her breasts went before her in a way that the figurehead on an old ship might once have, proud and decisive above the foaming waves. It hadn't always been like that and at sixth-form college there had been nothing to write home about. Tanya's mother called her daughter a late developer. But as developments went, even her mum had to admit that now Tanya's tits were Titanic.

Not the brightest button in the box, nevertheless Tanya got a 2:2 at Leeds and through some family fluke landed an interview and a job in PR in London. Her personality was like her chest, big, and it won over all whom she met. Some would describe her as 'bubbly', others as 'over the top'. No one could call her dull. Tanya excelled at her job and it was through no fault of her own that she found herself in the firing line when the call came for redundancies as the company floundered in the credit crunch. Like hundreds, thousands, of others Tanya joined the unemployed.

Never one to sit it out, Tanya took on various tasks that came her way. She worked in a charity shop and joined the amateur dramatic society to the critical acclaim of the local Watford paper.

"Miss Worsenot gave a convincing performance as the heroine in the company's latest offering of the Dracula Spectacular. In particular, her heaving bosoms lent a real sense of the fear of the vampire at her neck and Miss Worsenot can surely go on with confidence to greater parts."

The reviewer's words were prophetic and indeed, Tanya did go on to greater parts.

Her family weren't particularly impressed with the Page Three photograph, but Uncle Timothy approved although he didn't let on to his sister. As a result of the exposure, Tanya found herself courted as something of a minor celebrity and her appearance out shopping in Watford with her mother gained her several sideways looks, most of them from admiring men. Tanya didn't have time for men and, although she had boyfriends, she'd never felt the need to indulge any more seriously than the occasional snog. At twenty her mother told her she was still quite young enough to 'catch the right one when he comes along'. Tanya had no doubt that her mother was right. She also had ambition, an overriding sense that it was her destiny to be rich and famous and that pursuit left little time for developing frivolous relationships.

Her first move into her own business came just before her twenty-first birthday when she made an appointment with the local branch of NatWest Bank and went to see a business development manager. Sam was in his thirties and dressed in the regulation dark suit and tie, with a badge on his lapel so he looked the part. Tanya, on the other hand, looked more like someone who had just come directly from Page Three and several of Sam's colleagues were mildly disappointed that their first meeting on that Monday morning hadn't been with Tanya.

The business plan was simple enough. It involved Tanya's breasts and their ability to attract business. As she explained, "I'm not setting up as a knocking shop. More of a knockers shop if you like (here she laughed loudly at her own joke) but I think the idea has legs."

Sam thought the idea had a lot more than just legs but thought it best not to say so.

"I'm calling the business 'Tangible Assets' and propose to open my first branch in the High Street next month."

Sam looked a bit gobsmacked. Tanya continued.

"We'll be catering mostly for the male market and encouraging clients, we'll call them clients, to come into the shop for a touchy-feely experience."

"Touchy-feely?" asked Sam, not feeling particularly comfortable about where the interview was going.

"Yes," said Tanya. " Touchy-feely." There was a pause between potential new customer and perplexed banker.

"I know that men and quite a few women enjoy the topless female form and all 'Tangible Assets' will do is offer the chance for adults who want to, to come in and have a chat and a touch."

"Is it legal?" asked Sam in a voice rather too high-pitched and with eyes the size of oranges.

"It's not illegal. I've taken advice and what I'm doing is no worse than what The Sun newspaper or those top-shelf magazines do. The touchy-feely bit is done in private between consenting adults in 'Tangible tepees'. We're going to call it in tents therapy."

"Intense therapy?" asked Sam.

"Yep," said Tanya, not realising that she and the bank manager weren't exactly on the same wavelength.

Tanya produced an artist's impression of the shop. Its front looked like a cross between Ladbrokes and Argos with a hint of Waterstones and Starbucks thrown in. The words 'Tangible Assets' were in an interesting logo across the front window that looked like what it was trying to purvey. The letter 'g' in the word 'Tangible' was made up to look like the human ear and the three 'S's' in the word 'Assets' were formed in such a way as to look like the naked female form. The shop's interior was well lit and furnished with comfortable chairs and low tables and waitresses delivering coffee to the customers sitting at the tables reading magazines and browsing the 'Tangible Assets' menu cards. There were five tepees erected around the shop.

Sam studied the artist's impression and seemed impressed himself.

"Will it be like a club?" asked Sam, slightly more relaxed.

"No. Not at all. It will be a shop. We'll be selling nice coffee and charging customers for a touchy-feely session. Sessions will be strictly timed at one minute, two minutes or a maximum of three. Touchy-feely vouchers can be purchased from the waitress and will be charged at five pounds a minute. A regular cappuccino, we call it a C-cup, and a sixty-second touchy-feely session will cost six pounds fifty. A large cappuccino, a D-cup, and a one-hundred-and-twenty-second touchy-feely session will be thirteen pounds. Clients will be able to select the quality and size of the 'Tangible Assets' they are being touchy and feely with, and we'll produce menu cards of all the available assets on offer."

Tanya pushed a mocked-up menu card and the cash flow forecast across the table towards Sam who couldn't decide on which set of figures to focus.

"Given an eight-hour trading day, we should turnover somewhere in the region of £6,000, and that's working at only half capacity. That's five tepees working for four hours each at five pounds a minute."

Sam looked at all the figures in front of him. He looked impressed with both sets, although his attention was more firmly grabbed by the in-your-face set of five pairs of naked breasts, photographed in close-up and proudly reproduced on the laminated menu. His eye fell on the description of one set.

"Feeling these firm 34 double D's will be an experience that you'll remember forever. Treat yourself to a hands-on extravaganza that you'll never forget. Stroke don't poke, go gentle not mental!"

Sam had never seen a menu like it.

"I've worked out the worst-case scenario," said Tanya, leaning forward to point out that particular set of figures. "The best nets us about £15,000 in a full day's trade."

"What about your overheads?" Sam couldn't believe he was being serious about such an outrageous business proposition.

"To start with it'll be me and six willing, bright and well endowed girlfriends. That'll allow one girl for each tepee and two waitresses. We'll obviously change the rota regularly to give the girls a break and so they can keep themselves in perfect working order, so to speak," Tanya went off into another of her laughs. "Each worker in 'Tangible Assets' will be paid a percentage of the profits after expenses. It's as simple as that."

"And what's to stop... er... what shall we call it... er... hanky-panky," Sam was trying to be careful with his words.

"You mean what if the clients want a bit more than just a feel?"

"Well, yes. Precisely," Sam thought he'd found the Achilles heel.

"Each tepee is designed to fit just two people sitting down at either side of a table. Each 'Tangible Asset' in tents therapy session is filmed and the film, apart from acting as a record of the event, will be offered to the client at the end of the session as a memento for £10. If the client doesn't want it, it'll be destroyed. If a client gets out of hand (on hearing this expression, an extraordinary image conjured up in Sam's mind's eye) then the film will have recorded the event and the appropriate action will be taken. Apart from that, in each tepee the client's chair is discreetly wired up to a harmless but stunning electric shock system controlled by the 'Tangible Assets' counsellor. That's what we're calling the girls, and a press of the button will repel any unwanted or rough advances. Finally by paying for a touchy-feely session, each client agrees to be fastened into their seat for the duration. We don't want clients standing up during their sessions or leaning too far across the table. It's strictly a touchy-feely therapy and not a chance for a bit of slap and tickle."

Again the words that Sam was hearing played a dangerous game of slapstick with his thought-process.

"You seem to have thought things through, Miss Worsenot," said Sam, trying to shake off the images of erect manhood and slap and tickle.

"So what can the bank do to help?" (apart from provide one or two clients, he thought to himself).

"You'll see in appendix three, my cash flow predictions and the borrowing requirement. There is a set-up cost but we reach break even after two months' positive trading using the worst-case forecast."

Sam said nothing and looked from one set of figures on his desk to another.

"What 'Tangible Assets' will be doing is offering the community a very good and much-needed therapy service. We will be providing a unique, discreet and legal opportunity for people to feel the finest sets of breasts and talk with their owners, our counsellors, in the complete privacy of a relaxed High Street environment for a fee that is very affordable. Most men go through their whole lives without the chance to feel a really fine pair of breasts. 'Tangible Assets' will be making that dream a face-to-face reality."

Tanya sat back smugly having delivered her pitch.

Sam studied the cover of the proposal in front of him. "Tangible Assets," it read, "When feeling is believing!" was the strapline.

Of course the NatWest Bank declined the opportunity to back the venture. It was perceived by the managers who sat up the food chain from Sam as being 'too high risk'. More privately the view was expressed that if some Page Three girl was going to encourage the good men of Watford into her High Street parlour to drink coffee and agree to be tied to an electrically wired chair and only allowed to stroke the naked tits on offer to him across the table for a tenner, then what the hell was the real world coming to?

Tanya found the backing she and her friends needed from a private investor and the business opened as planned in Watford to much mixed media reaction and lengthy queues.

It didn't take long for Tanya to become the multimillionaire she had always wanted to be. 'Tangible Assets' was franchised in over thirty-six countries, and apart from giving rewarding and well-paid work to hundreds of woman of all shapes and sizes, the global business helped to counsel tens of thousands of men, most of whom became much better lovers and husbands as a result. The police, too, were secretly impressed with what one Chief Constable called the "knockers on effect". The level of sexual crime against women dropped noticeably when 'Tangible Assets' opened their doors in a neighbourhood.

Uncle Timothy, Sam from NatWest Bank and the Chief Constable are still regular customers at 'Tangible Assets'.

Tanya Worsenot had a breast reduction operation (down to a B cup) and received an honour from The Queen before both of them died.

You have a terrible fear of humiliation. You have been made to get on your knees and to clean streets with toothbrushes. Is the humiliation inflicted upon you by your peers any worse than that you inflict upon yourself? Burn elder and you'll warm to cyanide-fuelled flames if you don't look out. Many a freezing peasant has died a horrid death because of unsavoury fuel and unsavoury gruel, too. Never mind the cold. Looks are deceptive but I don't go by looks. Royal can be rogue and rogue might be royal. Those that are set over you, govern you, rule you, are not always chosen by you. They have an historic claim perhaps. Their forebears were in the right place at the right time. Born on the right side of the blanket. Or maybe they stole their position. Some may have earned it, but not many. You seem to tolerate them because better the devil you know and you might be able to replace them if they become too obtuse, stupid, foolish, unintelligent, dull-witted, ignorant, simple-minded, insensitive, imperceptive, uncomprehending, dim, dense, dumb, slow on the uptake, brain-dead, moronic, cretinous, thick or dopey, dozy or wooden-topped, boneheaded, glaikit, dumb-assed or chowderheaded. Some of you can put your mark against a different name and launch another candidate into that unenviable position. Like those obscure members voted in by someone somewhere, you don't know who they are or the cut of their jib, so it is with those that will judge you once your codes have been sorted. You didn't vote for them either but that's just hard cheese for eternity. Certainly better the devil you don't know because once through the Chamber, you won't have a bloody clue until it's too late and nothing you can do will ever, ever change the being that controls your every single tick and tock for eternity.

áꟓ-àã Pɱ : **Royal barge**

"Bugger this weather," said Philip, his gloved hand twitching angrily on the handle of his sword.

"It can't be helped," said his wife as she smiled and waved yet again at what she thought might be another passing vessel.

"If it gets much worse we won't be able to see a bloody thing." Philip wasn't going to be consoled.

"They must have called off the flypast," said Harry with a look of relief on his face. His pink beret was wet through and felt like a soggy cowpat.

"You warm enough, love?" William looked at Kate and even the glow from her warm red outfit looked damp.

"I put some thermals on, thank goodness," she replied.

"So did I," cut in The Duchess of Cornwall. "Nicked them out of your father-in-law's sock drawer."

The two Duchesses laughed and waved.

"Bloody ridiculous!" It was Philip again. "Can't tell if it's a stinkpot, a cutter or a bloody dragon boat."

"Why don't you go below, Philip?" suggested The Queen.

"Slip downstairs for a Chinky, you mean. Looks like a bloody floating Chinese restaurant." The Duke had said as much when he'd first boarded the red velvet and gold floating palace with its two absurd thrones. "Red velvet armchairs like something out of the back row of the local fleapit," he said to one of his grandsons as they explored the deck.

"They've worked very hard and it's not their fault the weather has turned a little inclement," said The Queen.

"Inclement you call it. Good God, woman, if this is inclement then my cock's a kipper."

Prince Charles laughed. "We're not far from Billingsgate fish market, Father," he added without thinking.

"You know I don't like that sort of talk," said The Queen, looking at her eldest son over her misty spectacles.

The royal party issued another wave and the rain responded cruelly.

"I've been standing here for over ninety bloody minutes, freezing my admiral's pip's off and if this bloody pageant doesn't come to an end soon I'm going to..."

"Oh do shut up, Philip. Stop complaining and wave," The Queen was being the boss.

"Wave after bloody wave," said Philip under his cold breath. "The Princess Royal drew the long straw on this parade. Bet she's tucked up, in the dry with a stiff drink." Philip just wasn't giving up.

Another burst of damp music hit the deck.

"I think it's the Royal Philharmonic, Mummy," said The Prince of Wales.

"Bloody Water Music is all we need," said Philip as he gazed into the swirling mists, a wet drip or two running in time to the music off his peaked cap.

"Lovely," said The Queen.

"If you like that sort of thing," said Philip. "Bloody Handel."

"Well, it's better that Elton John," said The Queen.

"We've got that dubious pleasure to look forward to tomorrow night," said the Prince.

"Well, let's hope and pray it pisses on his parade," said the Duke unkindly.

"Philip!" said The Queen abruptly. "I must insist!" and she raised another gloved hand and shook it in the direction of the music.

The newspapers had a field day. Of course they did. "Long to rain over us" was the firm favourite until the very last minute when somehow The Duke of Edinburgh slipped as he was moving off the deck. It looked as though Her Majesty had almost nudged him out of her way, but whatever had occurred, His Royal Highness took a tumble into Old Father Thames and was eventually fished out by the inflatable police launch once it had forced the excited Italian gondola out of the way. It was, so one of the river policemen later reported, the first time an Admiral of the Fleet had set foot inside their dirigible. One red top's searching headline quite simply read, "Royal Barge" and most of her disloyal subjects knew what it meant.

Not everyone loses his head, though, despite what those in charge of communication try to inform you. You believe what you are told by those who manipulate the truth to suit their own ends. It was always thus since early man discovered fire and smoke signals. In a crowded world where a whisper one minute becomes a tidal wave the next, you don't know who to believe. Fake news abounds but be true to yourself, my friend. Be true to yourself.

áś-āā ṔǸ: **1649**

I climbed those wooden, creaking steps, those I could not hear
for the crowd's clamour and I would not shake with the cold
for fear they thought me nervous when I was terrified as the
executioner, I could only see his darting eyes, shook me by the
hand and I tipped three gold coins into his to pay for a job well
done, even though, after my address to those nearby, he placed
the cold steel on the back of my neck, rested the edge of the
axe just where my collar might have been where she had once
kissed me so lovingly and where my children, the darlings, had
thrown their small arms around me to tell me how much they
loved their papa and now these hateful accusers, this misguided
tumult, was going to take off my head, cut their king in two, fillet
me like a common rudd using a rough fellow to wield their vile
instrument in an arc through the Whitehall air in one gory hack
in which proceeds some dipped their handkerchiefs and all for
what, so that I could come back and restore their faith in me and
monarchy for another four hundred years at least.

*Ye shall be judged: and with what measure ye mete, be it so. Drift all
you like. Because even Kings and Queens have to meet their makers,
take their chances, deliver their codes to the Chamber. Judge not, that ye*

be not judged. For with what judgement ye judge shall be measured to you again. Or something like that if you believe what is written.

áɔ́-àã ⲢⲢ : **Drift**

I love it when she reads me poetry in bed. It's an intimacy beyond intimate, if you can see what I mean. Her whispered words drip into my ear so that I close my eyes and sink into the pillow and let each soft syllable push into my auricle to beat out its rhythm on my eardrum and echo around my inner aural senses like cream folding over itself in a churner or, better still, the seaside on a tropical beach with those gentle waves climbing up the hot sand towards where I am lying half awake in the sunshine under that deep blue cloudless sky. I want to move to higher ground. I want to stay on the dry sand but then the waves reach me, curve around my body and melt away the supporting terra firma and leave me like an island in a place one moment wet with swirling salt water and then an outcrop surrounded by a glistening, sparkling, white, damp, sandy moat. It's difficult not to move, for when the cool sea water, fizzing with life and heat from the dry sand, finds its way up to the top of my legs and into that place between them, I want to cry out and pull away. My own short curls like fronds of silky seaweed are stuck fast to their pubic rock face, drenched but not dislodged, and they nod approval in tight unison. Like a spider crab, I am moved. I stir inside my bikini suddenly aware that the

279

sea is trying to undress me, starting to seduce me on its shore. It is making me wet. I do move, perch up on my elbows, but the waves persuade me to stay. One gentle caress after another they wash over me until I have become a sculptured part of the beach, half in and half out of the sand. I am flotsam, although borne from the land rather than the sea. I am debris. I sink into the rhythm. The waves wash over my smooth stomach and leave a sandy trail like light ground pepper against my nut brown skin. My belly button is a pool of salt water, a tiny, fragile oasis. The waves won't stop and I don't want them to. With each rush and then each retreat, they grow bolder and soon they reach between my breasts, overwhelm them and cause their summits, my pink nipples, to pucker and harden under their wet covering. Propped up on my sinking elbows I watch as my body is taken by the tide. I have made a brief impression but the sea is never impressed. More wet than dry, I am become like the salt water and float with its increased flow so that the waves lift me, carry me and then drop me. I rise and fall like a curtain in the breeze and am pulled further and further out of my depth; words no longer intelligible. While I float with the flow, I sink with the ebb and all too soon I find that if I try to make my own way, resort to my impulses, I flounder and flap gently. I could shout, scream and thrash about, but when you don't want to be rescued why throw out the wrong signal, why cause a scene? Where I had been safe, high and dry, my own island, I am now just a drop in the ocean. The strong current pulls me and I am helpless to do a thing but succumb to its force and I shudder, surrender and let out a brief cry that itself is drowned by the noise of the tremendous swell. Her words have washed over me, through me like electricity up a wire and she has had me all to herself, taken me like the sea takes its shore and I have let her because I love it when she reads me poetry when I'm dead.

Your Psalm 70 is rather a pathetic cry as in, "As for me, I am poor and in misery, haste thee unto me, O God." There can be much joy in living, great happiness and deep warmth with life and love. Love is apparently the greatest gift given to you. You make a lot of fuss and nonsense over it. It has all been coded and will continue to be so as long as writers, musicians and their lyricists have the inclination. Love is in the air, love is all around, love me do and love don't come easy, addicted to love, the power of love, what's love got to do with it and when a man loves a woman or puppy love, I'd do anything for love, I will always love you, crazy in love, all out of love, vision of love, all you need is love, sunshine of your love, you've got to hide your love away, can't help falling in love, can't buy me love, loves me like a rock, you give love a bad name, my love, crazy little thing called love, I just called to say I love you, love me two times, silly love songs, and I love her, feel your love tonight, love her madly, love you ,too, too much love will kill you, best of my love, bold as love, I love the dead, love street and love minus zero, love gun, the one I love, love of my life, only love can break your heart, whole lotta love, victim of love, words of love, it's only love, I need your love tonight, the way you love me, ain't talkin' 'bout love, I think I love you, I believe in a thing called love, love in vain, oh my love, love profusion, love in an elevator, love ain't for keepin', why can't this be love, love bites, higher love, crazy love, we found love, I'll have to say I love you in a song, you look so good in love, love walks in, love don't cost a thing, all my love, it's your love, love in the first degree, people need love, I was made to love her, I was born to love you, I can love you like that, all my love and love train, stone in love and love somebody, drunk in love, love the way you lie, make you feel my love, will you love me tomorrow, all my loving, old love, used to love her, this maniac's in love with you, a world without love, woman in love, love don't live here anymore, love game, let there be love, this ain't the Summer of Love, falling in love with you, don't fall in love with a dreamer, one love, you've got the love, love without end amen, hate it or love it,where did our love go, to sir with love, I'll make love to you, this guy's in love with you, best of my love, lovefool, baby love, love takes time, bleeding love, everybody loves somebody, so much in love, I knew I loved you, justify my love, I wanna love you, glory of love, your love is my drug, all out of love, come and get your love, hate that I love you, sometimes love just ain't enough, when love comes to town, Friday I'm in love, the deeper the love, love walks in, let my love open the door, stubborn love, if you love somebody set them free, love stinks and love is a battlefield, rhythm of love, cradle of love, sowing the seeds of love, big love, oh love, the crush of love, stand inside your love, love me dead, lucky in love, the people that we love and love is a long road. A part of little barefooted Gandhi's code said, "When I despair, I remember that all through history the way of truth and love have always won. There have been tyrants and murderers, and for a time, they can seem invincible, but in the end, they always fall." C.S. Lewis's code indicated that he thought that to love at all is to be vulnerable. Lock it up safe in the casket or coffin was his advice. Put it at the back of that wardrobe no doubt. Love is always patient and kind. It is never jealous. Love is never boastful or conceited. *It is never rude or selfish. It does not take offence and is not resentful. Love takes no pleasure in other people's sins, but delights in the truth. It is always ready to excuse, to trust, to hope, and to endure whatever comes.* So coded that scribe in Corinthians. The truth is you don't get to choose who you fall in love with. They may love you in return or they might mistreat you, ignore you or hurt you, but you stay with them. Why? It's not because you're stupid or you enjoy getting hurt. It's because you can see the good in them; it's because despite all the arguments they are the ones who make you feel a certain way that no one else can and you value that feeling. Because your brains won't allow them to leave, your minds and your hearts won't allow them to leave your lives. You are quite complicated and besides don't forget those sentiments that love is in the air, love is all around, love me do and love don't come easy, addicted to love, the power of love, what's love got to do with it and when a man loves a woman or puppy love, I'd do anything for love, I will always love you, crazy in love, all out of love, vision of love, all you need is love, sunshine of your love, you've got to hide your love away, can't help falling in love, can't buy me love, loves me like a rock, you give love a bad name, my love, crazy little thing called love, I just called to say I love you, love me two times, silly love songs, and I love her, feel your love tonight, love her madly, love you, too, too much love will kill you, best of my love, bold as love, I love the dead, love street and love minus zero, love gun, the one I love, love of my life, only love can break your heart, whole lotta love, victim of love, words of love, it's only love, I need your love tonight, the way you love me, ain't talkin' 'bout love, I think I love you, I believe in a thing called love, love in vain, oh my love, love profusion, love in an elevator, love ain't for keepin', why can't this be love, love bites, higher love, crazy love, we *found love, I'll have to say I love you in a song, you look so good in love, love walks in, love don't cost a thing, all my love, it's your love, love in the first degree, people need love, I was made to love her, I was born to love you, I can love you like that, all my love and love train, stone in love and love somebody, drunk in love, love the way you lie, make you feel my love, will you love me tomorrow, all my loving, old love, used to love her, this maniac's in love with you, a world without love, woman in love, love don't live here anymore, love game, let there be love, this ain't the Summer of Love, falling in love with you, don't fall in love with a dreamer, one love, you've got the love, love without end amen, hate it or love it, will you love me tomorrow, where did our love go, to sir with love, I'll make love to you, this guy's in love with you, best of my love, lovefool, baby love, love takes time, bleeding love, everybody loves somebody, so much in love, I knew I loved you, silly love songs, justify my love, I wanna love you, glory of love, your love is my drug, all out of love, come and get your love, hate that I love you, sometimes love just ain't enough, when love comes to town, Friday I'm in love, the deeper the love, love walks in, let my love open the door, stubborn love, if you love somebody set them free, love stinks and love is a battlefield, rhythm of love, cradle of love, sowing the seeds of love, big love, oh love, the crush of love, stand inside your love, love me dead, lucky in love, the people that we love and love is a long road.*

áǯ-àā Pṕ: **Global Warming**

He quite often got rather hot under the collar. But then Donald Global would. He'd developed a bad temper.

"Got out of bed the wrong side," was how his wife, Eve, described his mood some mornings when Donald was obviously not on top form. "Grumpy old bugger," was what she really thought.

Donald didn't used to be like that. Circumstances had made him. The wear and tear of life had got to him. The mortgage, the bills, the job, the sodding neighbours, speeding cameras and bloody parking tickets, the crap on the TV, immigration, potholes, Brexit, Mrs fucking May, soft judges, the lack of local police ("When on earth did you last see one in our street?"), litter everywhere and the price of petrol; everything had just piled up. He couldn't put his finger on the actual date when things had changed. They had, though. Rather like his thinning, grey hair, it had happened gradually. He thought it was somewhere between fifty-four-and-a-half and fifty-six that things had probably got worse. He didn't really enjoy sex with his wife anymore and didn't think about doing it with anybody else's either. His waistline could no longer be pulled in for any length of time and he had become pear-shaped. He looked stupid in jeans and ridiculous on any beach. But by far his biggest worry was climate change.

"Well, what can you do about it, dear?" said his wife to him when Donald read out loud anything pertinent to environmental issues reported in The Daily Telegraph.

"We just can't let the Third World do what we did. They can't be allowed to make the same mistakes."

"What? You mean we can use their oil, mine their natural resources, but we mustn't let them drive cars or have dishwashers."

"Something like that," said Donald.

They liked their holidays abroad. Donald spent hours leafing through piles of glossy brochures; putting Post-it notes on those pages he thought might be of interest. They'd been to Santorini in the spring, the remnant of a volcano set like pumice stone in the Aegean Sea. They quite liked it, but Donald thought that it was being ruined by tourism. In February they chose Zanzibar, the Spice Island.

When their battered minibus had been stopped on the bumpy dirt track en route from the airport to their resort hotel, the angry crowd terrified Donald and Eve Global. They were abducted and marched into the bush by a group of machete-wielding natives. The ritualistic way in which they met their end was taken straight off the pages of history. The Acting British Consul in Stone Town had never seen anything like it before. Donald and his wife were boiled alive, each cooked in an old oil drum filled with salt water and fish bones and heated up on a fire of broken wooden pallets, rubber tyres and old tree stumps.

You have destroyed your planet and, not content with your own vandalism, you are intent on wrecking the universe. The inevitability is death. Your own demise will reduce the timing of the event by a fraction of a fraction of a fraction because your avid consumption will become a memory, a footprint. By that print may those that follow understand the folly of your intent. If they heed the obvious signs then disaster may be slowed but sadly, because you have chosen the certain route to self-destruction, a deceleration will not be sufficient to prevent the end. Those who have paraded their pathetic signs, "The end is nigh!", have been correct with their prophecy. Little did they know and little have they done to put things right. Preachers often only preach, they don't do a lot more of real influence, if you get my drift. Those that have demanded their country back, space for their own brand of bigotry will, in time, vandalise the very thing they say they love so much. The only non-vandal, if there is such a word, is my master and your judge.

áś-àā ṔṔ: **Rollover**

Jake was feeling in a good mood so he bought two lucky dips from the nice girl behind the fag counter in Martin's the newsagents. He told her his pet joke, too.

"Man goes to a zoo but there was only one dog. It was a Shih Tzu."

The nice girl behind the counter wobbled with laughter. She handed Jake his lottery ticket and wished him luck. She wished most of her customers luck. Those that spoke politely to her, made an effort at conversation, showed they were human, not just impatient shoppers in a hurry.

"If you win the jackpot will you share it with me?" she said. She said it to lots of punters and they always smiled back at her. Some said, "of course, love," without meaning it, but most just smiled back at her. The young men thought that if they won, they'd get shacked up with Megan Hanson or any bit of decent totty, rather than the nice girl behind the fag counter. The nice girl behind the fag counter wasn't a looker. Some said, rather cruelly, that she needed to carry a government health warning. Jake, on the other hand, came from the school of you don't look at the mantelpiece when you're poking the fire. There was something he quite liked about the nice girl and he didn't care about health warnings. "If I win you can have half but you'll have to make an honest man of me," he said and the nice girl giggled at the idea. She liked Jake. As her customer's went, Jake was all right. She quite fancied him.

Jake didn't win. Only one of his numbers came up and he screwed up the phoney bit of paper-thin dreams and chucked it in the bin, the pedal bin next to the kitchen sink. The discarded knot of paper, the one that had been bought with so much optimism, lay scrunched up next to a damp Typhoo tea bag and a three-quarters-eaten fish pie still in its tinfoil dish. The little piece of printed hope had turned into no hope when the numbered balls spewed from Sir Galahad at the press of a button by the smiling, fat, Irish TV man who spoke those meaningless words, "Good luck, everybody."

Jake felt robbed. It had been a rollover, too. Twenty-three million pounds and he hadn't won a penny. Someone had, though, and the next time he called at the newsagent, the talk from one of the girls who worked with the nice girl was that the winning ticket had been purchased from them.

"Just imagine that," the girl who worked with the nice girl said to Jake as she passed him a packet of Marlboro Lights. "Some lucky bugger's won the lot and we sold them the ticket."

"How d'you know?" asked Jake

"Lottery HQ tell us," replied the girl who worked with the nice girl.

The local rag was full of it. Who, asked the headlines, was the mystery winner? No one came forward and within a week the search was forgotten and the headlines roared about a local lad who'd been killed in Basra.

On the Saturday evening, two weeks after the big jackpot, Jake breezed into the newsagents and waited until the nice girl was free. He'd got a plan.

"It was me," he said to her almost too quickly.

"What was?"

"It was me that won the rollover jackpot."

"You can't have done," said the nice girl with real surprise.

"I bloody can," said Jake. "What time d'you finish work because we've got some planning to do."

They met in the snug bar of The Rose and Crown. The nice

girl had a Cinzano and lemonade and Jake had his usual pint of lager. They got on well and after nearly too much to drink they walked back to Jake's flat with a large Domino's pizza to share.

After the feed, the nice girl let Jake take advantage of her. She undressed and the two of them embraced on Jake's old sofa and one thing led to another.

"Roll over," implored Jake as he wrestled with his shirt.

The nice girl let Jake have his way selfishly and in a matter of moments. Less time than it took to pick the lucky balls from Sir Galahad.

"Right," he said after he'd got himself dressed. "You'd better be going."

"What?" said the nice girl somewhat taken aback. "Not even a cup of coffee."

"Have a cup of coffee by all means. But then you ought to be going. By the way, I never won the lottery. I lied. I just wanted to shag you. That's all."

The nice girl looked at Jake with pity. Pity turned to disgust and then disgust turned to amusement. She started to laugh.

"What's so funny?" said Jake.

How fish got there

"Nothing really," said the nice girl who had already decided that she'd pay whatever it took to have Jake taken out and dealt with because she could afford to. "It's just that it was me that won the rollover."

Every town has a Jake and every bar, a Sue;
each nook has its cranny; a monkey for every zoo.
A Jonny for any dick; a ticket for those to try;
a full stop for mankind because you're all going to die.
But, do you know what, my friend? No revenge is as complete as forgiveness, and if it was down to me, I might forgive them all, if you get my drift. As with a gamble, a flutter, a wager, a bet, taking a chance, sticking your neck out, risking it, taking a flier, chancing your arm, having a punt or a leap in the dark, taking pot luck or speculating, hazarding a chance, putting your shirt on it, you always wish for something you cannot have. Everlasting life maybe, but then you might just find you've been had over a barrel.

áś-àā ṔQ: **Abbott's Bitter**

There was fierce competition for the pub. A property company
had brought the big, old place hoping to turn it into housing,
but their plans had been opposed by the locals, some not
without influence with the planning officer. It was a Grade II
listed building right in the middle of the village and only a few
miles from the centre of the city. It was a rambling place with
six lettable bedrooms and room to create more; space for a fifty-
cover restaurant and the kitchen to match, a large car park and
a 'beer garden'.

Rather than sell it, the property company decided to find a
good tenant for the place. They wanted their new tenant to turn
the old-fashioned country pub into something a bit special, so
placed the job in the hands of a couple of local agents. During
the search for new incumbents, the business ticked over with a
relief landlord and his wife just about satisfying the meagre local
needs. It was what could be called 'a drinkers' pub' with good ale
and cider, spirits if required, and a bar snack menu with things
like chicken and chips or ploughman's with the butter served
up in mini-sized, foil wrapped portions so that customers were
always asking for more butter please. The owners had visions

of increasing the turnover from £200,000 a year to more like £800,000. They wanted somebody with flair to turn the place from 'a bed and breakfast pub with grub' into 'a gastro-pub with style and comfortable bedrooms.' The property company was looking for somebody with money to invest in a serious makeover for the place. Low 'key money' proposed at £40,000 and an annual rental of 10% of turnover and a twenty-four-year lease made the place quite an attractive proposition. Even in times when more pubs were closing down than opening up, the Drover's Inn was an opportunity for someone with a bit of flair and hard work to turn a useful shilling. The agents had plenty of interest and a shortlist was drawn up of those thought to be most suitable candidates.

The Abbotts had set their hearts on getting the place. It had long been their ambition to find a run-down pub and turn it into a place people would want to visit, a place where good food sat easily alongside warm hospitality. The Abbotts could do it. Their enthusiasm and personal good taste would more than make up for their lack of experience. They were an outgoing couple with a wide circle of friends, all of whom would certainly patronise their new venture. The fact that Mr Abbott worked for a brewery must be to their advantage. They planned what they would do with the Drover's Inn, how they would change the décor, extend the bar, completely refurbish the bedrooms, gut and replace the kitchen and restyle the beer garden. They drew up their elaborate plans and went to see their bank manager who agreed that he'd lend them the money, £200,000, provided that they could give a personal guarantee and their property as security against the loan. The Abbotts didn't mind that in the slightest. They were keen as mustard and spent every hour planning what they would do. They prepared menus and selected fine wines for the new list. They planned a launch party, decided who they'd invite. They talked about the chef they were going to take on. Someone recommended one who was very good and they went to see him and offered him the job at £30,000 a year, with accommodation of course. They talked to an architect and got him to do some preliminary drawings of the proposed changes. They went to their accountant and with his help, prepared the financial models that showed them and the bank manager and the property company that they could make a profitable go of it. They kept their wage bill at less than 22% of turnover, their GP averaged 60% and even if it dipped to below 55%, the bottom line still looked good. They prepared a very professional presentation to the agents and the property company, a ten page document with lots of words, figures and images that would reassure the landlords that the Abbotts were absolutely ideal candidates for the business.

It went right to the wire. Second interviews were arranged and the Abbotts found themselves in the last two. They didn't sleep much the night before the final interview. They had put everything they could into getting the deal. The property company couldn't decide right away and the agents were divided about who should get the lease. After reappraising everything they had heard and seen, a decision had to be made and phone calls made.

"We're very pleased to be able to tell you that we'd like to offer you the lease for the Drover's Inn. There's a letter in the post confirming the detail," the agent's PA told an excited Mr Abbott on the phone on the Thursday night. The Abbotts were as chuffed as nuts. They celebrated by opening one of Mr Abbotts's fine old wines, went to bed as pleased as Punch and made love like they hadn't for several months. The following morning Mr Abbott quit his job as a senior manager at the brewery. They met for lunch at the Priory, the city's finest and splashed out on lobster.

"Maybe one day, our place will have a reputation like this," Mrs Abbott whispered to her husband over coffee.

On Monday morning the post arrived and with it a letter from the property company as promised. The Abbotts could tell it was from them by the slogan on the outside of the envelope, 'putting property & people first.' Mr Abbott opened the white envelope more as a formality than anything else that evening. They both knew what would be typed inside. Or thought they did.

It was a very close call but the other contender just had the edge because of his relevant experience. The Abbotts were dumbfounded. They simply couldn't believe their eyes. There must be some mistake, some awful cock-up. After all that, they hadn't been given the Drover's Inn to run as their own, or had they? What the hell was going on?

"But the agent?" said Mrs Abbott to her bewildered husband. Mr Abbott was on the telephone to the agent first thing on Tuesday morning.

"I am so sorry, Mr Abbott," said the agent "it seems that there must have been an administrative error and we telephoned you last Thursday and mistakenly gave you the wrong news. The letter you received is correct."

There was absolutely nothing that the Abbotts could do about it. They wrote a letter to the agent with a copy to the property company expressing their displeasure and demanding some recompense. They never received a reply. They rang a lawyer friend, but he said that in his opinion mistakes like those were unfortunate but not worth going to law over.

The Abbotts brooded over their misfortune. Mr Abbott tried unsuccessfully to get his job back, but had to work out his notice then leave as planned.

When the successful applicant took over the pub and pulled his first pint, nearly all the men that joined him that evening, including the directors of the property company and their agents, ended up in hospital having their stomachs pumped. Most were OK, but three died from the poison that had been put into the barrels of beer that in truth should have been named Abbott's Bitter.

How fish got there

How easily you give your trust; your faith. Now here's a question for you, all you knob-gobbling philosophers. Do you swallow or do you spit? Which would you rather do; choose how to live or choose how to die? A tricky one. Without doubt a real teaser. Some would have you believe that you don't have a say in either. It's all predetermined, they say. It's all written. Some book, that! And those you love or who love you; what about them? What about your best friend? Did you determine that friendship or was it fate that brought you close? Your choice is most often selected from humankind. Some of you would pick concubine or carbine; most others equine, feline or canine. In the end I will be your best friend or your worst enemy but sadly, you won't even have a say in that.

áʂ̃-àã Pʠ : **Gun Dog**

There is something rather reassuring about an obedient gun dog. Each owner will tell you that he has the very best of the breed because, as we all know, dogs take after their masters and in some cases vice versa.

John's new Labrador was something else. Sitting tethered by the side of his shooting owner, whenever a bird flew over, the dog would offer up advice; tips on how to deal with the shot.

"If that one was flying backwards, you'd knock its beak off," was how it started.

"What!?" said John with so much surprise that he missed at the next attempt as well.

"Why don't you take up tennis?" said the dog under his breath.

"You cheeky bugger!" shouted John and he kicked the black dog at his feet.

The Labrador learnt not to be critical just for the hell of it. The wrath of his owner would only invite unwelcome retribution. He decided that constructive comment would be a better course of action, and so began a relationship between dog and gun that made a perfect combination in the sporting field.

Not surprisingly, John's shooting accuracy improved almost at every outing thanks to the dog's considered instruction. John became a very good shot.

"You were under that by a gnat's cock," said the dog, adding "you must move your feet. Don't be afraid to move your feet."

John did move his feet and he swung when swinging was in order and always maintained his lead when following through the bird.

"Bum, belly, beak, bang!" growled the Labrador as John connected with another bird at least sixty yards away.

Now, the normal bond between a man and his dog relies on one of them, normally the man, always holding the upper hand. The best relationships are those where the dog does exactly what his boss wants him to without question and with total devotion. In exchange for obedience the dog receives a daily square meal, the occasional admiring glance and a pat; a rub down with a dirty towel when wet; the chance to run about in the countryside retrieving dead and, more often, wounded quarry, and periods of lengthy isolation being locked up in the back of a four-by-four. There are moments of sheer bliss when the owner's other half or offspring will make a fuss of the dog, but these are as rare as the scraps from the Christmas dinner table.

When a Labrador talks, familiarity breeds contempt; and so it was with John's dog.

"You missed in front of that," said the dog on the first drive of the day on a Devon shoot.

"Rubbish!" said John who was feeling more agitated than usual.

"I saw the pattern of the shot leave the gun and believe me, you were in front," said the Labrador in a way that John just knew was the truth.

"All right. All right," said John and he yanked rather too hard on the choke chain around his Labrador's neck.

"There's no need for that," said the dog, shaking his head.

"Look. You might think you're the dog's bollocks when it comes to shooting but you're just a bloody black bastard of a Labrador when all is said and done and not a very handsome specimen at that. Now sit there and shut up or fuck off and go annoy somebody else!"

Not another word was said and at the end of the drive the dog was let off the lead to go and pick up the dozen or so birds that John had despatched. The woods that ran behind his peg fell away to the valley bottom and the dog bounded off through the trees in search of his master's birds. He didn't come back. Despite John's high-pitched whistling and energetic shouting, the dog was gone.

"Well, we can't stay here, John," said the host. "We've got to move on to the next drive. I'm sure we'll find him before the day is out."

No one was quite sure how it happened. Standing at number eight on the end of the line and hidden from the sight of his neighbour at number seven, tucked as he was around the corner along the ride in a wood, John was really out of the shooting. He had a go at something halfway through the drive and at the end, after the keeper had sounded his horn to tell everyone that the drive was over, they found John slumped on the brown stained ground where his blood had soaked into the earth and, red on green, where it had congealed on the grass as a result of the dreadful shot that had blown half his face away. Sitting next to his master's dead body was Spyder, his black gun dog.

Every dog has its day. If, when you're in charge of your own affairs, you really want something, then normally that something can be yours for the taking. You need ambition, drive, determination, enterprise, initiative, eagerness, motivation, enthusiasm, zeal, commitment, a sense of purpose, vision, intention, goal, aim, objectivity, purpose, intent, a plan and a strong desire, passion, hunger, ruthlessness, timing, ego, confidence, a target, a dream, assertiveness, aplomb, courage, boldness, mettle, optimism, diligence, conscientiousness, assiduousness, assiduity, hard work, application, concentration, effort, care, industriousness, rigour, meticulousness, thoroughness, perseverance, persistence, tenacity, dedication, commitment, tirelessness, indefatigability, doggedness, talent, skill, expertise, adeptness, aptitude, savoir faire, prowess, mastery, accomplishment, competence, proficiency, dexterity, adroitness, deftness, know-how, ability and capability, intelligence and knowledge, sharp-wittedness, acuteness, acumen, acuity, cleverness and, smartness, wit and canniness, common sense and insight, discernment, understanding and perceptiveness, sagacity, perspicacity, nous and horse sense, savvy and street wisdom, understanding, persuasive powers and arm-twisting ability, a strong and yet charming personality, belief, faith, credence, conviction, direction and luck. And don't forget forcefulness, a degree of prudence, lots of foresight, dynamism, dominance, being oh so go-ahead and feisty to boot. You'll need brilliance, virtuosity, artistry, sheer talent and bucketloads of flair. Add dauntlessness, stout-heartedness, heroism, backbone, grit and don't forget bottle. It's nottle the bottle that'll give you the throttle; it's never the drink makes you think. You might be relaxed or even poleaxed: you'll swim but really you'll sink. So why are you surprised that it isn't easy? Oh ye feckless one, why is't you expect it on a silver platter?

áś·àã ṔQ : **Trophy wife**

The Honourable Angus was tremendously proud of his collection. Over the years he had harvested a herd of trophies mostly from Africa, but there was a smattering of taxidermy from South America and three tigers he had shot illegally in India. In pride of place over the big stone fireplace, firmly set between two magnificent lion's heads, was his rogue bull elephant, the tusks protruding into the room seven feet or so above the floor so that for a party piece he could, when encouraged by too much whiskey and the shouts of his chums, perform a sort of gymnastic stunt by gripping each tusk in his hands and lifting himself off the ground. The skill was to see how many lifts from the floor in front of the fireplace the Honourable Angus could perform before his muscles wouldn't let him do any more. The whole stunt wasn't always done just for show and would on occasion involve serious competition with anyone foolish or drunk enough to issue a challenge. The Honourable Angus, though, was so far unbeaten in the 'Jumbo squat thrust stakes', as he called the exercise or as his long-suffering wife named it, his 'tinkering between the ivories'.

"How much do you want to bet this time?" The Honourable

Angus was goading Jonny.

"A hundred notes," said Jonny with more confidence than his wallet should have allowed.

"Oh Jonny, don't be a fool. He's bound to beat you." The Honourable Angus's wife had a soft spot for Jonny and she knew her husband would win the bet. He was a bully when it came to being competitive.

"A hundred," Jonny confirmed the wager and the Honourable Angus removed his jacket ready for the trial.

It was another easy victory and the Honourable Angus managed fifteen lifts to Jonny's twelve. The two men slumped exhausted by their efforts into the leather armchairs in front of the fireplace.

"I'll bloody well beat you one day," said Jonny.

"I doubt it," replied the Honourable Angus. "But you're welcome to keep trying."

The two men drank far too much whiskey and the Honourable Angus's wife probably overdid it on the fizzy white and she tottered her way up to bed relieved that Jonny had decided to stay the night rather than risk the breathalyser. The Honourable Angus came up several hours later and collapsed onto the bed in a state of drunken dishevelment. His wife tried to undress him, but the decidedly unfriendly grunts and groans that he uttered put her off the job and she left him on his side of the big bed to snore with a token bit of the duvet over his dressed body.

She got up and went to the adjoining bathroom. She hadn't heard Jonny come up and decided to go and see if he was alright. She padded along the landing and found the spare rooms empty with no sign of any life. Even the stuffed marlin her husband had fought into submission looked lifeless, despite the taxidermist's artistic endeavours at breathing some life into the poor creature. The door to the guest bathroom was open and she peered into the empty room, calling Jonny's name in a half-whisper. Not receiving any reply, she tiptoed down the main stairs in her bare feet, fastening the pinstriped shirt, one of the Honourable Angus's old ones which she had adopted, more closely around her shoulders and neck. A dim light escaped from the slightly open drawing room doorway and she entered quietly.

At the far end of the long room she could see the figure of Jonny as he pulled himself up and down between the elephant's tusks. She stood quite still and took in the show before her. Jonny had no clothes on. It was, she began to realise, quite erotic watching Jonny, dear Jonny, straining with his back to her, the moisture on his body glistening in the warm glow of the table lamp that had sole responsibility for lighting the room. She could feel his efforts, see his sinews as they strained to lift and lower his undressed body. The bicep muscles on his arms tensed and relaxed as he went up then down, up, then down. His shoulder blades moved like metal plates beneath their taut skin covering. The hollows of his buttocks puckered, in then out, with every rise and fall. The Honourable Angus's wife felt as horny as the big elephant's tusks she saw Jonny, dear Jonny, swinging his neat, naked body between, so beautifully in front of her. She approached very quietly on bare tiptoe and when he had lifted himself up off the floor once more, reached around his hips with her outstretched arms to feel for that most sensitive area of Jonny's, dear Jonny's, anatomy. The effect of the Honourable Angus's wife's touch was electrifying. Jonny leapt and danced like an enraged cock salmon hooked on a fishing fly and fell to the floor, uttering the words "Fuck me!", a command that the Honourable Angus's wife didn't disappoint in carrying out.

And so it was that the Honourable Angus's wife and Jonny became lovers and plotters. In the very early hours, and under the watchful gaze of that vast grey head, the Honourable Angus's wife had the best sex she'd had for ten years. It seemed as though the rogue bull had become an accomplice; a willing participant in the ménage à trois in front of the fireplace.

"That was the best tinkering between the ivories I've ever had," the Honourable Angus's wife said to Jonny as the two of them sat spent together in the old armchair under the twinkling, smiling, knowing eyes of that old rogue bull and the two lions. What comes round goes around, the animals thought, and how appropriate it was that justice had been done and the Honourable Angus's wife had been stuffed and mounted and that the Honourable Angus himself would soon be taking his place somewhere in the hereafter.

Not every trophy has a winner, but girls who wink expect a dinner. But what if that signal is misplaced, misinterpreted, misconstrued or misbegotten? You seem to be living in an age of fear, promoted by those who communicate to you and nurtured by those you have put in charge. The climate of fear swirls around but is manifest in the main by the f in fear and fear of facelift, fear of facetiousness, fear of fact, fear of factions, fear of factoids, fear of factory farming, fear of fads, fear of faeces (shit scarred of them!), fear of faggots (or anything that thinks it's a meatball), fear of failing and of failure, fear of fainting, fear of fair play or fair trade, fear of fair-weather friends, fear of fairy godmothers (she's behind you!) or indeed fairyland (all around you!), fear of fairy stories (or multi-stories for that matter!), fear of fait accompli, fear of faith, fear of fajitas, fear of fakes, fear of falling, fear of fallacy, fear of fall guys, fear of falling-out and fallout, fear of false alarms and false dawns (and Rita's too!), fear of false economy, fear of falsehood, fear of false moves, and false pretences, fear of false starts and steps, fear of falsettos and fast talkers, fear of fame (although fear of being famous is way down the list nowadays), fear of familiarity, fear of family (especially when they make you an offer you can't refuse!), fear of famine, fear of fantasy, fear of fanatics, fear of fancy men or fancy women, fear of fanfares, fear of fanny (although once bitten twice shy), fear of fantasy, fear of faraway, fear of farce, fear of farewell, fear of farmers and farriers, fear of fascism, fear of fashion, fear of fast food (it can make you sick quick!), fear of fastidiousness, fear of fast-track, fear of fatalism or fate, fear of Father Christmas (a fat man with a beard coming down my chimney!), fear of fatigue, fear of fatty acid or fat anything, fear of fatuousness, fear of fatwa, fear of faults, fear of favours, fear of favouritism, fear of fear, fear of fearlessness, fear of feast days, fear of fecundity, fear of federalism, fear of feebleness, fear of feeding frenzies, fear of feeling, fear of Feldenkrais method, fear of felicitations or felicity (or Felix), fear of fellatio or fellow feeling, fear of feminism or femme fatales, fear of feng shui (which ever position you're in), fear of fermentation, fear of ferocity, fear of ferrets, fear of Ferris wheels, fear of fertiliser and fertilization (you like your eggs unfertilized thank you very much!), fear of fetish, fear of fiasco, fear of Fibonacci series, fear of fibre optics (you take it straight from the bottle), fear of fibrosis, fear of fickleness, fear of fiction (non-fiction is even more to be feared), fear of fiddle-faddle, fear of fidelity (especially if you're a forger), fear of fig leaves (and women offering you a bite from their apples) fear of fighting, fear of figureheads and figure-hugging (kiss me if you like but please don't hug me!), fear of filings and filth, fear of finality (you should be OK in life everlasting then!), fear of finance, fear of fine print, fear of finesse, fear of fire or firefighters (it's the way they pick you up), fear of firing squads (it's the way they put you down), fear of first aid, first nights, first refusals, First World; fear of fish fingers (fishy anything), fear of fishwives, fear of fission, fear of fisticuffs, fear of fitting, fear of five-a-side, fear of fixed assets or fixed-wings (helicopter your gold bars to the Faroe's) , fear of flagellation, fear of flaky pastry or flaky handshakes, fear of flamboyance, fear of flame-throwers, fear of flashbacks, fear of flatmates (especially when they haven't paid their fair share), fear of flavours, fear of fleas, fear of flesh wounds, fear of flexitime, fear of flibbertigibbets, fear of flick knives, fear of flight attendants, fear of flimflam, fear of flings, fear of flip sides, fear of flirts or flirting, fear of floaters or floating, fear of floods (unless your name is Noah), fear of floor managers and floozies, fear of floppy, floral Florentines, fear of floriferous florists, fear of flotsam, fear of fluffy flummery, fear of flushing (to hopefully remove floaters), fear of fly-by-nights (even in the daylight), fear of fly-tipping (or waiter tipping), fear of focussing, fear of fog (which won't let you focus), fear of folies à deux, fear of folie de grandeur, fear of folklore, fear of following, fear of follow-through (when you are miles from clean underwear), fear of fondling and fondue (the overactive Swiss again!), fear of fools, fear of foot-tapping, fear of forebears (Why? They're not around anymore), fear of force, fear of forecasts, fear of Foreign Legions, fear of forensics, fear of foreplay (why bother with it?) , fear of forfeits, fear of forgery, fear of forgiveness, fear of formaldehyde (certainly if you're Hirst's shark), fear of formality, fear of fornication, fear of fossil fuel, fear of foul play, fear of four-posters or foursomes, fear of fox-hunting, fear of fractions and fragmentation, fear of fragrance, fear of frailty, fear of fraternities, fear of fraudsters, fear of freaks, fear of free falling, fear of Freemasons, fear of free-range, standing or trade; fear of free will, fear of French knickers, polish or dressing; fear of frequency modulation, fear of friction, fear of friendlies, fear of frigidity, fear of frippery, fear of frolics, fear of frontbenchers, fear of frou-frou, fear of fruition, fear of frustration, fear of frying pans, fear of fucking, fear of fulfilment, fear of full bore or marks or house or moon or stop; fear of fumbling, fear of functioning, fear of fundamentalism, fear of fund-raising, fear of funerals, fear of furtherance, fear of futons (you may as well sleep on the floor), fear of future shock and, last but not least, fear of F-words. Why do you live in fear? Die in fear by all means but please, I implore you, do not live in fear! Commission that monumental mason or woodcarver. Give them the lettering and pay them so you can leave a mark for those that have left you behind. It'll make no difference other than line their pockets and make you feel good about yourself and the unreliable trophy.

áə̀-àā ρí: **Dead wood**

There's a wood not far from where I live. It is hundreds of years old and has been preserved so that people can go and enjoy it. A camping site right next door offers somewhere to stay for those that aren't local. A café, the 'Broadleaf Tea Rooms', is where visitors can order a pot of tea and some scones or home-made cakes. A small gift shop sells mementoes. Postcards and pencils, china mugs with stencils of trees on them, notepads to put by the telephone; that sort of thing. It doesn't cost an arm and a leg to visit the place. It's a good day out for the children, if the weather is kind, with an adventure play area and a woodland miniature railway. Father Christmas visits every December, and mums and dads pay a little extra so that their excited children can climb aboard the 'Santa Express' and get a wrapped present from the old man with the badly fitting white beard.

I can walk there. It's only about a mile away. I'm a 'Friend of the Wood'. For £17 a year I can visit the wood as many times as I like. So I do. I've been there six or seven times over the summer and have become familiar with some of the walks through it. Once inside, through the main entrance and past the woman taking the money from the motorists, it is a different world. The trees make the difference. They change the light. Even on the brightest of summer days, the green canopy filters the sunlight so that everything melts. What had been vivid walking down the country lane to get there, becomes less so in the wood. The colours change, become muted, as though I have entered an old, leafy cathedral. Outside there was a horizon: inside there is not. There is no real perspective, just a wall of dark green. A tree a few feet away could be fifty yards off and one in the distance perhaps only an arm's length away. Sudden clearings let the light fall in from the sky, so bright that it takes away sight. I stumble, trip over a tree root that is most obvious; most easy to see by those that can.

The temperature drops a degree or two. Defined paths are cut and worn through the trees where the earth is always damp and where the roots emerge and twist and wriggle their way, breaking cover. They then dive back into the ground, try to trip up the walkers and lie there like petrified snakes. The smell is different, too. There is the stench of death. Rotting things in the undergrowth; dampness and decay. Burst puffballs, leaf mould and fox pee. I can smell where 'Charlie' has been. I remember an old gamekeeper telling me years ago, wrinkling his red-veined nose up as though the Devil himself had urinated in that patch of bracken. The stillness in the wood is almost disturbing. The rustle of a grey squirrel and the squabbling of a jay cause alarm, make me jump. My perturbation makes my hair itch, not my scalp or head, but my hair and I feel uncomfortable in my skin; prickly, irritated, out of sorts. I stop by a tree that's older than me; taller with branches and leaves that appear to be harmonious and I rub my back up against the trunk's bark, like an old bear might. Me and the tree massaging each other; rubbing each other up the right way, it puts me back into a cool frame of mind, again in a good place. Trees can be like that; good for body and soul. High up in the tremulous leaves I can hear the sound of bees, legions of them humming as they work. I hum too, try to catch their pitch, but it's impossible; like breathing underwater or trying to spin a web.

At intervals there are new trees, individual young saplings, ring-fenced with old timber and with little inscribed plaques at their base. Each is dedicated to somebody. A name and a date with a few well chosen words. A tree has been planted in commemoration of someone who has died. What a nice idea, I think. A permanent memorial to someone loved. I wouldn't mind that when it comes to my turn.

As I leave the wood after my most recent visit I stop and ask the woman, the usual one taking the entrance money, how much it costs to plant a tree in memory of someone.

"What, dear?" she says.

"Your memorial trees. The ones with the names of people on them. I think it's such a good idea. How much do you charge for them?"

"Oh, there's no charge, dear. We just put them up when it's appropriate. It gives a lot of comfort to the grieving." The woman speaks quietly, taking me into her confidence.

"What a nice touch," says I.

"Yes. We think it is," she replies, "and here's a new one we'll be putting up later this week."

The woman reaches beneath her counter and hands me a memorial plaque. My name and date of birth are correct but I look perplexed over the date of my death, next Friday.

"Is there an inscription we can add, dear?" she asks in a hushed tone. "Just a few words perhaps; something to remember you by."

Here and now or there and then; it doesn't make much difference. You will immerse yourself in a virtual world ignoring the realities of life. Procreation, beekeeping and the nurturing of fish and spiders is what you have been created to do and everything else is coincidental. Remember, everything else is coincidental. So if you don't procreate, look after bees, fish and spiders, will you be brought to account? The lack of offspring is itself punishment enough, my friend. Your influence on those around you is just as important and will be judged accordingly. Such is life and you're all so disengaged with it, so immune from its vitality that you cannot really contemplate your own demise. Such is your arrogance or short-termism. It is the second certainty. Birth the first, death the second. What you do between the two certainties, what you make of life will determine your afterlife. You cannot say that is certain, but Eliza the list maker does. Maybe X among the many one day; maybe Y and even more the next. Both were funny in their ways; one with a tickling stick, the other with time. Big men; giants in your fields with interesting codes. One one day, the other the next. They wouldn't have planned it that way, had no idea that their paths would cross in circumstances far removed from tickling sticks and time. It takes all sorts. From here your importance looks miniscule. Although, in un mondo di ciechi un orbo è re. So understand or not, your codes (and I have given you fifty examples to be going on with) will find you out and when it's your turn to enter my Chamber, please don't be found wanting; Eliza will decode you, decipher you, decrypt you, work you out, solve your workings, interpret your musings, translate your secrets, make perfect sense of your life, get to the bottom of all your goings-on, unravel your mysteries, find the key to your inner being, crack you wide open, figure you out, twig everything and suss the lot, if you get my drift. What I'll never do is correct your codes. I'm just the marker, the invigilator, adjudicator, assessor, evaluator, appraiser and examiner and, I love it. You have been warned so Nema and nemesis my friends, Nema and nemesis!